PENGUIN BOOKS

THE BLOOD DETECTIVE

Dan Waddell is a journalist and author who lives in west London with his son. He writes about the media and popular culture, and has published ten non-fiction books, including the bestselling *Who Do You Think You Are?*, which tied in with the BBC TV series. This is his first novel.

D1392909

DAN WADDELL

The Blood Detective

PENGUIN BOOKS

PENGUIN BOOKS

Published by the Penguin Group
Penguin Books Ltd, 80 Strand, London WC2R ORL, England
Penguin Group (USA) Inc., 375 Hudson Street, New York, New York 10014, USA
Penguin Group (Canada), 90 Eglinton Avenue East, Suite 700, Toronto, Ontario, Canada M4P 2Y3
(a division of Pearson Penguin Canada Inc.)
Penguin Ireland, 25 St Stephen's Green, Dublin 2, Ireland (a division of Penguin Books Ltd)
Penguin Group (Australia), 250 Camberwell Road, Camberwell, Victoria 3124, Australia
(a division of Pearson Australia Group Pty Ltd)
Penguin Books India (Pvt) Ltd, 11 Community Centre, Panchsheel Park, New Delhi – 110 017, India
Penguin Group (NZ), 67 Apollo Drive, Rosedale, Auckland 0632, New Zealand
(a division of Pearson New Zealand Ltd)
Penguin Books (South Africa) (Pty) Ltd, 24 Sturdee Avenue, Rosebank,
Johannesburg 2196, South Africa

Penguin Books Ltd, Registered Offices: 80 Strand, London WC2R ORL, England

www.penguin.com

First published 2008
This edition produced for The Book People Ltd, Hall Wood Avenue, Haydock,
St Helens, WA11 9UL

1

Printed in England by Clays Ltd, St Ives plc

ISBN: 978-0-241-95346-4

www.greenpenguin.co.uk

This is for Emma.
See you in my dreams.

Acknowledgements

This book would never have been completed without the help of the following people. Firstly, my editor at Penguin, Beverley Cousins, whose patience and faith were greatly appreciated during the difficult circumstances in which I found myself writing the book, and whose expert editorial eye has since improved it immeasurably. Her assistant, Claire Phillips, also offered some helpful suggestions and alterations.

Secondly, I am extremely grateful to my agent, Araminta Whitley, who helped locate the real story in among my earliest drafts. She worked tirelessly to improve the book at every stage and was always at hand to offer advice, ideas and encouragement. Mark Lucas, Peta Nightingale, Lizzie Jones and the other wonderful folk at LAW also made vital contributions along the way. Thanks to you all.

I would also like to thank the following, all of whom helped in the writing of this book: Nick Barratt, resident genealogical genius; Professor Robert Forrest; Rachel and Paul Murphy; Lillian

Aylmer and Gavin Houtheusen at The National Archives; Christine Falder at DeepStore; Wall to Wall productions; and my family, especially Irene and my Dad, for their love and support.

Finally, and most significantly, my wife, Emma, who died of breast cancer while this book was being written. Without her ferocious loyalty and the belief she had in me, I would never have begun writing it. Or any other book, for that matter. I owe her everything. She lives on in the heads and hearts of me, my son and many, many others.

Wearing the type of lazy smile that often distinguished the half-cut from the sober, Bertie stepped out of the Prince Albert on Pembridge Road and immediately felt the icy blast of cold air on his face. It was invigorating; the rigours of a week's work, a bellyful of beer and the numbing warmth of the pub's fire had helped him forget how bitter it was outside, though word of it had been on the chapped lips of everyone who had come in for a drink. March, they muttered. Felt more like January.

After shaking his head to rid it of the fug of the pub, he glanced up at the clear, black sky. No fog; the wind had chased away the perennial smoke that blanketed the city at night. A nice change, he thought, to use his eyes and not instinct as he made his way home.

To his right he could hear the clatter of traffic on Notting Hill Gate. A man scurried past, head down, left hand holding his hat in place, the right gripping his coat across his throat. Bertie did not even button his; he did not mind the cold. He was warm-blooded. 'My little bed-warmer,' Mary liked to call him, as they closed in to form a crescent shape together under the covers. Sometimes in winter, when he got into bed, she would raise a chilly foot – she felt the cold terribly – and place it softly between his legs to warm it. Made him jump. 'Back off, woman,' he would tell her. But she would giggle and so would he. He was incapable of getting angry with her – and she with him, as she would prove in about fifteen minutes' time when he stumbled into bed near midnight with the smell of booze on his breath.

The thought of it – the thought of her – made him smile as he started weaving his way home along Ladbroke Road. The wind was at his back, blowing towards the Dale. Bertie was glad to have left that benighted place behind. Their life had improved immeasurably since he and Mary and the little ones had moved to Clarendon Road. It might still be on the edge of the Dale but it had felt like a fresh start. For the first time in his life he felt able to breathe.

He crossed the road, passing the Ladbroke Arms and the police station ahead of the crossing with Ladbroke Grove, the lamp casting a halo of warming light over the few policemen standing outside having a smoke. He nodded at them as he passed. Ladbroke Grove was quiet so he crossed without pausing, turned right and made his way up the hill. At the summit he toyed with going further on and turning on to Lansdowne Crescent, or cutting across the churchyard and down St John's Gardens. He chose the latter.

He went to the left of St John's, its cathedral-like spire pointing a bony finger into the darkness above him. As he passed the church he noticed something moving to his right. Some poor beggar seeking shelter from the wind, he thought.

Then it was on him; hot, rancid breath on his cheek.

'What the . . .'

Before he could finish, the blade was stuck deep in his ribs. The noise as it left his flesh sounded like a finished kiss.

The figure retreated into the darkness as swiftly as it had arrived. Bertie felt little pain, just bewilderment. His hands went to his ribs; there they felt the warm stickiness of his own blood. He sat back on the ground, as if pushed. He tried to call for help, but no words came. He raised his hands to his face and saw them slicked with his own blood. God save me, he thought, his breath becoming shallow.

'Mary,' he whispered, thinking of her lying there, waiting for him to slip into bed so she could warm herself on him.

He lay back on the damp grass, aware of the smell of moist earth and the last pitiful throbs of his heart.

Finally, he felt the cold.

I

Detective Chief Inspector Grant Foster, stiff from lack of sleep, dragged his tall, weary frame from his brand-new Toyota Corolla, feeling the familiar ache of being hauled from his bed in the middle of the night. Even though he had stopped smoking six months ago he felt a pang for nicotine. Arriving at a murder scene had been one of those occasions when he would habitually spark up; part of a ritual, a summoning of will. He cracked his knuckles and sniffed the cold air.

Dawn was approaching over London and the sound of traffic on the distant Westway was evolving to a constant drone as early workers joined late-night stragglers on the road. Despite the frosty tang in the air and the last blustery breaths of the fierce wind that had blown all night, a mild warmth hinted at the first signs of spring. In less than two hours the sun would be up and the late-March day would begin. But Foster was in no mood to be optimistic. When he sniffed the air, he noticed only one smell: trouble.

Detective Sergeant Heather Jenkins, her wild black

hair tied back in a ponytail, fell in beside him as they crossed the road towards the church.

'It's a nasty one, sir.' Her strong Lancastrian accent flattened the vowel of her final word.

Foster nodded. 'Certainly sounds like it,' he said, speaking for the first time. His deep, rich voice seemed to emanate from somewhere down around his boots. 'Unlike the drunk the other night.'

Both of them had been woken when it was still dark the previous Sunday morning to attend what appeared to be the suicide of a tramp in Avondale Park. Foster, supposed to be having a weekend off, though no one had seen fit to inform those on duty, had left it to Heather, gone back to bed and tried to get some more sleep. Unsuccessfully. So he got up and drove to the scene. Four days later, he still resented the intrusion.

Heather made a noise down her nose to indicate her disbelief that Foster was still angry, not quite a snort, more a sort of reverse sniff.

'You can't let that go, can you, sir?' she said.

'Our workload is bad enough without having to poke around the cider-drenched corpse of some loser,' he muttered without looking at her.

'You don't reckon that tramp is entitled to the same consideration we lavish on other people's deaths? We don't even know his identity: don't you think we owe it to him to find out who he is and whether he had a family?'

'No,' he said emphatically. 'But have you checked with the Missing Persons Bureau?'

She nodded. 'Nothing that seems to fit so far.'

'Probably yet another loser no one gave a stuff about. One less piss-stained wino for the lads on the beat to sling in the drunk tank.'

From the corner of his eye he saw her shake her head slowly.

They had reached the churchyard. Cresting the hill of Ladbroke Grove, overlooked by a crescent of handsome early-Victorian mansions, it made a curious scene. It certainly beat the council estates, pub car parks and patches of barren land where London's murder victims were usually found. Yet he felt uneasy because, during more than twenty years on the force, he couldn't remember another body being found on religious ground. As if that was a step too far, even for the most psychotic. He made a mental note to revisit this thought.

Detective Inspector Andy Drinkwater, hair neatly cut, lantern-jawed with chiselled features, was waiting for them at the cordon that had been put around the entire perimeter and was being guarded by a few uniformed officers. Foster often teased Drinkwater about looking like an ageing refugee from some long-forgotten boy band: he was an obsessive gym-rat, a teetotaller and, given his clear complexion, Foster suspected, with a shudder, he might even moisturize. This morning in his knee-length woollen overcoat and gloves, he looked every inch the detective.

'Sir,' he said, nodding at Foster. 'Heather.'

She smiled at him apprehensively.

'Morning, Andy. What we got?' Foster asked.

Over Drinkwater's shoulder, to the left of the church, he could see forensics settling in for the long haul. A white tent had been erected over the crime scene, tape bound around the perimeter of the churchyard, while an arc light illuminated the area.

Drinkwater sucked in air between his teeth. 'Not very nice, sir,' he said. 'Forensics are here. Carlisle too: he's having a look at the body.'

Foster's eyes narrowed. Pathologists rarely beat him to the scene.

'He lives nearby,' Drinkwater explained.

The three of them passed through the gate and made their way towards the tent.

'Victim's a male in his early thirties,' Drinkwater said, both he and Heather scurrying to keep up with their superior's giant strides. 'Looks like he hadn't been here long when two youths found him. They raised the alarm at Notting Hill, down the road, shortly before three a.m.'

'You've spoken to the kids?' Foster asked, still walking.

'Both of them were pretty stoned. But yes, I've had a brief chat.'

'How old?'

'One fifteen, the other just turned sixteen.'

Foster shook his head; what sort of parents let their kids out in the small hours of the morning? Probably the type of dad his force arrested by the score on a daily basis, and the sort of feckless mother whose maternal instincts had been doused by years of booze and drugs. Some people aren't fit to raise hamsters, he thought.

'They're not suspects in my opinion,' Drinkwater added, anticipating Foster's next question. 'But they're at the station if you want to speak with them. We've notified the parents. Both kids are pretty freaked out.' He paused. 'You'll see why. About the only thing they did say that might be interesting is that a drunk woman, a derelict, often used the part of the churchyard where the body was found.'

'Used it as what?'

'A place to doss down. They referred to her as Ciderwoman. Mad as toast, apparently. But they haven't seen her for a couple of nights.'

Foster nodded slowly. 'We need to find her.'

'So there *are* some tramps you're interested in finding,' Heather interjected.

He turned and looked down at her. At over six feet, he was several inches taller than her. She was bright and spiky and he liked the way she maintained a dark sense of humour at even the grimmest of scenes. It was a vital attribute for a murder detective.

The three of them stopped. They had reached the entrance to the tent. A gust of cold wind tugged at its moorings, making the corners flap.

'I always feel like I'm about to enter a freak show outside these things,' Foster muttered as he climbed into the white suit. Given his height, few of them ever fitted. This one wasn't too bad, though; nothing ripped when he put it on. 'Come on, then. Let's do this,' Foster said, stretching his arms to see how much movement he had. The younger detectives followed him in.

Inside, the smell of damp earth was strong, almost heady. Foster had to stoop forwards slightly, to prevent his head brushing the roof of the tent. He looked down at the corpse. His view of it was blocked by a crouching figure. All he could see was a grey trouser leg that had ridden up to reveal a gulch of pale flesh between it and the sock. The crouching man was Carlisle, the duty pathologist. He was checking the victim's pockets.

'Robbing yet another corpse, Edward?' Foster said.

The man, dressed head to foot in white, did not even look up. 'You would, too, on my salary,' he replied. Then he turned and grinned at Foster, but his eyes gave away the desperation of the scene. He stood up, revealing the corpse to Foster for the first time.

'Jesus Fucking Christ.'

'Yes, nasty business,' Edward Carlisle said in his plummy, public-school voice.

The victim was on his back. Mouth agape, thousand-yard stare; so much was common to most corpses Foster had seen. But what truly shocked him were the hands – or, rather, the lack of them. At the end of both arms were livid, fleshy stumps, jagged bone protruding.

'Very little blood at the scene,' Carlisle said.

'So he wasn't killed here?'

'No, I would say not. The body's temperature has dropped about twelve degrees, which at one and a half degrees per hour indicates he was killed around nine p.m. last night.'

'When was he found?' Foster said, his question addressed to Andy.

'Just after two forty-five a.m.'

'How about the hands, Edward? Severed post-mortem?'

Carlisle wrinkled his nose. 'Difficult to say. You'll have to wait for the autopsy.'

'Cause of death?'

'A single stab wound to the heart seems to have done the trick. The chest is also covered with several superficial cuts, some quite deep.'

'Why keep the hands?' Foster asked.

'Trophies,' Drinkwater said confidently.

It was a reasonable theory, Foster thought. His initial impression had been the same. But somehow it didn't ring true.

Heather, previously silent, piped up. 'There could have been a struggle, sir,' she said. 'The vic could have got fibre or skin under his nails. Perhaps the killer thought if they severed the hands they'd reduce their chances of being nicked.'

Another sound theory.

'Do we have an identity?' Foster asked out loud.

'James Darbyshire, according to his cards and driving licence,' Drinkwater said, reading from his notebook. 'There was a mobile, too; forensics have bagged it.'

'Good,' Foster murmured. Mobile phones were godsends to a murder investigation. 'I'll see you in a few hours, if that's OK, Edward.'

Carlisle nodded, eyebrows raised to indicate his concern at the tight schedule Foster was suggesting in his usual matter-of-fact manner. But he knew the DCI liked to have a look at the corpse before it was sliced and diced.

The three of them left Carlisle to his work and went back outside. Dawn was breaking. Once it was fully light, a fingertip team would search the entire churchyard. All three drew a deep breath, Foster more discreetly than the others, delighted to be out in the open air, away from the body. It was after some time with their thoughts that Foster ended the silence.

'I take it we've had a scout around for the missing hands?' he asked Drinkwater, who nodded.

'No sign,' he said.

'Well, make sure we get a team checking all the gardens and nooks and crannies around here. Perhaps they've been dumped elsewhere. Let's get a dog team out here too, see if Fido can dig them up. And when it gets light, get some people knocking on doors in all these houses overlooking the churchyard. Someone might have seen something.

'Where were the kids smoking?' he asked, looking around the small churchyard.

'Across the other side. I'll show you.'

They walked around the back of the churchyard. Drinkwater pointed to a set of stone steps leading down towards a door.

'Down there, by the entrance to the undercroft.'

Foster looked at it for a few seconds. 'So they wouldn't have seen the body being dumped from here?' he asked rhetorically. 'Did they hear anything?'

Drinkwater shook his head. 'Too windy. That's how they found the body. They were after a bit more shelter to skin up, so they went round the other side out of the wind.'

Foster nodded slowly. He was pretty certain they hadn't done it. Most teenagers may be lawless, disrespectful scroats, he thought, but they rarely butcher and mutilate grown men and then walk coolly into a police station to report the crime.

'Just what is an undercroft anyway?'

'A crypt. At least, I think it is,' Drinkwater replied.

'Not any more,' Heather said. 'My mate used to come here for antenatal yoga classes; then a baby massage course after the baby was born.'

Foster turned and looked at her. Ordinarily he would have used this as an excuse to wind her up, but the scene had left him too enervated.

2

The three large crows cawed as they played, wheeling and tipping one after another, their coal-black feathers standing out against the watery-grey sky. Nigel Barnes, his black duffel coat buttoned tightly to his neck, which was wrapped in a woollen scarf, and his battered brown satchel strapped across his shoulder and front so it sat on his right hip, watched them from behind his black-rimmed glasses, wondering how many crows constituted a murder. He thought it was more than three.

His attention wandered from the raucous crows to the sky. The sun, he felt sure, was trying to break through the canopy of cloud, the colour of dull aluminium. But, until it did, he was stymied, the small shaving mirror in his bag redundant. He sighed and brought his gaze back to eye level.

He looked at the gravestones in front of him. How many unfulfilled hopes and dreams lay in the soil? Hundreds. Thousands, maybe. Away to his left was a glorious, tree-lined avenue of dramatic and gaudy mausoleums, a testament to the Victorian obsession with death and mourning, lurid monuments to the dead and now forgotten, where the great and the good of nineteenth-century London were laid to rest, many of them above ground rather than below. Beyond, Nigel could see the gothic outline of the Anglican chapel, beneath which lay the catacombs. He had been down there once and loved every ghoulish second, particularly the moment when the guide conspiratorially said that if the embalmer failed to do his job, then the bodies crammed in there often exploded, made combustible by the waste gases of their decomposition. The whole group had laughed nervously, and shuddered collectively.

Kensal Green Cemetery was a favourite spot of his, rivalled only by Highgate Cemetery for macabre splendour. The Victorians knew how to do death. Unlike us, he thought; now we burn people and have little to do with the dusty aftermath. Genealogists won't have graves to go to in fifty or a hundred years when tracing future generations, no inscriptions to locate and decipher, just like they won't have letters to read and learn from, thanks to email. Nothing is permanent any more, for all time, he thought: it's all about now.

He looked around and through the trees bowing in the wind, the tangled bushes and endless tumble of overgrown, battered graves and statues. He could see no one else. Just him and thousands of dead. It was like entering a lost world. Only the faraway hum of traffic punctuated by the sound of sirens, London's incessant soundtrack, gave an indication of the century he was in. It felt good to be out in the open air, away from the exhaust fumes of the traffic-choked streets. There were few outdoor oases like this in central London, places of silent contemplation: the other cemeteries, of course, the odd residential square with its private gardens, and a few of the smaller parks, but that was it. Nigel knew that 150 years ago this cemetery was in open countryside. That was the whole idea. The teeming, crowded cemeteries in the middle of the city had begun spewing out their decomposing bounty, and the foul, fetid odour and miasma that resulted were the cause of disease, or so the belief was. So the newer cemeteries were built out of town – the one in Brookwood had its own mode of transport to export the city's deceased, the Necropolis Railway. But soon London's voracious appetite had swallowed the ground in every direction.

Nigel checked his watch: ten thirty. From his coat pocket he pulled a crumpled piece of paper torn from the notebook. 'Lot 103', it read. The grave of Cornelius Tiplady, Architect, 1845–85. His quest was to find whether this Cornelius Tiplady was the great-great-grandfather of his client. He wanted to see if the inscription on the gravestone mentioned some names that might link him to some of the other relatives he had found, and so confirm he had the right man. A poetic inscription might be a nice garnish to offer alongside the dry genealogical info he had unearthed, and to confirm a job well done. He needed to let people know he was back, working well. Rebuilding a business was not proving easy.

Lot 103 was off the beaten track and, as he suspected, in an unkempt part of the cemetery teeming with unruly grass, small trees and lichen, muddying his brogues as he ticked off the graves one by one. Few had escaped the ravages of the weather. He reached lot 103, took off his glasses and gave them a quick rub on the edge of his coat, put them back on and sank to his haunches.

The grave was unremarkable, standard for the time, a flat grey gravestone. No ostentation for the Tiplady family. But, as he feared, the words used to honour the deceased's two-score years had been rendered unreadable by time and decay. He could not even make out the name, bar the outline of a capital C, which did at least offer him the comfort that the burial records had been well kept and that somewhere beneath his feet lay Cornelius, or whatever was left of him. He ran his finger gently across some of the indentations, almost able to make out the other letters of the name, even if he could not see them. He noticed there was another jumble of letters below the name, though the inscription appeared brief. A family of few words, too, it seemed. Good.

Nigel removed his bag from his shoulder, unzipped it and pulled out his shaving mirror. He had bought it when he was a student, from a barber on Jermyn Street. He stood up, stepped to one side of the grave and, trying to avoid standing on the plot next to it, angled the mirror to the sky, turning it so that any reflection of light would be cast across the face of the gravestone. He had adopted this method before, to great effect, using the reflection of the sun to cast a shadow across the lettering and so create contrast. But then he had enjoyed the benefit of sunshine. Here he did not, and it was clear after only a few seconds that it was futile. He did not have a torch to magnify the effect of the light; that would require another person, and dragging people to graveyards on weekday mornings was a difficult sell. Luckily, he knew of another, less subtle method.

He put the mirror back in his bag and took a surreptitious glance around him. What he was about to do was not just frowned upon in genealogical circles, it was an offence right up there with defacing documents and licking your fingers before opening an aged manuscript. In the conservative, preservation-first world of family history it was tantamount to desecrating a grave, a subject of fevered debate in genealogical forums across the Internet.

Nigel ran his hand through his mane of black hair, pushing back the fringe that flopped over his brow. There was still no one in sight. Bugger it, he thought, old Cornelius is not going to complain, and neither are any of his family. It crossed his mind that he was standing in almost the exact spot where Cornelius's grieving widow and children would have stood mourning his death, but he managed to cast the thought out once more. Acid rain, bird shit, lichen, they had all inflicted worse damage on the stone than the substance he was about to use. And he did not have the materials with which to make an impression of the inscription. Instead, from his bag he produced a tin of shaving foam and a squeegee.

He shook the tin and squirted several lines of foam across the face of the gravestone. With his right hand he then smeared the foam across the stone so that the entire area was covered with a thin layer. Then he took the squeegee and wiped it gently across the stone from left to right, as if it was a window. The foam came away, except where it had lodged in the crevices of the inscription.

He stepped back. Now the legend was revealed, in menthol, the best-shave-you-can-get white.

Cornelius Tiplady 1845–85.

He was a consistent Member of the Church, a Friend of the Lord, ever an affectionate Husband to Jemima and an indulgent Father.

Faith was triumphant in his death. Sweet is the memory of such for we know they sleep to live again.

Jemima. That confirmed it. Cornelius and his final resting place had at long last been found. He now had enough detail on his life to produce a decent report for his client. He scribbled the epitaph in a notebook and put the materials back in his bag, then took the opportunity to scour the surrounding area. There was no one, only the distant, demented cackle of the crows and the wind rustling the trees.

Before he left, he cast a guilty look at the grave, illuminated with foam. The chemicals in it could leach into the pores of the gravestone and cause permanent damage. For the umpteenth time that morning he surveyed the grey sky. Forget the sun, he thought, what I need right now is some heavy rain.

3

Heather was waiting for Foster at the autopsy room in Kensington. It was approaching noon and he was running late, delayed by his interview with the two stoned kids who had stumbled across the body.

'Did they see anything?' she asked hopefully.

Foster's face gave her the answer immediately, incapable as it was of hiding disdain. His crumpled, creased face appeared to darken, his lip curled and the mournful brown eyes narrowed. An unlamented ex-girlfriend from years ago once told him he had an 'ugly/handsome thing going on', a phrase he still didn't know whether to take as an insult or compliment.

'They could barely recognize their own mothers,' he spat out. 'I've left them with an artist. They saw a few people on their way to the churchyard. But, given the strength of the skunk they were smoking, I won't be surprised if we get a sketch of Big Bird.'

They put on their masks, covering nose and mouth, took deep breaths and entered the pristine, stark white-tiled space. The smell of disinfectant hung in the air – almost, but not quite, managing to obliterate the underlying stench of death and decay. A couple of morticians busied themselves around James Darbyshire's handless, naked body, supine on the dissecting table. The sternum had not yet been cut. Foster was glad; he wanted to see the body as it was when they found it, before Carlisle peeled back the skin like fruit rind to reveal the flesh and internal organs. Sometimes, when Foster got there, those organs were sitting in metal pans waiting to be weighed or examined. He could handle death; he could stare at a corpse and learn from it regardless of the injuries it had endured. But the sawing and splicing involved in most autopsies never failed to sicken him, which is why he liked to have a look first and read about it later.

Edward Carlisle welcomed them with a quick nod and motioned for them to follow him towards the body. Foster turned to check Heather was OK; his eyes made contact with hers, but the look she gave back was impatient, as if his concern was grating.

'Here it is. Of course, I haven't yet rummaged around inside, but it seems clear, as I indicated earlier, that the cause of death was a single stab wound to the heart, here.' He pointed to a two-inch slit slightly to the left of centre of the victim's chest. 'I'll have more on that later. And as for the hands, I'm almost certain they were severed prior to death.'

Foster looked at Heather. This wasn't a case of mutilating a dead body. It was torture.

'What has interested me are these wounds here,' Carlisle continued.

Foster and Heather watched as his hands pointed out a series of scratch marks and nicks across the chest.

'I can only think they are the consequences of a struggle, but there are no defence wounds elsewhere, and the victim's shirt has not been damaged.'

'Not even by the stab wound?'

Carlisle shook his head.

'Then he wasn't wearing it when he was stabbed. Or when these cuts were made.'

Foster was standing to the right-hand side of the cadaver. He walked slowly, clockwise around the table, never taking his eyes off the body. When the soles of the dead man's feet were facing him, he stopped for perhaps a minute, his eyes fixed on the victim's torso. By this point Heather and Carlisle were more interested in Foster's perambulation than the corpse. He set off once more until he arrived back where he started. He leaned in for a closer look at the scratched and bloodied chest.

'Did you shave the chest?' he asked Carlisle, without looking up.

'No.'

Foster stepped back and examined the torso, tilting the angle of his head slightly as he did, first to the left, then to the right, then leaning over once more. He looked around the room, his eyes eventually alighting on an empty dissecting table that had been pushed against a wall to one side of the mortuary. He walked over and grabbed it, using his strength to free the table from its awkward position, and then wheeled it over to where the others stood.

Carlisle's eyes narrowed.

'Can I ask what you're doing, Grant?'

Foster held up his hand as if to say, 'Wait and see.'

Bit by bit he manoeuvred the table into a position parallel to the one holding Darbyshire's body, both edges touching, then he hauled himself on to it. He stood up and leaned over the dead man, his weight on his right leg. The table creaked under the strain.

He remained on his perch for some time, without speaking.

'Heather, get up here,' he said finally.

She hopped up beside him, while Carlisle shook his head in disbelief.

'These aren't defensive wounds,' Foster said. 'Look at the right nipple: above it is a long vertical scratch. Can you see that? Then look how it's topped with a small diagonal nick, or looks like it is. And beneath it is a horizontal scratch.'

Heather agreed.

'What does that look like?'

She stared at the wounds. 'A number 1,' she said, certain.

'Look at the others.'

Carlisle had joined her at the other side of the table for a closer look. Foster dropped to his knees. He pointed towards the middle of the chest, his finger tracing the lines of two slanted cuts, the hairless, paper-white skin almost delicately torn.

'See how they almost reach a point?' he said. Then he indicated a barely distinguishable graze between the two lines, like a shaving nick.

'That almost bridges the gap between the two wounds. It looks like a letter A.'

Foster continued his way across the man's chest, following the outlines of each cut and deciphering a figure or letter it represented. At the end, Foster reached under the gown and retrieved his notebook from his suit pocket. He wrote down five figures: 1A137.

'These cuts were made post-mortem,' Carlisle commented.

'In which case, they were for our eyes,' Foster replied. He turned back and looked at the body for the final time. Carlisle picked up a scalpel to show what he intended to do next.

'Fill your boots,' Foster said, gesturing towards the body.

They left the room before the first incision was made.

4

All promise had bled from the day. It was just after three p.m. when the investigating team gathered for their first briefing, and already the lights were on at West London Murder Command – officially known as Homicide West – an anonymous building next door to Kensington police station. Inside, the mood was grim but determined. Foster was standing at the front, beside the whiteboard. The victim's name was written on it; beneath that were pictures of his body. The top of Foster's giant, close-shaven pate shone in the strip light.

The team had been speaking to friends and family of the deceased. Some were still out, though not Heather. At least, as far as he knew. He couldn't explain her absence.

A few more details had emerged. Darbyshire was a trader who worked at a bank in the Square Mile. He lived out in Leytonstone, the city commuter belt, with his wife and two kids.

'This is what we know,' Foster declared slowly and

deliberately in his rich molten croon that demanded, and always got, attention. 'Darbyshire goes to the pub with three men at five thirty. An hour earlier, he called his wife and said he was going out with clients, but that was probably a white lie because all three were colleagues. They have four pints. One of them goes to buy a fifth. Darbyshire says he feels hot, faint. The pub is packed, cheek to jowl, so perhaps no surprise there. But he's only thirty-one and, apart from being a smoker, he's fit; he plays football every Sunday. Doc Carlisle tells me the heart looked healthy.

'We've interviewed his mates and he seems like a happy family man. His life revolved around his job, his friends, his family and West Ham United. He was liked at work, and he had no particular worries, financial or otherwise, as far as we can tell, so not much stress.'

Looking at Drinkwater, 'Andy, chase up toxicology and tell them to get their arses in gear. I want to know what was in his bloodstream as quickly as they can. Any medication, anything at all.'

Turning back to face the others, 'He told one of his mates he was going outside for a fag – which, if he was feeling hot and claustrophobic, is fair enough. He leaves. Then he disappears. It's almost seven p.m. The next time anyone sees him, he's dead and mutilated in a churchyard across the other side of London.'

Foster let his words sink in before continuing, 'At some point after leaving that pub, he comes into contact with his killer. The killer then either persuades him or forces him into a vehicle or a building, removes his hands and stabs him. Our killer is very strong, has help, or Mr Darbyshire is so incapacitated that our killer can sever his hands without too much of a struggle. He then does one other thing.' From the desk in front of him Foster held up a picture showing what had been carved on Darbyshire's chest. 'He shaves his chest and then carves a series of letters and numbers. Look closely and you'll see it says 1A137. Now the obvious question is: what does this mean?'

The question was met by silence.

'A reference,' someone suggested at last.

'A crossword clue,' came another.

This loosened them up, and a few ideas were floated.

'A chess move,' said one; 'a map reference,' said another.

'Hang on,' said DC Majid Khan, a young detective who fancied himself as a comedian. 'I think that's the order for a vegetable pakora and a chicken dhansak at the Taste of the Raj in Thames Ditton.'

The rest laughed.

'We need to investigate all of those,' Foster went on, ignoring Khan's attempt at levity. 'Our killer is trying to tell us something. When we work out what, we move a damn sight closer to catching him or her.' He cleared his throat. For the first time that day he was hit by a sudden feeling of exhaustion, but he repelled it. 'The kids who found the body say there's a tramp who lives in the churchyard. Ciderwoman, or whatever. Have we managed to find her?'

The answer was negative. They knew her real name was Sheena but she had not been seen around her usual patch lately.

'She's got to be somewhere. Probably on an alco-holiday, swigging Strongbow outside Camden Town tube. Let's keep on it. Any news on witnesses in or around the church?'

Again he got a shake of the head. That surprised him in one sense: the churchyard was by no means secluded. It was on the top of a hill on a busy thoroughfare, enclosed by tall residential buildings. On paper, a terrible spot to dump a body.

So why choose it?

'I want us to go through every single piece of CCTV footage from every camera in Liverpool Street from seven p.m. last night. That's where he usually got the tube home. Who knows, maybe he made it on to one. And let's go through all the footage from Ladbroke Grove, too.'

Suddenly Heather burst through the door, breathless. Foster looked for some sign of contrition, yet saw none.

'Sorry, sir,' she said. 'Tying up the loose ends on the suicidal tramp.'

The fate of the tramp found dangling from the frame of a park swing the previous Sunday morning had long since been superseded in Foster's mind by the Darbyshire murder. He felt a wave of anger.

'Give that bleeding heart of yours a rest. Put the tramp to one side and concentrate on this, please.'

'The least we can do is find out who he is, and who his family are. He has every right to . . .'

'Yes, he's got every right to equal consideration. But that doesn't mean he's going to get it. I wish I could find the fool who invented the concept of rights, and deprive him of them. Violently.'

Heather's eyes, never docile, blazed bright with anger. Her face was always quick to express emotion, but Foster knew she would soon calm down. Having a go at her in front of the others was not the most politic thing to do, but her mission to turn detective work into another arm of the care services occasionally grated with him.

The discussion moved on to the missing hands. A

search of the scene had failed to find them, or a murder weapon. The team split into camps: those who thought they might be trophies; those who thought it was a way of avoiding detection; and a third camp who thought it was neither, that there was perhaps more to it than the obvious explanations.

'What forensics do we have?' Foster asked.

'Initially, nothing really,' said Drinkwater. 'So far, the scene tells us nothing.'

The room fell silent. It was rare for forensics to fail to provide them with a few leads. Foster nodded slowly. It was as if the body had fallen from the sky. But the lack of evidence or clues wasn't insignificant.

'What the crime scene tells us is that our killer worked very carefully, thought it through beforehand. And it confirms that our victim was killed elsewhere.'

'Do we have any idea about motive?' someone asked.

Foster spread his hands wide; he had been giving this some thought. 'We can rule out mugging because there was still a fair bit of money on his body. And his mobile phone, too. Of course, we don't know the full story of his private life so there could be something there . . .' His voice tailed off. Foster already knew that the motive for this was one his mind had not yet considered. Something told him it was beyond the usual mundane language of murder:

drugs, money, rage and envy. 'Have we got mobile-phone records?' he said, changing tack.

Drinkwater told him they had retrieved the last ten calls dialled, received and missed from Darbyshire's mobile phone. Most of them had been identified as friends, family or work-related. The only call made or received after seven p.m., when Darbyshire was last seen in the pub, was to a number: 1879. The time dialled was 23.45.

'Have you spoken to pathology?' Foster asked.

'Carlisle reckons that Darbyshire was dead by then.'

'Any theories about that number?' It sounded to him like it could be for message retrieval, or the number for the network.

'We rang it, from several different networks. All of them went dead,' Drinkwater said.

It seemed the whole room reached for their mobile phones and starting staring at their keypads.

'What sort of phone was it again?' Foster asked.

'One of those slim, dinky ones with the flip-up screen. Clamshell. Girl's phone. Khan's got one,' Drinkwater added, with a smirk.

So had Foster. A murmur of amusement went round the room.

'Seven, eight and nine are on the same row,' said Khan, examining his own keypad. 'They easily could have been pushed accidentally. Where was the phone?'

Drinkwater looked into the middle distance; with his left hand he patted his left suit pocket, while his right tapped lightly on the right-hand side of his chest.

'Inside breast pocket, right-hand side,' he said eventually. 'If the key guard wasn't on during the struggle, if there *was* a struggle, or after he was killed and the body was being moved, the buttons might have been pushed. The dial button, too.'

'Sounds the likeliest option,' Foster agreed. 'But stick the number up on the whiteboard. Get back in touch with his wife and his bank; see if this number means anything to them. It may be the start of an account number, or a PIN number. We need to know.' Foster rubbed his face, then ran his right hand over his head. 'Darbyshire had drunk only four pints. He would've been merry, not arseholed, so how did the killer get him off the street in the first place? A 31-year-old man isn't easy to lure into a car. Unless you're giving him a lift. We have to accept the killer may have had some help. How many hits did we get, Andy?'

Earlier that afternoon they had fed details of the murder into the computer to sift through suspects who had been cautioned, charged or convicted of stabbings and were out on the streets.

'About two thousand,' Drinkwater said.

Each of them would be checked out in the coming days and weeks. A fair bit of mystery surrounded the workings of a murder inquiry, but most of it was simply a long, methodical slog.

'Find out how many had, have had, or still have cab or minicab licences,' Foster ordered. He clapped his hands together. 'The rest of you know what comes next,' he added, winding things up. 'We need to crawl all over James Darbyshire's life: his movements, his habits, his daily routine. Scour his credit cards and bank details; interview his friends, relatives, girlfriends, boyfriends and colleagues; check his emails; look at what sites he visited. Any porn, anything a bit dodgy, then I want to know.'

The team got up, a few stretching, some starting conversations while others hit the phones.

'Can I say something, sir?'

The hubbub died down. It was Heather, her face still reddened from anger. Foster's first thought was that she may publicly challenge him for having slapped her down when she arrived late for the meeting. But he knew she wouldn't be that stupid.

'Go on,' he said.

Everyone turned to look at her.

'I must have missed your discussion about the letters and numbers carved on the victim's chest,' she explained. 'But I've got an idea about them. It's been bugging me ever since the post mortem.'

Foster realized the colour in her cheeks was not anger, it was excitement. 'Yes?'

'Have you heard of genealogy?'

He thought for a second. He knew it; old people filling the last few days before death came knocking by tracing their dead relatives.

'Yeah,' Foster said. 'Bloody stupid hobby.'

A few of the others laughed.

'Whatever,' Heather said, ignoring them. 'My mum traced our family tree a few years back. But you sort of need to leave the house, and the best place to do it is in London, not Rawtenstall. She came down to see me and we went to this place in Islington where they have loads of indexes for birth, marriage and death certificates. Place was heaving; no room to swing a cat.'

Get to the point, Foster thought. 'Where does it fit with the Darbyshire killing?'

'When you want to order a certificate, you have to fill in a form. On that form you have to give the index number of the certificate you want. You follow?'

'Go on.'

'The index numbers are like the reference we found; a mixture of letters and numbers.'

Foster could see some of the others nodding their

heads, murmuring assent. It sounded a better idea than the ones proposed in the meeting.

'How are you going to check it out?' he asked.

'My mum gave up on it. She thinks London is a den of iniquity and depravity and won't come down again. Anyway, she hired some guy who does it for a living and got him to do it for her. Turned out we come from a bunch of peasants. Nothing juicy. On the way over here, I gave her a call. She still has his number.'

'Give him a call, but don't spill any details over the phone. Arrange to meet.'

They had nothing, Foster thought. This might be the break they needed.

5

Nigel was sitting at a table for two in the canteen – no one would ever be so bold as to describe it as a café – of the Family Records Centre in London's Clerkenwell. He had chosen a small square table for two against the wall, rather than a large round one for four, so reducing his chances of being forced to share his personal space with a soap-dodging amateur keen to swap stories about an elusive ancestor who had lost a leg at the Somme.

Located in the basement of a modern, functional beige-bricked building tucked away apologetically at one end of Exmouth Market, rows of tables filled the room to one side, glass lockers and coat racks to the other. There were no black-clad baristas serving coffee seven different ways; only a few vending machines touting tongue-scalding, mud-coloured water. Another machine sold sandwiches, limp and curled inside their plastic wrapping. The average age of people who used the centre was probably twice that of any other meeting place, family history being the preserve – with a few exceptions – of those for whom death is no longer a distant possibility but an imminent certainty.

The Family Records Centre is a Mecca for genealogists and family historians, housing the indexes of almost every birth, death and marriage that has taken place in England and Wales since 1837, as well as copies of every census taken between 1841 and 1901. Nigel used to love delving into the indexes, looking forwards to a day losing himself in the bureaucratic traces of the long departed, but now his presence there was a constant source of disappointment. Eighteen months ago he had left, vowing never to return, and adamant that he would never again spend a whole day researching the family tree of some middle-class dilettante who was not interested in the stories of the past, the narrative arc of their ancestors' lives, all the stuff that fascinated Nigel, but who simply wanted the information to help produce a chintzy, beautifully drawn family tree to hang on their wall. Eighteen months ago he had headed off to the sunlit uplands of academia – real research. Now here he was back doing the bidding of others.

At three thirty on that chilly late-March afternoon, Nigel was idling away time that would have been better spent among the indexes. The day, he thought to himself, had not been a bad one. Even the elderly gentleman on the next table, who was peeling an apple so slowly that, by the time he had finished and was ready to eat it, the flesh had turned a rusty brown, was struggling to spoil it. He had phoned in the discovery of Cornelius Tiplady's grave to his client, much to her delight. Then, before coming to the FRC, he had stopped off to do a few hours' research for another client, a Mrs Carnell, at the National Archives in Kew. Now he was trying to work out, and keep the smile off his face as he did so, what he was going to tell her when he called her later that day to inform her that he had discovered the truth about Silas Carnell, an ancestor of hers, who had died at sea in the 1840s, and about whose heroic death she had paid to know more.

The thing was, Silas's death wasn't heroic. It was anything but. True, Nigel had unearthed naval records that confirmed the sailor had met his demise at sea. Though not in combat. Silas had been hanged as punishment. His offence? He'd had sex with one of the goats brought on board to provide milk. Any port in a storm, Nigel thought. Bizarrely, Silas was not the only one executed; the goat's throat had been slit.

Intending to waste more time by having a fag outside, he was just fishing out the rolling tobacco and papers from his pocket when his mobile phone startled him by coming to life. It was years old, the size of a small brick; he saw no need to trade it in, and his provider (or whatever name they gave themselves) had long since given up on trying to get him to upgrade. Given the choice, he'd downgrade – to not having one at all.

He debated whether to ignore it. The number was unfamiliar. And, quite rightly in his view, speaking on mobiles was frowned upon in the FRC; those who did were at risk of being assaulted by fuming septuagenarians armed with half-peeled fruit. But the only other person in the room had just disappeared into the toilets, so Nigel decided to risk it. He needed all the business he could get.

'Nigel Barnes,' he said.

'Hello, Mr Barnes.'

The voice was female, the accent broad but not one Nigel could place.

'This is Detective Sergeant Heather Jenkins of the Metropolitan Police. Sorry to ring out of the blue like this.'

The police? What did they want? He scanned the last few weeks of his life in a millisecond and failed to come up with any misdemeanours. He felt his throat constrict. Surely not . . .

'Not at all,' he whispered eventually.

'We're wondering if you could help us with a case we're investigating.'

He felt a sense of relief mingled with excitement, undercut by the suspicion that this was a wind-up. 'What sort of case?'

'Murder.'

Nigel's mind scrambled as he sought the appropriate response. 'Yes,' he managed to blurt out.

'Good. Look, it's not something I'm comfortable talking about over the phone. Is there any chance I could come to see you? Maybe at your office?'

This presented Nigel with a dilemma. His 'office' was the crowded sitting room of his flat in Shepherd's Bush.

'I'm currently away from my office for the day, Detective Sergeant,' he lied.

'Oh,' came the disappointed response.

'I'm at the Family Records Centre.'

'Oh, I know that,' the detective said.

Lancashire, Nigel thought to himself. Her accent's definitely Lancastrian.

'Is there a discreet place where we could meet?'

Nigel's brain kicked in at last. The canteen was a no-no: in thirty minutes it would be four o'clock and time for afternoon tea. The place would be crammed with the cardigan-wearing hordes wielding thermos flasks and potted-meat sandwiches. There was only one place he could think of.

'There's a coffee shop on Exmouth Market. I

know the owner and I'm pretty sure he'll let me use the downstairs for an hour or so.'

There was a pause at the other end of the phone. When the detective's voice returned it was stripped of its courteous veneer.

'Well, if you can guarantee us some privacy, then OK. Does four thirty suit you?'

Nigel said it did, and the detective hung up. He swept his documents into his bag and left the canteen, praying that Beni would be willing to close half his café – or he'd look a complete fool.

Foster and Heather drove to Exmouth Market in his car. The interior still bore the leathery smell of the showroom. It was an aroma he loved, and one of the reasons he had managed to come up with a scam that persuaded the Met to give him a new set of wheels annually. From one of the many car magazines he bought each month, he'd learned that almost every solid surface in a car was held together by adhesives and sealant. Research suggested that the gases given off by the compounds may even be addictive, and every time he sat behind the wheel of that year's model, he could well believe it.

On the way across London they spoke about genealogy. Heather said she wanted to know more about her family, how they lived, the struggles they endured;

Foster just sneered. To him, it was a bit like stamp collecting, or grown men building a train set in their attic with hills and signals and sheep and stuff. He couldn't care less who his ancestors were; all you needed to know was that your great-great-great-grandfather wasn't firing blanks.

Foster found a meter near Exmouth Market and parked. He completed the entire manoeuvre one-handed, spinning the steering wheel furiously first one way and then the other with an open palm. He could sense Heather looking at him, not without disapproval. But she drove like a vicar, as he often told her. Hands at ten-to-two, like a seventeen-year-old out with her dad for her first drive.

They found Beni's almost immediately. It was a spartan, wooden-fronted coffee shop that thrived on the lunchtime trade, but was in the process of winding down for the day.

'Can I have a decaf latte please?' Heather asked.

'God's sake,' Foster muttered, but she failed to hear. Or ignored him again.

The jovial, rotund man with thick hairy arms nodded. 'And you, sir?' he asked Foster.

'Black coffee, please. Hot as you can make it.'

'We're looking for Nigel Barnes,' Heather said to the barista.

'Downstairs,' he replied, motioning towards a

narrow staircase in one corner of the café. 'The smokers always sit downstairs.' He looked them up and down, clocking their suits and demeanour. His eyes narrowed. 'You're not police, are you?'

'God forbid,' Foster muttered.

Nigel was waiting, wondering if he'd picked a good place to meet. When he'd spoken to DS Jenkins on the phone, the only discreet place he could think of was the sparsely populated room beneath Beni's café. The handful of people who used it were smokers, allowed by Beni to continue feeding their habit out of sight, if not smell, of the other clientele. He came here every morning on his way to the FRC for a cig and a scan of the newspaper. But now he was wondering if a windowless dungeon filled with the scent of stale smoke was not, after all, the best place to meet a female detective. All of a sudden the place seemed seedy.

She will have experienced worse, Nigel thought. He shifted nervously in his seat, nursing his coffee, waiting for the arrival of DS Jenkins. He had tried to imagine what she might look like – she had sounded young, perhaps around his age, early thirties – but he'd given up when all he could muster were images of sour-faced ball-breakers whose femininity and softness had been eroded by years of work in the brutal, relentlessly male world of crime and detection.

Two people descended the stairs, something in their bearing marking them out as police officers. The female was wearing a tight-fitting black trouser suit. Her black corkscrew hair was tied back, her kohl-lined eyes suggested chilliness, and his fears appeared to be founded. Her aquiline nose wrinkled on meeting the polluted air. But on seeing him, and realizing, as the only person in the room, he must be the person she wanted to see, she broke out into a beaming smile that breathed life and warmth into her entire face. The smile was genuine, not forced. He felt himself smiling back.

Ms Nice, he concluded. Presumably that meant the tall, thickset figure, bored and looming at her shoulder, holding their drinks, was Mr Nasty. DS Jenkins introduced him as DCI Grant Foster and, once he had put down their coffee, Nigel felt his enormous paw grasp his own less-weathered, per-spiring hand and grip tightly. The detective was over six feet in height, his head closely shaved, he guessed in response to a receding hairline, with a face that looked like it had seen a few fights. Unlike his female colleague's, the smile was fleeting and perfunctory.

Nigel sat down, both officers facing him.

'Bit airless down here,' DS Jenkins said, wrinkling her nose once more. 'The smoking room, I presume.'

Nigel nodded. 'Beni realizes there's a few of us desperate souls who like to combine . . .'

Nigel realized his unease over meeting here was not only caused by chivalry. Beni sold sandwiches, so the existence of this room was against the law. The DS saw the penny drop.

'Don't worry,' she reassured him. 'Secret smoking dens are the least of our worries.' She looked around, taking her bag off her shoulder and laying it on the floor beside her feet. 'Actually, I like it,' she said. 'It's got character. I'd rather have places like this than one of those soulless chains any day.'

'There's been a coffee shop on this site since the seventeenth century, give or take a few decades,' Nigel said.

'Really?'

'Yes. I mean, don't get me wrong, the coffee isn't that great, but at least it tastes like coffee. And it rather lacks for comfort in here, but it makes me feel better to know I'm supporting an independent place with a bit of history, rather than some faceless, corporate monolith.'

She smiled at him once more. 'Hear, hear.'

'You're a genealogist, then?' DCI Foster asked, cutting in impatiently, as if he hadn't heard the preceding exchange.

'More of a family historian,' Nigel replied.

'There's a difference, is there?'

'Only a bit. But you wouldn't believe how offended some people feel if you get it wrong.'

'Much money in it?'

Nigel shrugged. No, he thought. 'It's a living.'

'How do you get into something like that?'

'It depends,' Nigel answered. 'I did a history degree at uni, and during the summer holidays I did some research for a guy who traced people's family trees. I did it full time for a while. Then he dropped dead of a heart attack while giving a talk at a conference on early medieval finance, so I took over the business.'

Last year I tried to get out of it, he thought. But, like the Mafia, I was sucked back in.

'And enough people actually pay you to trace their ancestors?'

'Yeah. Genealogy's a very popular pursuit. The third most popular on the Internet. Behind porn and personal finance.'

Foster's face showed surprise.

'Or wanking and banking,' Nigel added. His face reddened immediately, unaware of how police officers reacted to smut.

DS Jenkins stifled a laugh; Foster smiled weakly.

Nigel felt the urge to smoke. The craving was too strong to ignore. He picked up his cigarette papers from the table. 'Mind if I . . . ?'

Heather gave her head a quick shake. He thought maybe she did mind. He felt a twang of disappointment for inciting her disapproval. But it would look pathetic to put away his fixings now, so he looked at Foster, who was staring intently at Nigel's pack of tobacco. In the absence of a complaint, Nigel plucked a paper from the packet.

'You ever traced your family tree at all?' he said as he placed a wad of tobacco in the crease and started to roll it out expertly between the forefinger and thumb of each hand.

Foster shook his head.

'My mum did,' DS Jenkins said. 'She hired you to do it for her.'

Nigel's eyes shot up from the cigarette he was rolling. 'Really? When?'

'Two or three years ago. That's how I got your number.'

Funnily enough, the reason they had chosen to call him, and not someone else, had simply not crossed his mind.

'Jenkins,' he said to himself. He could not remember and wondered whether he should pretend to, but realized she was sharp enough to know instantly whether he was bullshitting.

'It's all right. I don't expect you to recall my family tree,' she said, helping him out. 'I bet you've traced your family tree back to the Domesday Book or something, haven't you?' she added.

He shook his head. 'I can't trace my own father.'

'Your father?' Heather said, eyes widening.

'It's a long story.'

'Your mother's side?'

He shook his head once more. 'As I said, it's a long story.'

'Oh.' A wary look crept across her face.

'History has a habit of putting obstacles in your way,' he explained. 'It's one of the reasons I liked the job.'

Neither Heather nor Foster appeared to notice his use of the past tense.

'You get a real sense of achievement from helping people overcome those obstacles, track down relatives and ancestors they knew nothing about.'

Heather smiled at him. 'I can imagine you do.'

'I'm also interested in surnames: their origins, their meanings.'

'Really? What does Jenkins mean?'

'Kin of John. Or Jones, perhaps. "Kin" is Flemish in origin, but it's one of those names that doesn't really indicate an area or locality. Too popular, really. It was the forty-second commonest surname in America in 1939.'

'What about him, then?' she said, indicating Foster. 'What does his surname mean?'

Nigel pulled a face. 'Literal meaning is difficult to pin down, as is origin, the study of surnames being inexact, to say the least.'

'Fair enough,' Foster said, sitting forwards. 'About why we're here . . .'

'Oh, go on,' Heather interrupted. 'What about the name Foster?'

'There are several possibilities. It could be derived from a forester, a man who is in charge of a forest. Or someone who lived near a forest, or worked in a forest.'

Nigel thought it politic to leave out another explanation: one of Foster's ancestors was either a foster child or a foster parent.

'Fascinating,' Foster said, as if it was anything but. 'Now can we get on?' He looked at his colleague.

She spread her arms wide, as if to say, 'It's your show.'

'This morning we discovered a man's body. He'd been murdered. At the scene we discovered a reference written by the killer. We believe it refers to a birth, marriage or death certificate. We thought you could help us out.'

Nigel lit his roll-up and inhaled deeply. 'Could I see the reference?'

Foster shook his head slowly. 'No. But I can tell you what it was: 1A137.'

'Small "a" or capital?' Nigel asked.

'Capital.'

'Should strictly be a small "a". But it could be the reference for a birth, marriage or death certificate for central and west London issued between 1852 and 1946.'

'Why those specific areas? And why those dates?'

'Every district was given an index reference. Between the dates I mentioned 1a was assigned to Hampstead, Westminster, Marylebone, Chelsea, Fulham and Kensington.'

'The body was found in Kensington,' Heather said, looking across at Foster. 'Think there's anything in that?'

Foster rubbed his chin slowly. 'I don't think we can ignore it. Is there any way you can tell whether it's a birth, marriage or death certificate?'

'It could be any one of them,' Nigel replied.

'So could you go off and locate the certificate with this reference?'

'Yes, no problem. But we'd get thousands of results. This is simply a reference to a registration district and a page number. If I'm going to have any chance of finding the certificate quickly then I need to know an exact year, preferably a name. The Family

Records Centre has indexes going back as far as 1837.'

Both detectives sat back, frustrated. Heather took a sip of her coffee, while Foster stared at Nigel. The DCI sat forwards once more.

'We found the victim's mobile phone,' Foster said. 'The last-dialled number wasn't a telephone number; it was punched in after his death. We thought it might have been pressed by accident, when the body was moved. But perhaps it was put there intentionally.'

'What was the number?'

'1879.'

'1879,' Nigel said thoughtfully.

'Is that enough for you to go on?' Foster asked.

Nigel grimaced. 'Yes, but it won't be quick. A lot of people will have been born, married or died in 1879 in central and west London.'

'How long will that take?'

'A day. But then you have to order the certificates and wait for them to be copied and posted.'

'Can't we just go to the local register offices?'

'That reference is a General Register Office index number, not a local office one. It would be of no help there. If this *is* a reference to a birth, marriage or death certificate, then it was discovered through the central index.'

'Who handles that?' Foster asked.

'The General Register Office in Southport.'

'Southport? What the hell is it doing there?'

'London isn't the centre of the universe, sir,' Heather said.

'It is when you work for the Metropolitan Police.'

There was a pause while Foster thought. Nigel watched him earnestly. The DCI drummed his right finger on the table.

'Heather, get on the phone to headquarters. Get them to ask Merseyside Police to send a couple of officers to the GRO.' He turned to Nigel. 'What do they need to do?'

'Commandeer a couple of staff to pull the full certificates – once you've identified the ones you need – and pass the information on to you as quickly as possible.'

'Got that, Heather?' Foster asked.

She went upstairs to make her call. Both men watched her go.

'How busy are you at the moment?' Foster said.

'Relatively.'

'Well, can I hire you and your staff to hunt down these references for me?'

Nigel's cheeks flushed. 'There's a problem with my staff.'

'What?'

'I don't have one. Not at the moment. I . . .'

55

Foster held his hand up to stop him. 'Don't worry, Mr Barnes. I'll get you some help. They'll be with you first thing. What time does this records centre let people in?'

'Nine a.m.'

'They'll be waiting for the doors to open.'

Nigel experienced a feeling denied him for some time: excitement. For the first time in months, he couldn't wait to start a day's work.

6

It was after ten p.m. when Foster returned to his terraced house on a quiet, unspectacular street in Acton, too late to even think of going to the pub. He parked and then switched the engine off, but not the electrics so he could continue listening to the music. He didn't know the song; it was piped through the stereo via his personal music player, a small metallic gadget no bigger than a matchbox. There were more than a thousand tracks on it, few of which he knew. One of the guys at the station had downloaded them for him a few months before. You didn't have to build your own record collection these days, merely annex a friend's or even a complete stranger's off the Net. He couldn't remember what had happened to the boxes of vinyl he assembled as a teenager. His first single? 'Indiana Wants Me', R. Dean Taylor. The simple fact that the protagonist was on the lam infuriated his father, which is probably why he treasured it so. God knows where the record was now. He made a mental note to download it.

The car was warm, the lights on the dash illuminated

against the dark. He felt cocooned, as if he could recline the seat and sleep for hours. But, when the song finished, he turned the volume down to a murmur, picked up his mobile and called Khan to tell him to meet Heather at the FRC the next morning. Khan did not sound too enamoured at the prospect but Foster was beyond caring.

He climbed from the car, walked up the small paved path to his front door and unlocked it, flicking on the lights in the hall. He was relieved to see and smell that Aga, his Polish cleaner, had been that morning. He thumbed through some mail, found nothing interesting and added it to a growing pile of similar letters, then hung his coat up, took off his tie and jacket and went straight through to the kitchen, where he pulled the cork out of a half-drunk bottle of red wine that stood on the pine table in the middle of the clean tiled floor. He filled a vast glass. It was a '62 Cheval Blanc that had tasted a damn sight nicer the previous evening, but was still drinkable. Taste didn't matter so much: these days he needed at least a few glasses to ease his mind and body's nightly fight against sleep.

The wine wasn't his. None of the bottles were. His father, once he had retired from the force, sought a new passion and found it in wine, specifically Bordeaux. He collected bottles from all the best vintages, laying them down proudly, cataloguing them in a ledger. Occasionally, on special occasions, he would tootle off to the cellar, blow the dust off one he thought may drink well, open it up and serve it to his guests, offering alongside it a description of the vintage, the maker, whether it had been a good year and why, and some of the wine's characteristics. Then he would sip and savour just one glass during the course of a meal, sometimes making it last a whole evening. Among the last phrases he remembered his father saying to him – before he took the cocktail that ended his pain – was, 'Look after the cellar, son.'

'Sorry, Dad,' he muttered as he took another large slug, wincing at the acidic bite created by being left open twenty-four hours.

He wandered out of the kitchen and back into the hall, then turned into the sitting room. Occasionally, when he walked through the door, he detected a lingering hint of the lavender that formed part of the small bowls of potpourri his mother had left dotted around the place. They were one of the first things he threw out when he moved back into the house, on that drab November day a few weeks after his father's death. And they remained among the last. The walls bore ghostly imprints, grey-white traces of now unwanted photographs and pictures. The sideboards were bare apart from a few well-thumbed magazines, the odd book and a couple of empty candleholders. The only photograph on display in the room – in the entire house, as it turned out – was of Foster at his wedding, grinning with an insouciance he no longer recognized beside his best man and best mate, Charlie. They had been inseparable.

He cast his eyes around the room. Seven years ago he'd moved in. It still looked like he was lodging.

He thought about the day, the murder, the body; then he thought about Barnes. He'd asked Foster whether he was aware of his own family history. He wasn't, and he'd said as much. What was the point? But Barnes's question reminded him of his father. Of those last few days. That was his significant family history.

He headed over to the bureau in the far corner of the room, the place where his father used to sit and pore over his paperwork, glasses perched on the end of his nose, a cigarette balanced on the rim of an ashtray, spiralling smoke. He lowered the lid for the first time in years, the past leaping out. There was a cup with his father's pens, a half-shorn pad of writing paper, a Metropolitan Police paperweight detailing his years of service, 1954–1988, a letter opener in the shape of a sword and a photograph of Foster in short trousers, with his mum on Camber Sands. He stared at it for a few seconds then closed the bureau lid. Closed the past.

He collapsed on to the sofa and turned on the television, immediately muting the sound. He was tired, but he knew he was not yet ready to sleep. First he needed to switch off mentally, which meant emptying his head of all the thoughts swirling around in it.

They had nothing. The killer had left no detail, no trace, clue or weapon at the scene. No witnesses had yet come forward. There was no obvious motive. They had a reference carved on a chest, a number left on a mobile phone, a missing, severed pair of hands. That was all. They were still fumbling for a way in. Foster wanted to find the detail, the piece of information that would flick the switch and illuminate the investigation.

The house was silent, save for the odd creak from some shifting floorboard or the rattle of an ageing radiator. The first spots of rain spattered against the bay window. Foster took another hefty slurp of wine, and then went back into the kitchen to make sure there was more. There was: he could see the bold vermilion lettering of a Petrus, albeit one of the 1980s bottles, which he found a bit underwhelming compared to the complex vintages of other years, but that was why it was one of his favourites among his dad's collection. Who wants wine that tastes the same every year? Not him, and not least when there were another six years downstairs to drink.

The wine was doing some good, smoothing the edges. He looked around for something else to do, an activity to help the wine take his mind off the day so that he could sleep, wake up in the morning and get this case out of neutral. He sat at the kitchen table and fired up his computer, a sleek silver laptop dormant. Then he uncorked the Petrus and poured himself a glass without allowing it to open up, an act he knew would make oenophiles swoon. It tasted tight. He knew he should buy in some lesser-priced, easy-drinking wines for times like these, but he never remembered. He glanced at the clock on the wall. It was nearing eleven.

The computer was primed and ready for action. He opened his Internet connection and was straight on to the Net. Once online, the question was where to go. None of his favourite distractions appealed: Formula One racing websites, luxury car dealers and makers, spoof news sites. He checked his email but found only unsolicited invitations to enlarge his penis. As he pondered what to do, the images of the day seeped back into his mind, like smoke under a door.

One detail in particular: Why would someone not only commit murder but also sever the victim's hands while he was still alive, if not to inflict maximum pain? Someone truly hated Darbyshire.

His mobile rang, vibrating and trilling next to the bottle of wine on the sideboard. He answered it.

'Sir,' Drinkwater said.

'Yes, Andy.' Foster admired his young colleague's stamina. He'd been the first at the scene that morning and was still at it.

'Notting Hill have picked up the tramp who lived in the churchyard. Sheena Carroll, aka Ciderwoman. She went back to the churchyard for the night. They've got her at the station now.'

'What state is she in?'

'Roaring pissed, apparently. I could go and have a word with her tonight. If I don't get anywhere, we could always try again in the morning.'

Foster was tempted to let him handle it. It meant he could get some rest. If the call had come ten minutes later, he might have already been asleep. As it was, he was dressed and still – hopefully, at least – under the limit. And he knew he could force himself to stay awake for another hour or two.

'I'll meet you at Notting Hill in half an hour,' he said eventually.

*

Foster walked into the interview room at Notting Hill police station and was almost floored by Ciderwoman's pungent scent, an unholy trinity of booze, grime and urine. She was sitting at the table, slouched back in her chair. Guessing her age was impossible. Her ravaged, pink face might have been anywhere between forty-five and sixty-five. Her sagging skin looked as if it had tired of being attached to her body and was heading south. Her black hair was matted and few of her teeth were their original white. She looked up at Foster when he entered and scowled, her piggy eyes boring into him.

'What the fuck do you want?' she spat out, the words tumbling into each other as they fell haphazardly from her mouth.

Inwardly he smiled: he knew immediately that she was a frazzled, cantankerous drunk, and not mentally ill – though it was too early to gauge the effects of a two-litre bottle of cheap cider a day on her psyche.

'And what the fuck are you keeping me here for?' she asked before he could answer. Her voice sounded as if she had been gargling with gravel.

'Well, you might be able to help us, Sheena,' he explained, sitting down. 'Which'd be a first.'

'It'll cost you a fucking cigarette,' she said.

'That's a price I'm willing to pay.' He turned to

Drinkwater and motioned for him to purloin a few fags from someone who smoked.

'So, how can I help, Officer?' The last word was hopelessly mangled.

'You'll have noticed that your bedroom is closed to the public. That's because we found the body of a man there earlier today. In exactly the same spot where you usually doss down. He'd been murdered.'

'Nothing to do with me,' she said instantly.

'Didn't say it was, did I, Sheena? Does anyone else doss down there?'

She shook her head vigorously. 'Wouldn't fucking dare,' she said. 'It's my pitch. The only other people who go in there are a couple of kids. Smoke dope in the middle of the night.' She smiled, a train wreck of a smile – all mangled, with yellow teeth or blackened stumps. 'And the little bastards never give me any.'

There was a wheezing, rattling sound that seemed to emanate from the ground. It was Ciderwoman laughing. It culminated in a coughing fit, which ended with her spitting violently into her hand just as Drinkwater walked in with a couple of John Players. Once she had wiped her mouth, Ciderwoman tugged both from his hand and lit one. She inhaled mightily, like a diver about to go under.

'Yes,' Foster said, once the charade was over. 'They found the body. The question is, Sheena: where were you? I've been led to believe you sleep there every night. Why not Tuesday night? Or last night, even?'

In three large drags she had smoked almost half the cigarette. She blew the smoke upwards. 'Because I was told not to,' she said.

Foster leaned forwards. 'By who?'

'A man.'

'Which man?'

'How the fuck should I know? Some gadgey like you.'

'What do you mean? Did he look like me?'

She shrugged. 'Can't remember,' she said, taking another drag.

'What did this guy say?'

She paused to think. 'He said there was going to be some sort of clean-up. That they were gonna come down like a sack of shit on all the people sleeping rough, so I'd better clear off for a couple of days.'

'And you believed him?'

'Why the fuck not?' she said, looking indignant. 'He said he worked for Shelter, or something like that, and he didn't want to see me banged up.'

'Did he show you a card?'

She shook her head. Before she extinguished her cigarette, she put the second one in her mouth and lit it with the stub of the first.

'When was this?'

'I've only been away for two nights, so it was . . .'

'Tuesday,' Foster said, helping her out.

'If you say so.'

'Listen, Sheena, we think the guy who spoke to you might have been linked to this murder. Can you remember anything about him?'

She puffed silently on her cigarette. 'It was early afternoon,' she said. 'I'm never at my best then. He wasn't wearing a suit, because I would've thought he was the Old Bill and told him to fuck off. No disrespect.'

Foster made a gesture with his hands to indicate none was taken.

'He was dressed sort of casual,' she added.

'Any distinguishing features?'

She thought some more. 'He didn't smoke,' she added hopefully. 'I think I asked him for a ciggie and he said he didn't smoke.'

That narrows it down, Foster thought.

'He gave me a quid, too. Or, at least, I think he did.'

'Really,' Foster said eagerly. 'Do you still have it?'

'What the fuck do you think?' she said. 'I don't have much in the way of savings.'

He knew there was nothing more to be garnered from the conversation. 'My colleague will go through a description with you,' he told her, avoiding

Drinkwater's eye. 'Try and remember as much as you can.'

He got up and left. Outside he sucked in the night air. The black sky was clear, though not clear enough for him to make out the stars above the London smog. He remembered his unease that morning over the use of a churchyard as a dumping ground for murder, and how it did not seem right – not with all the houses overlooking the scene. Now he knew the killer had cased the place because he knew how difficult his task would be.

Yet he still went ahead with it.

7

Nigel was sweating as he bustled his way along Exmouth Market, lazily coming to life in the chilly spring sunshine. He was late. The centre would already be open and he was wasting police time. I'll blame the tube, he thought, not the fact that my alarm clock requires winding, and last night I forgot.

As he reached the edge of the market, where it met Myddelton Street, he could see Heather, hands on hips, standing by the steps and ramp that led to the entrance of the building. He increased his pace even further, his satchel bouncing rhythmically on his hip so that, by the time he reached her, he could feel his clammy shirt sticking to his back. He was struggling for breath.

'Sorry,' he gasped.

Her look was one of amusement. Her gaze was not directed at his sweating brow, however. It was below that.

'You're wearing tweed,' she said simply.

He was. Grey herringbone jacket over an open-necked striped shirt, navy-blue cords. He thought it best to make an effort, even though the jacket was second-hand, and leave behind the jumpers, jeans and duffel coat.

'Is that OK?'

She nodded and shot him a smile. 'It suits you. You've got that bookish, floppy-haired thing happening.'

She was wearing a short black skirt, black tights and a pair of black knee-length boots. Nigel was worried a few of the older gentlemen who used the records centre might keel over.

'Have you two finished swapping fashion tips?' A young confident-looking Asian man in a suit, his hair gelled back, had joined them.

'Nigel, this is DC Khan,' Heather said.

The men shook hands. Despite her reassurance, Heather's look and comment had made him feel self-conscious. Given that he had yet to cool down, he wondered if his face had reddened.

'After you,' he said, and pointed his hand towards the door.

Once inside, security checked Nigel's bags and they made their way into the main area. The place was already filling up.

'I never thought this place would be so busy,' Khan said, surveying the bustling interior. 'It's like Piccadilly Circus.'

Nigel nodded. 'You should see it at a weekend. Fights break out over files.'

'They don't look like the sort of people who get in a ruck,' Khan said. 'More likely to bore you into submission.'

Nigel smiled, yet felt mildly insulted. Yes, he was often scathing about the sorts of people who pursued their ancestors fanatically; the type more comfortable retreating into the silent, quiescent world of the dead, rather than dwelling in the awkward, insolent present. But the world today was awash with information about the wealthy, the famous and the tawdry. Somebody has to help remember the anonymous ordinary men and women, who make the world turn.

'So what's the brief?' Khan asked, rubbing his hands together.

They moved across to one of the enclaves housing around twenty years of bound, red birth-certificate indexes, arranged chronologically on solid wooden shelves.

'I'm going to go through the birth indexes; you'll do marriage and, Heather, you're going to do death.'

'Very appropriate,' Khan muttered darkly.

'The method for searching the files is the same,' Nigel said, eager to get started: he knew he could rattle through the birth files in a few hours.

He pulled a bulky file off the top shelf, its leather cover battered and torn by use, and put it down on an upturned V-shaped wooden desk with a lip at the bottom to prevent the volume slipping off.

'This is the birth index file for 1879, the first quarter, January to April,' he said, pointing to the print on the spine.

He opened the first page. Both Heather and Khan leaned in for a closer look. The page was smudged and grey from thousands of fingertips tracing down it in search of an elusive name, the bottom right-hand corner stiff and brittle from where people had wet their fingers to be better able to turn the page.

'Luckily for us, the entries for 1879 have been typed so they all fit in one volume.'

'There are loads of names on that page,' Khan said, without relish.

Nigel shrugged. 'The entries are listed alphabetically: first the surname, then the Christian names. But the columns we are interested in are the district and page number, 1a137 in this case. Whenever you see that number, jot down the details and make a note of which quarter it's in. Is that clear enough?'

'Think so,' Heather said. 'Does that apply to them all?'

'More or less. Your death indexes have an extra bit of information: age at death. Write that down, too. DC Khan, your marriage index will be the same as this index.'

'Hopefully with fewer names,' Khan replied.

Three hours later, Nigel went downstairs to the canteen. Heather and Khan were waiting for him. Both seemed animated.

'How did it go?' he said, sitting down.

'Heather's in shock,' Khan explained.

'Why?'

'I can't believe how many kids died at birth,' she said, eyes wide. 'On every page, there must have been at least one where it said zero under "age at death". Unbelievable. God, we have it easy. I mean, my mate Claire had a kid six months ago, and she was in labour for more than forty hours. *Forty!* Eventually she had an emergency Caesarean. If that had been a hundred or so years ago then the baby would have died.'

'She probably would have, too.'

Heather nodded and bit her lip. 'Shocking. And while I was facing up to the horrific reality of infant mortality in Victorian England, Simon Schama here was jotting down all the silly names he came across.'

Khan picked up his notebook. 'Listen to this: Smallpiece, Shufflebottom, Daft . . . Daft! Come on, if your name was Daft, you'd change it, wouldn't you? But this is the best one: Fuchs. For Fuchs sake!'

He started to laugh. Nigel smiled. Heather's face remained stern.

'You're a big bloody kid, you know that?' she said, though a smile was playing on her lips. She turned once again to Nigel. 'He's like this now after less than a year as a detective. You just wait: in ten years' time he'll be as jaded and cynical as Foster.'

'But I'll have more hair.'

'Have you finished your searches?' Nigel asked.

Heather shook her head. 'I'm up to September, but that's only because the April to June file is missing.'

'Being repaired?'

'Yes, I asked at the information desk and they checked. It'll be back next Monday, all being well. Let's hope what we need isn't in there.'

'That's quite common,' Nigel said. 'They get touched by a lot of grubby hands every day.'

'So does . . .'

'Don't even think of cracking that joke, Maj,' Heather interrupted, raising a finger in warning.

Khan adopted a mock-angelic look. 'Would I?'

Heather ignored him.

'I've nearly finished,' he added.

'Well, I *have* finished so I can give you both a hand,' Nigel said.

Heather looked at him, eyebrows raised. 'That was quick.'

He shrugged. Nigel did not want to tell her that he had once searched through 163 years of indexes in 5 hours; or that he had once traced a bloodline back to 1837 in a single day, relying on his speed and a few hunches.

'Who's going to phone them through to Southport when we're done?' he asked.

'I'm going to fax them from the office here,' Heather explained. 'I'll do them all together, so we'll hang on till we're all done.'

'Hello, Nigel.'

The voice was behind his right shoulder, out of his sight, but he recognized it instantly.

'Hi, Dave,' he said, before even looking around.

Sure enough, it was Dave Duckworth. Overweight, perennially sweaty, monobrowed Dave Duckworth. He had worked with Nigel at the agency before the old man died.

'So, Nigel, I hear Branches Agency, like Lazarus, has risen from the dead.'

Their paths had not crossed in the three weeks since Nigel had returned.

'You hear right, Dave.'

Dave wore a look of fake surprise. 'So am I to infer that the wisdom of a certain N. Barnes failed to take the world of academia by storm?'

'Something like that.'

Dave smiled broadly, then nodded at Khan and Heather. 'But, it appears that you have been sufficiently remunerated as to actually hire some staff.'

Nigel could see Heather's eyes narrow. Hers was the type of face that was quick to display emotion. She both daunted and fascinated him.

Before Nigel could introduce them both, Dave leapt in. 'I jest, of course.'

Heather's smile dripped insincerity. Nigel could tell she thought him a creep. He couldn't fault her judgement of character.

'I know you're police officers,' Dave added.

No one said anything.

'It's the talk of the FRC, how you rolled up with half of CID. What's the undertaking?'

'I think you'll find that's confidential, Mr . . . ?' Heather said.

'Duckworth. Dave Duckworth,' he said, thrusting out his right hand. 'If you require any further expert help, then don't hesitate to give me a bell.' He pulled a couple of his cards from a brown leather wallet.

'Thank you, Mr Duckworth,' Heather responded icily. 'Mr Barnes is doing a good job but we'll bear your offer in mind.'

'Please do,' he said, beaming a smile, before turning

to Nigel once more. 'Could we have a brief tête-à-tête?'

'I'm busy, Dave.'

'Ten seconds. No more.'

'Excuse me,' Nigel said to the detectives.

He followed Duckworth to the wall by the locker rooms, wondering what it was he wanted. Something to do with money, he guessed. It was Dave Duckworth's god. His whole career, his whole life, was dedicated to making it. Jobs were not judged by the quality of the research, but by the quantity of the payment. Nigel never sensed any love of the past in Dave, the thrill of the search, an interest in the stories of the dead, only a need to obtain as much work, and therefore as much cash, as possible. No one knew what Dave spent it on. He dressed cheaply, had no social life to speak of, and was notoriously thrifty. Nigel pictured him sitting at home in his fetid flat counting piles of coins with a thimble.

'I really am in the middle of something, Dave,' Nigel said, wearily.

'I know. You're in the middle of a murder investigation.'

For a second, Nigel was speechless. 'How do you know that?'

Dave, infuriatingly, tapped his nose. 'That's for

me to know, Nigel, and you and your friends to find out. More pressing is, what do we do next?'

'What do you mean?'

Dave leaned in closer, breaching personal space. Nigel didn't like it: there was a strong smell of rancid coffee on his breath.

'I mean, how about we inform one of my contacts among the fourth estate, brief them as to what's going on here and receive an emolument for our trouble?' he whispered.

'How much do you know, Dave?'

'That it's something to do with the murder a couple of nights ago in Notting Hill.'

'I still don't know how you know.'

'That doesn't matter. As I said, the question is what happens next.'

Nigel straightened himself up. He looked across; Heather was staring at them both.

'What happens next is this: I tell you to fuck off, Dave. I've got a job to do.' He left Duckworth and went back to the table.

Heather gave him a look of concern. 'Everything OK?' she asked.

Nigel took a deep breath. 'Yeah, he's just an old colleague.'

'You don't exactly seem to be the best of friends.'

He shrugged. 'Small world, professional genealogy

and research. All chasing the same money, things get a bit competitive.'

He held back from telling her that Duckworth made most of his money these days doing the bidding of national newspapers. Whenever someone became news, the tabloids would be on the blower, asking him to research their family history, see if there were any skeletons in the closet, or help them track down other family members to speak to. Before leaving for the university, Nigel had worked for the press a few times, though he'd always loathed himself for it. But the money compensated for that.

'How did he know we were police?'

'I don't know. Perhaps someone at the GRO, or in the centre here.'

She shook her head. 'No one knows about the reference outside the team. Apart from you.'

Heather had swiftly mastered the art of making Nigel feel uncomfortable. As if realizing this, her face softened and she gave him a warm smile.

'Don't worry, Nigel. We don't reckon you've told him. Christ, we only told you eighteen or so hours ago and you've barely been out of our sight since. Perhaps you could use your skills of persuasion to find out his source?'

'Consider it done,' he said earnestly. 'I don't think he knows about the reference or he would have told me. He's the sort of guy who can't hide things, especially if he thinks he can lord it over you.'

'So what did he want?'

'Talked a bit of shop.'

Khan intervened. 'We should tell Foster. Warn him that the press might get this.'

'Get what?' Heather asked. 'All he can say is that detectives were at the Family Records Centre. It means nothing. We could be tracing our family trees for all he knows, some sort of police genealogy drive. Let the little creep do his worst.'

DC Khan stood up and went to the Gents. Heather looked at Nigel.

'So what was that about the "world of academia"?'

He enjoyed her interest in him, but she was veering too close to an area he wished to avoid. Nothing Duckworth said seemed to have gone unnoticed by her.

'Eighteen months ago I gave this up. It wasn't panning out the way I expected. I got an offer to work at Middlesex University, setting up a course in family history. Things didn't work out,' he explained, not wanting to go into any more detail.

'You got fed up with genealogy?'

'Running a business doing other people's genealogy.'

'But you're back doing it.'

Yes I am, he thought. Except now I'm working for the police on a murder case and it feels like a shot at redemption.

'Come on,' he said. 'Let's find the rest of those certificates.'

8

By early afternoon Heather had faxed through the references for 457 birth, death and marriage certificates. The most Nigel had ever ordered at the end of one day was seventeen. It had taken four days before he could collect the copies. The 457 were all found, copied and faxed through to West London Murder Command in less than two hours.

Nigel was told to meet at murder squad HQ in Kensington at four p.m. He was there ten minutes early. He announced himself downstairs to a woman on the desk and was told to take a seat. He had nothing to read and there was nothing on the table for him to flick through, but then this was hardly the dentist's.

Heather finally emerged from a lift and passed him through the security gate. They ascended several floors, stopping at an open-plan office. Only a few people were milling about, some on the phones, a few more staring at their computer screens. Nigel expected more activity, hubbub, not the sort of inertia you would witness in a provincial insurance office.

The only giveaway that this was the incident room at the heart of a murder investigation was at the back of the room: a large whiteboard, which was attracting Nigel's appalled fascination long before they turned right and started walking towards it.

A series of photographs was arranged on it, two rows of two, surrounded by notes scribbled in red pen. As he neared he could see the pictures were of a person, a body. Darbyshire's. Nigel had never seen a corpse before. Without thinking, he stopped, stomach lurching. The first picture top left was of the dead man's corpse at the scene, clad in a pinstripe suit. Only the pallid, lifeless face and the pale blue lips gave any indication that the man had not just passed out. The next was more graphic. Taken from a position just below the victim's feet, Nigel could clearly make out two ragged stumps, white bone protruding where the hands had been removed.

His eyes fell on the next picture, a close-up of a naked chest, showing a small scar. The knife wound, he assumed. The last was of a series of marks and cuts; he could make out no order until he realized that it was the reference he'd been working on that day.

Nigel turned and looked at Heather.

She held his arm, squeezed it softly, then turned away. 'Come on,' she urged gently.

Nigel fell in behind her, casting a last glance back at the whiteboard.

They went to the left-hand corner of the office, across a small corridor and through a large door. The meeting room was bare apart from a wooden table in the middle. DCI Foster was there, sitting on one end of the table, scanning a certificate. He nodded at Nigel, his glance flickering with concern.

'You look like shit,' he said.

'We just walked past the whiteboard,' Heather explained.

'Sit down there.' Foster pulled out a chair with his foot. When Nigel sat, he got up, reached over to the tray in the middle of the table and poured a tea. 'Sugar?'

Nigel shook his head, the images still haunting his mind. 'I've never seen a dead person before,' he mumbled.

Foster put the cup in front of him.

'It gets easier,' Heather said. 'But not much.'

'I think I'll stick with death certificates. Less messy,' he added, looking up at her.

'Definitely less messy,' she repeated. Again the smile was warm. Other than the thrill and the excitement, he was finding another reason why he wanted to stick around this murder investigation for as long as he was allowed.

Nigel sipped a lukewarm mouthful of tea as Foster pointed to another man in the room, who Nigel hadn't noticed. He was tall, well-built, in his mid-thirties, blandly handsome.

'This is DI Andy Drinkwater.'

They shook hands.

DI, Nigel thought. Detective Inspector. A rank below Foster, one above Heather.

'DI Drinkwater and DS Jenkins will be helping you go through this pile of certificates. I have to do a press conference with the victim's widow in front of a mass of reptiles, all of them wanting to know one thing: Did she do it?' He peeled his coat from the back of the chair. 'And before you ask. No, she didn't.'

Nigel felt the shock at seeing the whiteboard's contents begin to wear off. The surname of the detective to whom he'd just been introduced finally registered with him. 'Your surname's Drinkwater?'

The detective eyed him suspiciously. 'Yes,' he said slowly.

'I've never met a Drinkwater.'

'Really,' said Drinkwater slowly.

'It's not a common name any more. Do you know what it means?'

'No.'

'It's a very interesting name,' Nigel said.

'It'll be about the only thing interesting about Andy,' Foster interrupted. He'd paused at the door, wanting to hear the etymology of his junior's surname.

Drinkwater gave him a sardonic smile. 'Why's it interesting?'

'There are two theories: either your ancestors lived in such poverty that they could not afford to buy beer, they could only drink water . . .'

'Or?' Drinkwater asked, curiosity aroused.

'Or your ancestor was such a drunk that he was given the name "drink water" ironically.'

'It's not ironic any more,' Foster said derisively. 'Andy here doesn't drink, spends his time working out and running on treadmills with all the other pod people.' He grinned. 'That's made my day.'

Foster left for the press conference.

Drinkwater was smiling. 'Thanks for that, Mr Barnes,' he said half seriously and sat down.

On the table were three piles of paper: birth, marriage and death certificates.

'Nigel, you take the marriage certificates.'

'Are we looking for anything in particular?' he asked.

Drinkwater shrugged. 'Anything that has anything to do with the murder. The name, Darbyshire, or the location, St John's Church: there might be a few who got married there. Put them to one side and we can have another look at them.'

He picked up a certificate and the room became silent. Nigel could hear voices coming from else-where, the persistent ringing of phones, but the three of them sat and sifted through the documents with-out saying a single word, reading and rereading, checking every name, every address, every witness on every form for any link. During the course of the next few hours, several links began to turn up: Drinkwater found the birth certificate of a girl who lived on St John's Crescent; Nigel a couple of marriages that took place at St John's Church. These formed the basis of a meagre pile requiring further inquiry. Heather found nothing relevant; it was heavy going. Many of the causes of death listed on the certificates were conditions she had never heard of, described in terms no longer used.

Nigel found it enthralling. The thrill of the chase had always been the job's main attraction, yet here the rewards were even greater, the purpose more noble. He scanned each document. His pile was reducing more quickly than the other two. For a second he thought he might be going too fast, but then he realized he was the only one used to reading the handwriting and scrutinizing the documents at a glance. Yet he had not come across anything he deemed significant and wondered whether he should have subjected the discarded documents to closer scrutiny.

'Bingo!' Heather shouted, startling the other two.

'What?' Drinkwater asked.

She held her finger up to quieten him as she reread the form. 'Bloody hell,' she said, inserting an emphatic 'a' between the 'b' and 'l' to show her surprise. 'Jesus!' She scrabbled in the pocket of her jacket on the back of the chair and found her mobile. She dialled quickly.

'Tell us what it is, Heather,' Drinkwater demanded.

Without speaking she tossed the certificate in front of him. 'Sir, it's Jenkins,' she said into the phone. 'Get back here as soon as you can. We've found it.'

Nigel watched as Foster, lounging on the table, his tie pulled loose from his neck, read the death certificate.

'It's got to be it, hasn't it?' Foster said eventually, looking at Heather and Drinkwater.

The certificate belonged to an Albert Beck, a 32-year-old tanner of Clarendon Road, North Kensington. He had been found stabbed to death in the grounds of St John's Church, Ladbroke Grove on 29th March 1879. The day James Darbyshire's body had been discovered.

Foster stared at the certificate, pulling at his bottom lip.

'We need to see if we have anything in our archives about this crime,' he said at last.

Drinkwater scribbled in his notebook.

Nigel had been quiet ever since Foster arrived. 'Much of the Metropolitan Police archives were destroyed in the Blitz. I think you'll find that the records from the second half of the nineteenth century were decimated.'

Foster nodded. 'Thanks. But get someone to check it out, Andy.' He turned to Nigel. 'The killer must have seen this death certificate, or known of it in order to have led us to it, correct?'

Nigel nodded.

'And you said this reference was from the central index. Does that mean he or she could only have ordered it from the Family Records Centre?'

'Not necessarily,' Nigel replied. 'There are several websites where you can browse the indexes online, though it costs you; or you can order online from the GRO.'

'Anywhere else?'

'There's always a possibility they already owned the death certificate.'

'What do you mean?'

'It's in the family; they could be related to the dead man. Or it could simply have fallen into their possession.'

'Let's discount that for now. For all the other possibilities, the person would have had to order it and get it sent to an address?'

'Unless they paid for it at the FRC and collected it a few days later.'

Foster went back to scanning the document, as if it would yield more secrets the longer he stared at it. 'Well, that gives us something to work on,' he said to his two officers. 'We need to get someone along to the FRC, get hold of any CCTV footage, find out if anyone else has ordered this certificate, who they were, OK?'

Drinkwater left the room.

Foster looked at Nigel. 'There is something else you can do for us, which sort of relates to your last theory about how the killer got hold of the certificate. Is it possible to trace someone's family going forwards? Not their ancestors but their descendants?'

Nigel nodded. 'It's called the "bounceback technique". You go back in time to trace the path of someone's family to the present day.'

'So you could trace the living descendants of Albert Beck?'

'No problem.'

'Will you go and do that?'

Nigel had his bag and coat in his hand before Foster finished his request.

The last train chased into the night. He could hear the great clank and wheeze of its infernal engine while he stood, waiting, at the dark secluded end of the street, his eyes fixed on the Elgin. The warm orange glow of its light poured out, illuminating the dark wall of the convent across the street. The door occasionally flapped open and the drunken chatter and laughter would waft its way towards him. He jerked his head sharply to the right, feeling his neck click. He'd watched them come and go, many of them, but not yet the perfect one.

The one that strayed.

The sulphur stink of the underground train was in his nostrils. He shuddered. Out of curiosity, he had ridden it once. It was worse than he imagined: Hades on wheels. It had been the previous summer. The weather intolerably warm, barely a cough of wind to chase away the heat and smoke. He descended the stairs at Baker Street with fear in his heart. The first rush and roar of the train, the hot blast as it steamed in, all of it damn near had him running back up the wooden steps; but he ventured on.

Underground, in that coffin on tracks, he knew the devil was with him. The decadent, the godless, the drunks and the whores; it was their chosen chariot. Around him men smoked their pipes, the smoke billowing through the airless carriage, mingling with the foul odour of the gas lamps. As they passed west they were plunged alternately into bright, eye-blasting light and profound darkness. He lasted two stops in the fetid atmosphere before he thought asphyxiation would claim him. At Paddington he emerged, gulping in great lungfuls of air. I'll go to Hell when the Lord tells me and not before, he vowed, and had not been anywhere near it since. He wasn't alone in his fear; most people he knew hated the thing.

Then he saw him leave. The perfect one. He stepped out of the pub, staggered forwards, righted himself, and then lurched to the side. He kept out of sight as the man stuttered across the Grove. Great drunken fool could barely lift his head. The drunk reeled towards the station; he stepped from the shadows to follow. He wondered where the chase would lead; north of the station, into the farmlands and fields of Notting Barn? That would be perfect: they were building streets there, rows and rows of townhouses for the rich folk brought in by the underground and its feeder railway.

But no. Just before the station, the drunk took a left. He kept his distance, was able to give thanks to another night without the fog, but quickened his pace when he saw they were reaching the area where the lights became scarce. The man swayed and he felt himself smile; this was too easy.

His quarry crossed the road, away from the track, to the verge beside the underground line. There was dark sodden earth. Away from the light, he found it hard to find him, but his eyes adjusted and he could see why the drunk had listed towards the dark: he needed to urinate. He stopped and looked behind: nothing, not a peep. The drunk was staggering over the verge, up a dirt track that would soon be a road. The empty husks of a few houses were around them, silhouettes in the pitch-black night. He watched the man stop near a wall and could hear the drill of urine hit the sopping ground.

From his pocket he pulled the knife, clutching it tight in his hand. His last few steps were bounding and cat-like, swallowing the ground between them. The drunk was shaking himself dry, unaware of danger, lifting his head to drink in the night air. As he did so, his pursuer wrapped his left arm around his throat, dragging him back, and the knife was plunged deep into his chest. He barely made a noise, other than a grunt, before he sank to the ground.

His night's work done, he slipped back into the tar-black night . . .

9

By the time Nigel left the station on Friday, the Family Records Centre was closed. When the doors opened on Saturday morning he was waiting outside eagerly. He was relishing the day ahead, wondering what secrets and lies would be disinterred. The new guy – Phil, Nigel thought his name was – was behind the customer inquiries counter, whistling the tune to 'One Day At A Time' by Lena Martell. Nigel nodded as he walked past.

'Made quite a stir yesterday,' Phil said.

'Who did?' Nigel answered innocently, even though he knew exactly what Phil was referring to.

'Your friends from the Met. What's the crime?'

'Nothing much,' Nigel lied. 'Just helping them out with a bit of research.'

Phil nodded while leafing through a pile of documents. He still hadn't looked at Nigel.

'Good work if you can get it, eh?' he said, finally making eye contact, his face round and friendly.

'I suppose,' Nigel said, wondering if Duckworth had been his less than reticent self.

Phil went back to sorting his pile of documents. As he wandered over to the birth indexes, Nigel could hear Phil begin whistling the first few bars of 'Coward Of The County' by Kenny Rogers.

He was looking forward to the search, intrigued by what he might discover. It was this sense of expectation that he enjoyed most about the job. Like a potato plant, the best part of family history lies beneath the surface. By digging deep, the stories of the dead, silent through the years, could be told once more.

Yet immediately he faced a problem. Given his age on the death certificate – thirty-two – Nigel thought Beck might have been born in 1846 or 1847. Yet he could not find the birth of a single Albert Beck during those years. This was no surprise; it was not compulsory to register births, marriages and deaths until 1865, so not everyone did. Scanning the marriage indexes from 1865 onwards, Nigel had better luck. In September 1873 he had married. A call to the police hotline at the GRO revealed his wife was named Mary Yarrow.

Nigel used this information upstairs at the FRC. The 1881 census is held electronically on a database on one of the terminals in the census room, which houses all the censuses from 1841 to 1901. He knew that Beck, being dead, would not be listed, but he hoped that his widow, and whatever children the couple had, would still be at the Clarendon Road address. He could then acquire the ages of their children and track them through the following census returns, discover who they married and whether they had any children of their own.

'Where are you, where are you?' he muttered to himself as he keyed in the search terms, a familiar refrain of his at the beginning of a quest. He was waiting for that one discovery, the detail, the name, the entry that would help him unravel the past.

There it was, on Clarendon Road. Mary was listed as head of the household. There were two children: a daughter, Edith, who was five on census night 1881; and a son, Albert (at least the name lived on), who was three. Interestingly, a John Arnold Smith, thirty-four, was listed as a lodger. Nigel guessed he might be the new man in Mary's life. Life as a widow with two children in mid-Victorian England would be tough, almost impossible to survive without the mercy of the parish, the looming gothic turrets of the workhouse casting a shadow over every step. A man around the house was essential. However, living in sin was not a fact you wished to advertise, hence the reason they would have neglected to tell the census numerators.

Part of Nigel hoped his hunch was wrong; if Mary was living with, and then chose to marry, her 'lodger', her surname and that of her children would have changed to Smith, making tracing their descendants virtually impossible because of the millions and millions of Smiths who would have been born, married or died in the next 125 years.

Back downstairs he searched the indexes of 1881 onwards for the marriage of a Mary Beck and John Smith. Unfortunately, he found it, in the summer of 1882. A new address was given for the couple, in Kensington. Nigel went back upstairs to the 1891 census and managed to track down the Smiths. The couple appeared to have had two children of their own, but one of the Beck children seemed to have disappeared. Edith was there, aged fifteen; yet there was no mention of Albert junior. Nigel managed to solve that mystery with a quick check of the death indexes: young Albert had died of tuberculosis in 1885, aged six, leaving only Edith from her first marriage.

Life was not proving kind to Mary. Nigel could picture her, weatherbeaten face drawn, aged before its time, the misery of losing first her husband then her only son etched across her features in the downward turn of her mouth and the dullness of her eyes. But she would have borne her tragedies and her life of quiet desperation with dignity and without self-pity, because so many like her did. These people did not parade or exhibit their emotions; nor did they seek to blame anyone for their misfortunes. Stoicism, forbearance, sobriety – these were often the words that sprang to his mind when he was blowing the dust off long-forgotten lives, in sharp contrast to the emotional incontinence he perceived in the modern world.

Only Edith was left of Albert's offspring. At least it narrowed his options. Given she was fifteen in 1891, he calculated that she would be twenty-five in 1901 and there was every chance she would be married by then. Before he searched the marriage indexes – and the idea of dredging through hundreds of thousands of Edith Smiths to find the right one made his heart sink – he gambled on her not being married by 1901. He typed in the Kensington address and there they were: Mary Smith, John Arnold Smith, Edith Smith. Perhaps Edith was not marriage material, Nigel thought. He pictured a plain, dowdy young woman, lonely and unloved. He hoped he was wrong and that eventually she had married, and not simply because it would prolong the search.

His only option was to trawl the marriage indexes for the next twenty years, until 1921, when Edith would have been forty-five and too old to bear children. It took him two hours to list the details of the nineteen Edith Smiths who were married in the

Marylebone district between the Aprils of 1901 and 1921. He went outside and phoned these to the GRO, and mentioned that he was looking only for an Edith Smith whose father's name on the marriage certificate was given as either Albert Beck or John Smith, a railway signalman. They said it would take some time to pull nineteen marriage certificates. Three-quarters of an hour later he got the call to tell him that neither of the two possible fathers' names was recorded on any of the certificates. Edith Smith was almost certainly a spinster; the pitiful picture he had created in his mind wasn't fanciful.

He went down to the canteen to clear his head of the names and the dates before ringing Foster. He got himself a plastic cup of scalding brown water and sat down.

'Hello, Nigel,' a voice said hopefully.

Nigel turned and was greeted by a man in a brown suit with slicked-back hair. He knew him. Gary Kent, a reporter from the *London Evening News*. He'd hired Nigel a few times to poke around in people's pasts. He expected to bump into Duckworth, unsavoury as the prospect was: but he'd hoped never to encounter Kent again.

'Hello, Gary,' he said suspiciously.

'Been a while, hasn't it?'

'It has.'

'I hear the job at the university fell through.'

'Been speaking to Dave, then?'

Kent tapped his nose theatrically. 'So does that mean you're back in use?'

Nigel shook his head. 'No, straight genealogy for me.'

'Well, that's not strictly true, is it? You're working for the cops.'

Duckworth, Nigel thought. He said nothing.

'Look, I'm interested in the story,' Kent said. 'Why have the Met hired you to work on the Notting Hill slaying?'

'My indiscreet days are over, Gary. No comment.'

He knew Kent would not leave it there.

'There must be some sort of family history angle there. You know I'll find out: the cops are leakier than a Russian submarine. You might as well make a few quid from it while you can.'

'I'm not saying anything. Not today, not tomorrow. Not forever. My days being your lapdog are over.'

Kent shook his head ruefully.

'Duckworth's cleaning up all the press work. You really want that fat toad lording it over you every time you see him?'

'He's welcome to it.'

'What happened at that university to make you so holier-than-thou all of a sudden? Maybe I should make a few calls, have a poke around. There could be a story in it, particularly now you're working for the forces of law and order.'

Nigel wondered whether he knew, whether he had already made those calls. 'Do your worst, Gary.'

Kent shrugged and sucked in air between his teeth. 'Shame. As I said, this genealogy game is pretty popular. Our newspaper might be looking for someone to do a piece or two about it. Maybe troubleshooting a few readers' problems, some sort of ancestral agony aunt. Pains me to say it, but you could do all right if they need a photogenic young expert: twinkling blue eyes, good cheekbones, full head of hair, pair of glasses that make you look clever.'

'Flattery will get you nowhere, Gary.'

Kent just stared at him, nodding as if he understood exactly what Nigel was doing, as if every word confirmed his expectations. 'You obviously feel some loyalty to the police,' he said, tossing his business card on to the table in front of Nigel. 'Which reminds me. You must pass on my regards to DCI Foster.' He turned to leave, but looked back over his shoulder. 'Tell him it's good to see him dealing with deaths outside the family for a change.'

Nigel was intrigued by Kent's comment. He went outside and waited for the hack to leave before he called Foster.

The detective answered the phone with a growled 'yeah'. He sounded distracted. Flustered, even.

'His descendants died out,' Nigel said succinctly.

'What, all of them? How?'

'Nothing suspicious. He had two kids: one died of TB when he was six; the other never married. I suppose there is a chance the daughter had a child even though she never married, but that would be impossible to trace, given the surname is Smith. The wife married again and had two more kids with another man. I could trace them, I suppose . . .'

Nigel's voice trailed off. Despite his desperation to remain involved, he hoped to God that Foster would not make him do that: he was looking at two or three days' backbreaking work, ploughing through thousands and thousands of Smiths; and he suspected it would be in vain.

'No, they're not the link. Beck wasn't even their dad. I can hardly see them passing the story of his murder down the generations. Knock it on the head for now.'

'One more thing.'

'Yeah,' Foster said, impatiently.

'I've just been tapped up by a reporter from the *Evening News*. Gary Kent.'

Foster sighed.

'Told me to pass on his regards.'

'Forget him. He's a creep. Right now, to be blunt, I couldn't give a rat's arse. Did he know about the reference?'

'No, he didn't mention it and I didn't tell him anything. But he knows I'm working for you.'

'Bully for him. If any more reptiles come crawling, tell them to shove it, too. And don't fall for the money thing: newspapers will always find a way not to pay, so you won't see a dime.'

There was a pause.

'Detective, I was thinking: the Metropolitan Police archives have been destroyed, so there are no details of the murder.'

Foster murmured his assent.

'The National Newspaper Library has copies of every single local and national newspaper going back a couple of hundred years. There's a good chance it will have been reported in the press in 1879. I thought it might be worth digging the reports out.'

'OK, sounds good. The one in Colindale? Is it open on Saturday?'

'Yes, until four.' He glanced at his watch. It was coming up to one p.m.

'Will you have time?'

'Let's see,' Nigel said.

'Look, I tell you what. I'll get someone to give this

place a call and see if we can get it to stay open a bit later. Would that help?'

'It would.'

'Consider it done. Give me a call if you turn anything up.'

The line went dead.

10

Thanks to the vagaries of the Northern Line, it was approaching two thirty when Nigel exited the station at Colindale. The sun was out, offering even this ignored and unloved part of London a healthy glow. Nigel turned right and strode with purpose down Colindale Avenue, a soulless strip of road, eating up the forty or fifty yards to the newspaper library. It was built in 1903 as a repository for yesterday's news, and opened to the public in 1932, a dirty red-brick building that still wears the austerity of the period.

Once inside the main reading room Nigel was hit by the familiar, rich, almost sickly smell of fading, worn paper. Becoming immersed in the bound volumes of newspapers was like entering a portal to the past. Here he was able to flesh out the stories of the people he hunted, their times and the events that shaped them. Inquests, court reports, obituaries, news reports, all these were genealogical gold. At the FRC, the act of looking through indexes rather than original forms removed you from history: at Colindale, you climbed a ladder and dived in.

Nigel found a seat. The whole archive is the size of several football fields – almost every single British newspaper, local and national, printed since 1820 is housed there – but the area given over to researchers is not much bigger than a penalty box. The main room has barely changed since 1932: the stark white walls, the wooden clock that has never shown the right time and, most of all, the fifty-six original reading tables. These were, to Nigel, objects of beauty. Not the tables themselves, but the reading stands perched on them. Made of brass in art deco style, each possesses a strip lamp – turned on by a switch that flicks with a satisfying thud – the table number and wooden frames, chipped and tattered from decades of use, on which to stand the huge bound volumes. If not for the odd, usually neglected computer terminal and the hysterical whirr of rewinding microfilm reels from the neighbouring room, it could be any time since 1932.

Nigel went to the inquiries desk first.

'Hi,' he said to the timid woman sitting behind the counter. 'Nigel Barnes. I believe someone from the Metropolitan Police might have said I was coming.'

He winced at how formal his introduction sounded. Her eyes lit up.

'Oh, yes,' she said eagerly. 'Ron on the order desk is expecting you. He'll be helping you out.'

A minute or so later a proud-looking fat man, hands the size of shovels, was greeting him. He had a stubbled chin and an enormous stomach that strained against his T-shirt.

'Sorry about keeping you here,' Nigel explained.

'Don't worry, mate,' Ron said. 'I only had a night in front of the TV with the wife planned; frankly, you're doing me a favour. Now what do you want first?'

He started with national newspapers: they carried stories of murder, the more gruesome the better, while the local papers were unpredictable. They came and went quickly, and often carried nothing more than market times and the price of apples. He asked for March 1879 copies of *The Times*, the paper of record. Although it was unlikely the murders would be in there, it was worth a try; he also ordered *The Daily Telegraph* – then *The Times*'s cheaper, down-market rival – and finally, the *News of the World*, which served up a weekly diet of murder and sin even in 1879.

Ron disappeared into the depths of the repository. Nigel went to his seat and waited, trying to stop himself checking his watch every other minute. The reading table would be superfluous. All the volumes he'd ordered came on that most dreaded substance: microfilm. Nigel hated it. Scanning through endless reels of the stuff on badly lit screens coated in inches of dust, developing repetitive strain injury by having to rewind whole reels manually, threading the crumpled, creased pieces of film over the rollers and not under, it was as much fun as gouging his eyeballs out with a teaspoon.

When they came, he took the boxes through to the room filled with microfilm readers, huge machines with screens the size of 1950s televisions. He teed up *The Times* first. For the week following the murder, it carried nothing. Not for the first time, Nigel marvelled at the verbosity of the Victorian press. In one edition there was a report of a parliamentary debate that must have comprised more than 15,000 words, the newspaper columns densely packed, unbroken by illustrations or advertisements. How anyone read it without losing the will to live was beyond him.

Relieved, he turned next to the *News of the World*. The *Screws* was founded in 1843 and quickly established itself as a primary source of salaciousness, mining the magistrates' courts of London for stories of murder and adultery. If Albert Beck's death had not made its pages, then it was unlikely to have been reported by anyone else. The microfilm reel carried every edition for 1879. It was his intention to scroll briskly through January but, as always, he found it impossible to avoid being consumed by the past. As he spooled sedately through the weekly editions his eye was caught by wonderful, evocative yet matter-of-fact headlines: 'Atrocious Outrage Near Bristol' and 'Threatening Attitude Of Nihilists'. The front page of each edition had a list of 'Jokes Of The Week' culled from other publications, so unfunny they seemed to have been filed from another planet – which, in effect, they were.

He found the first edition for April. There was a report from the Zulu War and a report on the exploits of the Kelly gang in Australia. He was about to scroll down to the next page when, at the bottom, he saw a headline that made his heart stop.

KENSINGTON: THIRD HORRIFIC MURDER

The story beneath read:

The bodies of all three men lay in pools of blood on the ground, a demon having wielded a sharp instrument to open them up. Up to one o'clock yesterday North Kensington had no clue as yet to the motive or identity of the fiend whose deeds have sown considerable terror within the local community. The first victim was named as Samuel Roebuck, a brickworker of Notting Dale, whose mutilated body was discovered in the fields near his home.

The man had last been seen drinking on the evening of Monday March 24th, and the police initially believed the killing to be the consequence of a drunken altercation. But then on the morning of Saturday March 29th, the stabbed form of Albert Beck, a tanner, of nearby Clarendon Road, North Kensington, was discovered in the undergrowth of St John's Church by a passer-by close to Ladbroke Grove. He leaves a widow and two small children in penury. The third victim was named as Leonard Childe, a 38-year-old blacksmith of Harrow Road, North Kensington, who leaves a widow and four children, the eldest being just thirteen. He was discovered during the early morning of Tuesday April 1st, near to Notting Hill station. Police authorities have called for calm in the area and are said to be closing in on the ghoul who perpetrated these wicked acts. Those who have witnessed any suspicious activity among relatives or neighbours, such as the sighting of blood-drenched clothes or lunatic behaviour, are entreated to present themselves at North Kensington police station to provide information.

Nigel finished reading, then left the room, headed down the short flight of stairs, all the time dialling Foster. By the time he made it out of the doors the phone was ringing.

Foster answered straightaway.

'I've found a report of the murder of Albert Beck.'

'What does it say?'

'The killer struck three times. A body was found on Tuesday 25th, Saturday 29th, and Tuesday 1st April.' He paused. 'April 1st is tomorrow,' Nigel added.

He heard Foster sigh. 'I'm aware of the date,' he drawled. 'That's not the only thing that bothers me. If he's following this pattern, then he killed someone last Saturday and we haven't found the body. Where were the first and third victims found?'

Nigel trawled his memory. Years of scanning documents had given him almost photographic recall.

'The first was Brick Field, Notting Dale. The third near Notting Hill station.'

'Find out as much as you can about each of the killings, in particular the spot where they were found. Call in when you have something.'

Foster collected his jacket from the back of his chair and put it on. He went through to the incident room and clapped his hands to get everyone's attention.

'Listen up. I've just had Nigel Barnes on the phone: he's found a newspaper report from 1879 about three killings in North Kensington in the space of a week. The second killing was of Albert Beck.'

'The *second*?' Heather said.

Foster nodded. 'That's not the only surprise. The

third victim was murdered on 31st March 1879, the body found the next day.'

A silence fell across the room.

'So this is what's going to happen. Andy and Heather, get a team to Notting Hill Gate. That's where Barnes says the third body was found in 1879. Scout it out, get plain clothes on the street, digging up the roads, begging for small change, whatever you can think of, as long as it's low-key: just get some bodies around there. Find a place overlooking the station if you can and keep an eye on it. I'll come and join you there later.'

'What about the first killing?' Heather asked. 'If he's followed the pattern . . .'

'I'll deal with those who might already be dead. You try and stop someone else joining their ranks.'

11

The mortuary attendant, the only person on duty that evening, at least until the inevitable victims of a Saturday night in the city were wheeled in later on, looked ill at ease when DCI Foster strode in purposefully.

'Can I help?' he asked, blinking furiously behind his wire-rimmed glasses.

'You can. I want to see every body that was brought in last weekend. The ones you still have, anyway.'

'Did you ring and ask about this in advance?' he asked nervously.

'Look,' Foster stopped himself. 'What's your name, son?'

'Luke.'

'Luke, I'm in the middle of a murder investigation. It is extremely important that I see those bodies and that I see them immediately. Now I'm going to walk in there and have a look. I think it's best you don't try and stop me. Agreed?'

Luke nodded slowly.

'Good man.'

Foster left him at his desk and barged through a set of double doors that led downstairs to the cold store. He could feel the temperature fall as he went further into the depths. At the bottom was another door. Locked.

'Luke!' he shouted. He could feel a draught coming from somewhere, he guessed the hidden approach where hearses and ambulances came to load and unload.

The young man scurried downstairs and punched a code into a keypad to one side of the door. There was a click and Foster pushed. He was inside. The air was chilly, though not freezing. He exhaled and caught a fleeting glimpse of his breath in front of him. Rows of cabins filled either side of the room, leaving a wide central area in the middle where a few tables stood. Only one was in use; Foster saw a black body bag. It wasn't empty.

'That one's waiting to be prepared for the tray,' Luke said, noticing where Foster's eyes were straying. 'Alcoholic,' he added, as if that explained the delay.

At the far end of the room was a chrome mechanism, a lift, a sort of dumb waiter that delivered the body to the autopsy room upstairs. Next to it Foster saw a large whiteboard. On it were the numbers of each cabin, written beside the surname of the deceased.

'Do you have any record of when these people died, or when their bodies were brought in?'

'It's in the register.'

'Get it, please.'

Luke departed while Foster went to a dispenser and put on a pair of latex gloves. By the time he'd worked them on, Luke had returned, his breathing slightly heavier, with a large black book in his hands.

'What dates interest you?'

'For a start, I want to have a look at everyone who was brought in late last Saturday night or on Sunday, regardless of when they actually died.'

Luke put the book down on one of the unoccupied metal tables, running down the page with his finger, then flicking it over. Foster wanted to grab it and look himself but, as he was about to, the technician spoke.

'Right, we have Fahey.'

Foster looked at the whiteboard. Couldn't see the name.

'Released to the funeral parlour on Thursday,' Luke added. 'Road traffic accident.'

Foster made a note of which funeral parlour.

'Gordon.'

This one was on the wall. Cabin 13. Foster went

over himself and pulled hard on the handle and the drawer slid out. He unzipped the bag to reveal a man, slightly overweight, in his early fifties, he guessed. His colour was pale blue and his jaw hung open. Foster looked closely at his chest and torso, then lifted both arms. When he found nothing, he summoned Luke and asked him to help sit the body up. With much effort, Foster carefully inspected his back. There wasn't a blemish on the whole body.

'Heart attack?' he asked Luke, who nodded.

'At home on Saturday night.'

'Perhaps he won the lottery,' Foster said, zipping up the bag and shunting the cabin back into its home.

The next name on the list was Ibrahim.

'This one's in the deep freeze. Number 30,' Luke said.

Great, Foster thought, just what I need. There was always at least one cabin where the temperature was 20° below. It stored bodies that required freezing to prevent decomposition. Then, when they were needed, for a second autopsy perhaps, they were thawed out with hot water from the boiler.

'Is this a keeper?' he asked.

Luke shook his head. 'No, it was in an advanced state of decomposition when it was found.'

'Marvellous,' Foster muttered.

He pulled the door open and dragged out the tray.

The bag was smaller, not body-shaped. He opened it carefully, breathing deeply.

The cold prevented the stench from overpowering him, but what he saw almost did. The body was in bits. An arm here, a leg there, the torso in the middle, the head missing; it was green, not pale blue, and had obviously been maggot food for some time. Foster recalled the case. Another team was on it; probable honour killing was the word.

He picked up the severed stumps and examined them carefully. His nose caught a whiff of rotting flesh, so he started to breathe through his mouth. He checked every part, lifting them all up apart from the torso, which he flipped over like a burger, but there was nothing else. With as much haste as possible, he bundled the body parts back into their cover and out of his sight.

Next on the list was a John Doe. Luke said this one was brought in on Sunday morning. His age was difficult to gauge, though late forties had been the estimate. The face was sagging under the weight of death, black hair tangled and the black-grey beard unkempt. Foster did a double take. It was the tramp whose suicide they had been called to the previous Sunday, the one that Heather had been taking so personally.

He was about to zip it back up there and then, but

something made him carry on looking. The chest was clear, the stomach too. He picked up the left arm, saw nothing; then the right, nothing apart from a few track marks. Obviously a junkie . . .

Tilting his head to one side, he looked once more at the punctures on his arm. Small nicks, all the world like the scars caused by injecting smack. But then they appeared to coalesce, to join together. He peered more closely. There it was: two slanted red cuts, a small cut bridging them. An 'A'. It was even less distinct than before, and done with less care, but it was possible to make out the other marks, letters and numbers. The same letters and numbers they had found on Darbyshire: 1A137.

He owed Heather an apology.

He put the arm down. 'Cause of death,' he shouted to Luke, his eyes still fixed on the body.

'Strangulation seems the likeliest option.'

'Anything from toxicology?'

'No. But there were signs of heavy drug and alcohol abuse.'

Foster completed a clockwise lap of the body.

He picked up one of the man's limp feet by the ankle. Strange, he thought. This guy's feet are in immaculate condition. He couldn't have been on the streets for too long. Most tramps' feet are knackered: covered in corns, bunions and blisters, filthy and stinking. It didn't make sense. Unless the guy used to be married to a chiropodist. The hands were soft, too; smooth and uncalloused like a clerical worker's, not the gnarled hands of a derelict who slept on the streets, smoked tab ends from the gutter and drank meths.

Something didn't add up.

Nigel had asked Ron for microfilm copies of the *Evening News* and the *Evening Standard*. It seemed to take him an eternity to return. Nigel sat there, cursing his name and his bulk, the building empty and quiet apart from the silent hum of a distant generator. Darkness was beginning to fall and the huge bowls of light, suspended by chains from the ceiling, cast a sepulchral glow across the main reading room.

I need to do something, he thought. He got up and wandered into the second, smaller room. To one side of that was the microfilm reading room, a dark space bereft of natural light, lit only by an occasional lamp and the illumination of the reading screens. Nigel had spent hours of his life in here, spooling through centuries of copy.

To his left, away from the microfilm readers, was a bank of computer terminals, a few of which were allocated for searching recent issues of the national newspapers by keywords. He sat down at one, hit a key and the screen burst to life. There was nothing on this database that would be much use to the investigation, it only went back a decade or so at most. It was the recent past, but still he fancied losing himself in it for a short time.

He wondered how high-profile a cop Foster was. In the search field he typed 'Detective+Grant+ Foster' and hit return. The machine chuntered reluctantly then produced its results: nineteen hits. The first few were reports of murder investigations in which he'd been quoted. But it was the seventh that caught Nigel's eye: 'Top Cop Cleared of "Killing" Father'.

The story was nearly eight years old. Nigel clicked the link immediately.

A Scotland Yard detective suspended after being suspected of murdering his father in a mercy killing has been cleared and reinstated after no charges were brought against him.

Detective Inspector Grant Foster, 39, was arrested two months ago after his father, Roger Foster, a retired detective, was found dead at his home in Acton last July. His son made the call to the emergency services reporting his father's death.

Last month an inquest into Mr Foster senior's death recorded an open verdict. The coroner said at the time: 'It is clear that Detective Inspector Foster helped his father end his life. It is not the duty of this inquest to decide whether that help was criminal. That is a matter for the police and the Crown Prosecution Service.'

The news that DCI Foster will not be charged and will return to his job has already attracted criticism from anti-euthanasia compaigners.

Last night, Adrian Lewis, Conservative MP for Thewliss, said: 'I'm not sure what message this sends out to the general public. It is not for us to decide whether someone has the right to die – it is our Lord's decision. I do hope this isn't a case of one rule applying to members of the public, and another to members of the Metropolitan Police.'

Nigel sat back to absorb what he'd read. Regardless of whether he had been charged, there seemed to be an admission that Foster in some way assisted his father's death. In that case, how did he keep his job? Nigel checked his watch. He could plough on and find more stories, but it had been half an hour since Ron had descended into the bowels of the building and time was getting on.

Back in the reading room there was no sign of life. He decided to go and find Ron himself, hurry him up, get an estimate for how long it would take. He walked across the reading room to the double doors through which the attendants disappeared when they retrieved an order. Nigel had always wondered what lay behind them. A vast cavernous hall stacked with shelf upon dusting shelf of yellowing files? He opened the door and stepped on to the landing of a brightly lit staircase. In front of him was a lift.

He pushed the button and it opened immediately. He half expected Ron to step out, clutching his microfilm or file. But it was empty. He entered and looked for the list of buttons on the wall. There was only one: B. He pressed it, the doors closed and with a slight judder the lift began its long descent.

It juddered once more when it hit the bottom, and with a weary clank the doors parted. Nigel was faced with an area with three exits: one ahead, one to the left, the other to his right. Which to choose? The window of each door was frosted, so he could not peer through. There was no light behind the glass on either side, but the path ahead appeared to be lit. Ron must be down there, he thought.

He opened the door to a long corridor, its walls uninterrupted by doors or windows. At the far end was another double door. Nigel hesitated. What if Ron wasn't down here? What if he was upstairs wondering where the hell Nigel was? He should turn back. But, no, he was certain Ron was down there and he needed those newspapers. He started to walk, his footsteps the only sound.

He reached the door, dark green and swinging slightly on its hinges. He pushed at it slowly and was immediately hit by the unmistakable, sweet waft of ageing paper and dust. But the area beyond was inky black. Funny, he thought. If Ron is down here, then why isn't the light on? The corridor light behind him was on, the only source of illumination. He shrugged and stepped through into the darkness. He reached with his left hand to the wall inside the door. His hand touched something cold and hard. Steel, he thought. He patted the area around the door hinges, finally locating a switch. He turned it on.

It took him a while to fully realize the dimensions of the room in front of him. Then he saw that it was a long, low tunnel. He looked up. He was an inch under six feet tall, yet the ceiling could not have been more than two feet above him. There were metal shelves either side from floor to ceiling, containing bound volumes of various newspapers. He thought of Ron and smiled. How did he fit down here? He must weigh twenty stone. Perhaps that's why he had taken so long. Perhaps, like an adult Augustus Gloop, he had become wedged in one of these tunnels.

Nigel knew enough about the newspaper library

to realize that this was one of the four storage units. These were more than 260 feet long. Nigel believed it: he was unable to see the door at the far end. But he could see rows and rows of files. This is what becomes of yesterday's news, he thought. Not wrapping chips, but bound together in silent volumes in this tomb.

There was the sound of a door shutting. Ron, he thought. He called his name out, though it emerged only as a hoarse whisper, which caused him to cough, choking on the dust generated by twenty-eight miles of shelf. When he finished, there was silence.

'Ron,' he said, louder this time.

No reply. Had the sound of the door closing come from behind or in front? It was difficult to tell. It must be the front, he decided. He peered down the long tunnel in front of him, waiting to see Ron's bovine figure heave into view.

Another door closed. That was definitely in front of him. He stepped away from the door at his back and called again. His uneasiness increased. I should have stayed upstairs and waited, he told himself. The door behind him opened without noise, but he sensed it, a waft of musty air at his back. He spun around.

'*Shit!!!*' he screamed.

Ron dropped the microfilm boxes he was clutching to his chest.

'Jesus,' he said, putting his hand on his heart.

Nigel held his hands up, more out of reflex than anything else. For a few seconds, neither man could speak.

Ron broke the silence. 'What the hell are you doing here?' he said, his face turning from surprise to anger.

'I came looking for you,' Nigel said eventually. 'I thought you . . . I don't know what I thought, actually.'

'You scared the crap out of me,' Ron said.

He bent down and collected the microfilm boxes. Nigel helped him. When the boxes had been located and picked up, both men looked at each other.

'Sorry,' Nigel said. 'I'm a bit jumpy. Like I said, don't know what I was thinking.'

Ron shrugged. 'Well, promise me you'll leave the collecting to me, eh?'

Nigel nodded.

Ron handed the films over to him. 'But you can take these up,' he said. 'I need a fag after that.'

Nigel made his way back to the reading room with the reels. He delved first into the *Evening News*, finding reports on each of the murders, each filling increasing space as a connection between them was made. But in the report of the third murder, and the shock and fear it had spread throughout Kensington – or 'dread and consternation', as the *Evening News* described it – there were no further details on the location of the body, only mention of it being found near Notting Hill station. He checked the next day's paper to see if any more mention was made. While there was a large report about how terrified local residents were, again no exact location was given.

He loaded the *Evening Standard*. It was as if the same reporter had penned both sets of articles; they were identical in detail and length. He scanned every report, soaked up every word, but there was nothing new for him to pass on to Foster. He sat back and rubbed his eyes. He checked his watch; an hour had passed in seconds, peering at the dimly lit screen in a dark booth. He noticed the familiar signs of a headache settling in behind his eyes, and he decided to go outside and grab some air to clear his head.

He told Ron, who was back at his station.

'I'll join you, mate,' Ron said jovially, obviously having forgiven him for his trespass. 'Need another fag.'

Nigel had put his coat on. Ron wandered down in just his T-shirt. Outside the front entrance, he lit his cigarette while Nigel watched a few cars flash past, not interested in a roll-up. He pulled his mobile from his pocket and switched it on.

No new messages. Not that he expected to be the first person to be told when they arrested the killer.

'Low battery' flashed up on his screen. He cursed himself for failing to charge it that morning and turned it off once more to save what little power he had.

'How's it going?' Ron asked, exhaling with force.

Nigel looked at him apologetically.

'I know you can't tell me the details, but you can tell me whether it's going well, can't you?'

'It's going ... OK. Just got microfilm eyes, that's all.'

Ron nodded in sympathy. 'You know how they used to get the papers flat enough so they could be filmed?'

'Can't say I do.'

'Iron. Used to have a team of women that flattened them with domestic irons.'

'Really?'

'Straight up,' Ron replied and took another enormous, loud drag on his cigarette.

Nigel realized he had to get more specific in his search. 'I need the *Chelsea Times*,' he said.

'I'll get down there and get it for you once I've finished smoking this,' Ron offered. 'Might take me a while, though. It's not life or death, is it?'

Nigel smiled. 'It could be.'

Foster was in his car, reliving the memory of the previous Sunday in Avondale Park in Notting Dale when he'd been called to the scene of the tramp's death. There had seemed little remarkable at the scene when he first arrived there. The rain had fallen steadily throughout the night, and he remembered the trees appeared to be bowing under the weight of water. The tramp had been found hanging from the frame of a children's swing, though he had been cut down by the attending officer in a vain attempt at resuscitation, so Foster did not see the body in situ.

He'd been back to the office and collected some pictures. The rope, the swing, the tramp's body, the area around the scene. None of it looked in any way out of the ordinary. The rope had been sent to forensics for examination and Carlisle had been summoned to do a second post-mortem. Foster had called the park keeper, who had found the body at dawn, and been assured, as he had been the previous week, that no one had witnessed anything strange or different the day or night leading up to the body's discovery. Yet the park had been closed at five p.m., which meant the killer must have dragged or hauled the body into the park by some means. Foster had walked around the park perimeter and could see no obvious way in.

The question that bothered him was: Why was there no stab wound? Barnes had told him that all three victims in 1879 had been stabbed. So why hang the first one?

They needed an ID. He had asked for dental records to be prepared and compared against those on the missing persons database, but that would take time. So, here he was in his car, kerb-crawling through the streets of Ladbroke Grove and Notting Hill, armed with a stack of pictures of a dead man. He started by St John's Churchyard. Pieces of police tape attached to the railings still fluttered in the wind. But the churchyard itself was empty.

He drove along Portobello Road; the market stallholders had long since packed away their stalls, though the detritus of a busy Saturday still littered the road. He parked up when he reached the railway bridge, at the northern, darker end of the street. It was here the winos liked to hang out, in and around the alleys, buildings and dark corners that constituted life under the Westway.

He checked Acklam Road, a pedestrianized street running parallel to the overhead motorway. There was no sign of anyone, homeless or not. He crossed back over Portobello and walked beside the Westway towards Ladbroke Grove. There was a small park called Portobello Green, a haven for local workers eating their lunch by day, and for the chaotic and confused drifters drinking fortified wine by night. He pushed the gate that led into the park, and heard it creak. From the other side he could hear voices, people laughing and shouting. As he got closer he could see a group of homeless gathered around one park bench, falling quiet as he drew near, recognizing him as trouble.

The person he wanted was sitting in the middle, the others circled around her, like children hearing a story.

'Good evening, Sheena,' he said, as silence fell.

Ciderwoman was wearing the same clothes as on their previous meeting. In the late dusk, and away from the harsh lights of the police station, she appeared less grimy. Her eyes, yellow and narrow, stared long and hard at him for some time before informing the brain.

'What the fuck do you want?' she said, remembering him at last. She looked at the gnarled old man next to her, bald head, bushy dirty-grey beard, sucking on a cigarette as if his life depended on it while he rocked forwards and back. 'This one's a copper,' she slurred. 'Asked me about that murder in the church.'

'Sorry to gatecrash the party when it's going so well,' Foster said. 'But I'm afraid I need your help again, Sheena. The rest of you might be able to help me, too.' He pulled a copy of the photo of the dead tramp from his inside jacket. 'Do any of you know this guy?'

Ciderwoman snatched the photo from his hand and put it within an inch of her face. She shut one eye and tried to focus. Foster pulled a small torch from his pocket and flicked it on.

'This might help.'

He gave it to Ciderwoman. She held it unsteadily in one hand and shone it on the picture.

'He's fucking dead,' she said eventually.

'I know that. Do you recognize him?'

She looked again. The others had crowded behind both her shoulders to take a look. She passed the torch and picture to a few others.

'Never seen 'im,' she said with certainty.

The photo did the rounds: no one else had seen him either.

'If he did hang around this part of town, would it be fair to say you'd know him?'

She cracked her tombstone smile. 'If he'd hung around here, it'd be fair to say I'd probably shagged him,' she said, then let rip with her wheezy, gasping laugh.

The rest joined in.

That's an image that will take some time to dispel, Foster thought.

*

Nigel was browsing the online catalogue when Ron returned, a couple of bound volumes under his arm, wheezing with the effort. No microfilm, Nigel thought with some relief. He took them from him and placed one volume on the reading stand. He pushed his glasses back from the tip of his nose and opened the front cover. The pages were dry as sandpaper and as stiff in his hand. It felt wonderful; he could almost sense the years falling away. He flicked giddily through the pages, until he reached the edition of April 2nd.

He thought wrong. There wasn't a single word. The newspaper consisted of two pages, both filled with advertising, grocery prices, a trade directory and other minutiae of Victorian life. Any other time it would have been a fascinating insight. But not now. He needed news.

Ron had shuffled away towards his station. Nigel called him back.

'Can you get the *Kensington News and West London Times* for 1879?' Nigel asked.

'Never heard of them,' Ron said mournfully.

'It's one newspaper,' Nigel replied. 'A weekly.'

Ron ambled slowly out of the room, back towards the depths.

Half an hour later, Ron returned with another bound volume. Nigel found the edition for April 4th.

The murder spree was front page. It concentrated on the worried reactions of Notting Hill residents, including a number who believed the killer to be some sort of golem. One 'eyewitness' had described seeing a man 'more than seven feet in height, hair overgrowing his visage' in the vicinity of the first murder.

Nigel read the report carefully. Nothing was new until he reached the point where the reporter had managed to find a talking head who claimed to know the person who had found the body. The man, unnamed, had been taking an early-morning walk beside the Hammersmith and City Railway when he came across the body near the station.

He rose to go and ring Foster. Then he stopped: Notting Hill Gate was underground. Unless this guy lived in a tunnel, what the hell was he doing walking alongside the track?

Nigel sat back down. Hammersmith and City Railway. Which line was that now? The Hammersmith and City Line still ran, of course, but it didn't go to Notting Hill Gate. That was on the Central Line. He thought the Circle and District Lines ran through it too.

He needed a reference book. He checked a few of the shelves, but they had nothing useful. The Internet, he thought. He went to the library catalogue and clicked the Internet icon. His first search term was 'London underground'. A minute later he had 369,000 results to choose from. The first was an online journey planner; the second was the Transport for London official website. He clicked that. For what felt like an age nothing seemed to happen. Just when he was about to try again, the page appeared. He clicked the link marked 'tube'. He scanned the page as quickly as he could, looking for a link to the network's history. He could not see anything about history. On the browser, he clicked 'back' to the list of search results.

The next result was more promising. It was 'Underground history: the disused stations on London's underground'. It concentrated on the 'ghost' stations on the tube: the platform you can see, if your eyes work in the dark, between Tottenham Court Road and Holborn on the Central Line, which has been closed since 1932, and used to be the station for the British Museum; or Down Street on the Piccadilly Line between Green Park and Hyde Park Corner.

He clicked back on the browser once more. He entered 'Notting Hill station' and hit return. The first listed site was Wikipedia: a free encyclopedia, the entries submitted by punters. He clicked it and read the short, bland entry.

Notting Hill Gate tube station is a London underground station in Notting Hill. On the Central Line it is between Holland Park and Queensway, and on the District Line and Circle Line it is between High Street Kensington and Bayswater. It is in both zones 1 and 2. It opened on July 30, 1900 and is most famous for its proximity to Portobello Road, the site of the movie *Notting Hill*, the Notting Hill Carnival, and the Portobello Market.

July 30, 1900? Nigel read it again and again. But the date didn't change. Was it a typo? Or was it right? If so, where the hell was the station before then? It existed, he had read about it in several newspapers. But where was it? He thought of Foster and his team waiting to pounce at Notting Hill Gate. He looked at his watch. It was nearly ten p.m. I'll give it another ten minutes, he thought.

He typed in the address for Google and entered the search term 'History of the London underground'. The first hit was a site that offered a history of the tube decade by decade, beginning with 1860–69. In 1863 it told how the Metropolitan Railway was opened between Paddington and Farringdon Street, stopping at Edgware Road, Baker Street, Portland Road (now Great Portland Street), Gower Street (now Euston Square) and King's Cross. No mention was made of Notting Hill.

The next page told the story of how the independent Hammersmith and City Railway opened between Paddington and Hammersmith in 1864 as a feeder for the new underground system. Locomotives ran on the overground track and then entered the underground system.

> The intermediate stations on this new railway were Notting Hill (now Ladbroke Grove) and Shepherd's Bush.

Before he had even finished the sentence, Nigel had dug into his pockets, grabbed his mobile phone, dialled it and put the phone to his ear. It rang twice and went dead. He looked at the screen: blank. He checked his pockets: he had a fifty-pence coin. That would last seconds – landline-to-mobile phone calls devoured money. He ran down the stairs to the payphone, picked up the receiver and called Foster.

The phone rang. And rang.

'Pick the bloody thing up,' he hissed.

'*This is DCI Grant Foster. I can't answer my phone . . .*'

'It's Nigel,' he said after the beep, not wanting to waste a word. 'You're in the wrong place. You need to be at Ladbroke Grove station. It used to be called Notting Hill. My phone is dying. Go to Ladbroke Grove. I'll go there . . .'

Then his money ran out.

Emergency calls were free. He punched the number in.

'Fire, ambulance or police?'

'Police.'

He was put through.

'I need to speak to Detective Chief Inspector Foster,' he said before the telephonist had asked what he wanted. 'It's really, extremely urgent. I really cannot stress how urgent it is.'

Foster was looking through a pair of binoculars from the seventh floor of a drab, watery-grey office block that towered over the area surrounding Notting Hill Gate tube station. Drinkwater had hired the entire floor because it gave them a clear sight of Kensington Church Street, Notting Hill Gate itself, and then the residential area behind. The floor was empty, save for a few desks, chairs and phone leads, and bore the stale smell of an unloved place of work.

It was Saturday night and the street beneath Foster was teeming with locals and tourists, on their way to overpriced bars and restaurants. His team was in position, primed and ready to go. An armed response unit was on standby, comparing guns in the far corner of the office. Two officers were posing as homeless by each exit of the tube station. An unmarked car was parked on Uxbridge Street, which ran parallel to

Notting Hill Gate, behind the Coronet and Gate cinemas. Another was parked on the other side of Notting Hill Gate, on Pembridge Gardens.

Foster's radio crackled into life. He could see there was a commotion across the other side of the street. A woman was screaming outside one of the high-street banks and a group of people had gathered around her.

'Come on!' Foster shouted and sprinted from the room.

He ran down the stairwell, Heather and Drink-water behind him. They tumbled out on to Notting Hill Gate.

'What's happening, people?' he barked into the receiver.

No reply.

The three detectives ran across the road. Officers were converging on the group outside the bank.

A group of rubberneckers were staring at an hysterical black woman, who was shouting at the top of her voice, 'He took my bag. He took my facking bag.'

Her friends were consoling her. None of them, or any of the gawpers, seemed impressed that a simple bag snatch had attracted the attention of half of west London's police. An officer in uniform further down the street was walking towards them, clutching a teenage boy by the arm, the woman's bag in the other.

'Give 'im here,' the woman screamed. 'I'll tear his facking head off.'

Even from ten feet away, Foster could see that her fingernails were up to the task; the threat was uttered with absolute conviction. The teenager looked terrified. Foster's eyes scanned the length of the street. All seemed normal.

'Still all quiet?' he said into his radio.

The answer came back that it was.

Foster holstered the radio. 'Let's get back inside,' he said. His breath had shortened, the anticipation and adrenalin still coursing through his body.

In the chaos, he failed to hear his phone ring.

Nigel had given up trying to speak directly to Foster. The woman who took his call treated him like a crank. He tried to urge her to at least pass the message on to the incident room, but she kept asking him for a phone number and location, believing he had witnessed a murder and not that he was foreseeing one, or its aftermath. When the call ended, he knew he could not afford to wait and see what happened, to find out whether the message had got through; he needed to get there, to the scene of the potential crime.

He left the library, hoping to hail a black cab. The road outside was dark and silent – little chance of a taxi passing by. He ran to the tube. Within five minutes a train came. He rode it southwards to King's Cross. When he got there, his first instinct was to get a taxi, but on a Saturday night at the gateway to the north he may be waiting ages; it would be just as quick to ride the Hammersmith and City Line to Ladbroke Grove.

It was almost eleven thirty when he tumbled out at Ladbroke Grove. Drinkers, revellers, winos and nutters thronged the area in front of the tube. The place stank of chip fat, booze and piss. People passed on their way from bar to club, or spilled from the tube to their homes. A nearby bus stop swelled numbers. Car stereos blasted out cavernous bass tunes, young couples laughed and argued. Nigel normally did all he could to avoid being in such places at a time like this. But here he didn't care: he stood for a few seconds and wondered which way to head – apart from one squad car parked a hundred yards down the street, there was no sign of any police presence.

He walked up the grove, under the railway bridge. A tube rattled into the station above. He stopped once more to look around. Nothing unusual. He started walking again, to where he didn't know.

Then he heard a scream.

It was a piercing, wounded cry that tore through the night. At first he put it down to a drunken fight, but it continued. No one else seemed to notice, or felt it too commonplace to act.

Nigel felt his blood thicken.

The screaming was coming from the right, behind the tube station. There was a short alley, along the side of a bar. He headed down it. The pavement widened into a road. Above him loomed the monstrous concrete Westway; the white noise of its traffic a background thrum. Yet the screaming got louder. Nigel quickened his pace to a jog. Fifty yards down the street, he could see a young woman. Her arms were spread wide and, as she screamed, she bent double with the effort. Beside her a car was parked diagonally in the road, its driver's door open and headlights shining. From the billow of fumes from the exhaust, he could see the engine was running. Nigel sprinted towards her.

The woman didn't see him coming; she just continued to scream. As he arrived, she backed off. He had his hands up to show it was all right, for her not to panic. He looked around but couldn't see what she was screaming at. Her shouts decreased to a whisper. Her left hand went to her mouth; her right hand pointed to a garage door, half open. The beams lit the door; the gap beneath was in darkness. Nigel walked towards it. All he could see was white graffiti on the door: 'Fuck Chelski'.

The street was deserted. Nigel licked his parched lips and bent down to see under the door. Too dark. The woman had stopped screaming and started to keen.

Nigel got up and walked to the door. He took a handkerchief from his pocket and used it to take hold of the handle. He began to lift carefully, inch by inch, so that the car headlights and the floodlit glow from the Westway slowly illuminated the interior of the garage. He was hit with a pungent combination of oil and turpentine. As the light grew, the shape of a body was revealed. A young woman. Nigel let go of the door and checked to make sure it wouldn't fall. Then he stepped inside.

Close up, he could see she was blonde, dressed in jeans and a shirt of several colours, torn open to reveal a pair of bloodied, mutilated breasts. The blood around them seemed to have solidified, become gelatinous. She was laid on her back, arms stretched out. Nigel's eyes went to her face. It was pristine, untouched. But where once her eyes had been, there were instead two gaping holes, congealed blood and matter garnishing the empty, cavernous sockets that still seemed to stare, baleful and black.

Nigel knew the scene would stay with him until his final breath, that it would play in his mind like some macabre screensaver whenever he closed his eyes at night. He stepped out and slowly lowered the garage door, as if to try and protect what remained of the young woman's dignity.

Two or three people had gathered in the road; one was attempting to calm the woman. Another was on his mobile phone.

'You all right, mate?' one black guy shouted.

Within a few seconds the crowd was in double figures.

Nigel nodded. Slowly he sat on the ground in front of the garage door, blocking the path to it.

In the distance he could hear sirens.

12

The monotone whirr of the police helicopter above echoed through the night, its searchlight swaying and lurching futilely on the surrounding streets. It was too late, Foster knew that. The killer had slipped in, dumped his cargo and retreated back into the vast anonymity of the city. All the while he and his team had been waiting at the wrong tube station. It did not top his list of worries – there was a killer still to catch – but he knew that fact, regardless of whether the murder could have been prevented, would not be welcomed by his superiors. Particularly if it came under the baleful scrutiny of the press. Following the investigation into his father's death, Foster had exhausted much of the goodwill he had accumulated with the top brass as a detective; he had few remaining allies, if any.

He stood in the middle of Malton Road. He had lost count of the nights when he had stood on some godforsaken street in the wee small hours of the morning, illuminated by the stark glare of arc lights, over the body of some poor unfortunate. When you've watched your father take his own life to prevent himself from being wracked by future agonies, some of the venom is drawn from dealing with the murder of strangers. Yet this woman's death hit him in the pit of his gut. They had matched the killer's stride only a few hours before he was due to strike, and that had been too late.

Foster looked at the woman, her eyes cut out and her chest torn apart. Carlisle was examining the body. Noticing the detective, he glanced up and the pair acknowledged each other, their tight faces conveying the bleakness of the scene. Neither spoke. Foster cast his eyes around the garage while Carlisle completed his checks. He saw nothing out of the ordinary.

'I'd say she was in her late twenties, early thirties. Time of death was around five or six last night,' the pathologist said eventually.

Foster nodded. That answered one of his main questions.

'Cause?'

'Too early to say. Presumably one of the wounds to the chest, but I'll need to get her back for a proper look.'

'The eyes?'

'Could have been pre-mortem. I hope, for her sake, it was post. They were removed carefully, with some precision and not just gouged out, which would indicate she was at least unconscious. The optical nerve remains but is severed.'

An eye for an eye, thought Foster. Darbyshire had lost his hands. Was the mutilation symbolic, rather than ritualistic? Had this woman's eyes seen something, or Darbyshire's hands performed some act that required them both to be severed? And where did that leave the 'tramp' whose body remained intact?

'What about the chest wounds?'

'Yes, interesting. Seems like he has carved the breasts open. She had silicone implants. They have burst, hence all the mess. When we get her back I'll remove what's left, see if we can get a serial number. There are no other forms of identification on her anywhere. Other than a rather distinctive tattoo on her right shoulder blade.'

Foster bent down. Carlisle carefully rolled the woman so he could see her right shoulder. There was a symbol of some sort, obviously professionally done. It appeared oriental. Foster sketched it in his notebook.

'Know what it means?' he asked Carlisle.

'No. But I'm pretty certain it's Japanese. I spent some time out there years ago. Fascinating place.'

'That the only markings you've found?'

'Yes. Aside from the chest, of course.'

Foster stared at the bloodied mass that was once

the woman's breasts and upper chest. It was impossible to make out any deliberate markings. He would
have to wait until she was cleaned. Yet the state of
the chest, the severity of the wounds, did not indicate
careful precision. It suggested frenzy.

The missing eyes did not.

He was getting a feel for how the killer worked.
First, the subject was sedated in some way. Then, in
the case of Darbyshire and this young woman, he
severed or removed parts of their body before carving the reference. Whether they were still under
sedation was unclear but they must have been
restrained. Then he stabbed them through the heart.
In this case something had interrupted him, or upset
him, which explained the bloody mess.

'He could've started carving the reference and got
a shock when the implants burst,' Foster said to
Carlisle. 'Then got angry.' He paused. 'But I suppose
we all prefer our breasts as God intended,' he added
darkly.

Carlisle's face betrayed a flicker of humour.

They turned to leave the garage, Carlisle stripping
off his gloves.

'Did you get a chance to have a look at the
unnamed tramp at the mortuary?'

'Not yet. It's waiting for me as we speak. A fun
Sunday in store,' Carlisle said.

'For all of us.'

It was almost three a.m. And yet, at the perimeter of the tape they had set around the entire stretch of road, Foster could still see a few sightseers gawping. Andy Drinkwater was standing to one side of the crime scene, in conversation with an officer.

Foster told Drinkwater the result of Carlisle's preliminary examination.

'So if she died around tea-time, he dumped the body there tonight. Or, rather, last night,' Drinkwater added, checking his watch.

'Seems so.'

'But what if we'd got the right tube station? We'd have caught him.'

'He was banking on us getting the wrong one.' He paused. 'And he was right,' Foster added. 'How's Barnes?'

'He's at Notting Hill with Jenkins. She's going through what happened with him. He's a bit shaken up.'

Who wouldn't be, Foster thought. One minute the guy is peering through his thick square specs at history books, the next he's staring at the carved-up corpse of a young woman.

'Any witnesses yet?' he asked Drinkwater.

'Only the woman who discovered the body. She got back from a dinner party at eleven thirty. We've checked that and the story stands up. The garage door was open. Thought she forgot to lock it. Opened up and . . . there she was.'

'The lock was jemmied open, wasn't it?'

'Yes. But it was in a right old state. Wouldn't have required much effort.'

'Did she own or rent it?'

'Rented. From a guy in Acton. We're on it; we've got a name.'

'Which is more than we have for our victim. Get me someone, anyone, who speaks or, better still, reads Japanese. I don't care if it's a fucking sushi chef. Just as long as someone is here soon.'

Less than an hour later, a young police translator, still blinking the sleep from her eyes, was waiting for Foster at the perimeter of the scene with Drinkwater. She was Japanese, or her parents were. Her soft voice was unaccented English.

'Thanks for coming at such short notice,' Foster said, mustering a smile. Her handshake was soft and limp. She attempted a smile back but he could see she was terrified. She was more used to sitting in interviews, explaining police procedure. Here she was at a murder scene.

'What's your name?'

'Akiko,' she whispered.

Foster explained what they wanted. 'I need you to have a look at her shoulder and see if you can decipher the meaning. I have to warn you: her body is in a bad way. I'm truly sorry you have to do this, Akiko.'

He led the way to the garage. He made sure he stood behind Akiko as she got closer to the body, putting one arm around her to stop her if she fell. Foster had asked that the victim be placed on her side, covered with a blanket.

'Kneel down with me,' Foster said.

While he could see her trepidation, he also sensed Akiko was more resolute than her fragile frame suggested. They both bent down and Foster flicked back one corner of the sheet revealing the shoulder and a few strands of blonde hair. He pointed to the tattoo.

Her response was instant.

'It means "light that shines".'

'You sure?'

She nodded.

'Does that have any special significance?'

She thought for some time. Then shook her head.

Foster replaced the blanket and stood up. 'Thanks for doing that. Sorry you had to go through it.'

'It's OK,' she said, turning to leave, but then swinging round to face Foster. 'It's very fashionable at the moment to be tattooed with the Japanese translation of your name. Quite a few celebrities do it.'

Even after years of policing in west London, where parents named their children Alfalfa and Mezzanine, Foster had yet to come across anyone called Shining Light.

13

The morning sun was too watery to cast more than a weary light into the sitting room of Nigel's flat in Shepherd's Bush. But even a blinding sun found it difficult to illuminate a room brimful with objects and books, occupying every corner and empty space. The musty smell of old books filled the air; Nigel possessed few that weren't second-hand, used and yellowing, their covers and binding tattered and torn. As well as being balanced in perilous, towering piles on the floor, volumes were scattered across his computer table and filled two floor-to-ceiling wooden bookshelves, their titles rendered even more indecipherable for being hidden behind a mass of ornaments, knick-knacks and photographs. There was no method to it, which is why he was scrabbling on his knees to find a book of names.

'Well, at least you're not the sort who stores his books and CDs alphabetically,' he heard Heather mutter, though he did not reply, so intent was he on finding the volume he needed. Shining Light was the name Foster wanted. He felt certain Eleanor, taken from the Greek, bore that meaning and had told Foster that. But when Heather took him home, with instructions to rest from Foster, he was keen to find out for sure.

'Are these ancestors of yours?' Heather asked.

She was holding a photograph from Nigel's mantelpiece, a family portrait. Father was standing sternly at the back, beard bristling with pride. His left arm was cradled in the elbow of his wife, who was seated. Her hair was tied back, her eyes so bleached of colour by the print she looked almost ghostly. Beside her was a serious-faced boy in a buttoned-up frock coat holding a hoop, while the two girls were seated; the elder, a mirror of her mother, holding a bunch of flowers, the younger mournfully staring with wide brown eyes at the camera, her frilly white shirt in joyous contrast to the monochrome solemnity elsewhere. All, apart from Father, looked as if they had just received the worst news of their lives. It was a picture Nigel loved.

'No,' he said.

'Then who are they?'

'The Reeve family.'

'And they are?'

'I have no idea.'

'So how do you know the name?'

'It's written on the back in pencil. It was taken in 1885.'

'So how come you have it?' Heather asked, gazing intently at it one more time. She was frowning.

'I like it. These people took their family portraits seriously.'

'I can see that. No saying "cheese" back then.'

'Most people wanted to convey an image of being serious, dependable and honest. You didn't do that by smiling.' He took the picture from her. 'I like to wonder what happened to them all. The younger girl with the sad face, especially. To be three or four, however old she is, and to seem so daunted by life. It was a different world.'

'I suppose you don't know enough to have traced them.'

'Don't know where they lived, otherwise I would have. Without that detail it'd be impossible.'

Nigel returned the picture, conscious all of a sudden of the thick layers of dust that had accumulated on top of most of the surfaces in his flat.

'How did you get it?' Heather asked.

'It fell out of a book I bought. I got it framed.'

'What about this?' She was holding a picture of a football team. The men, all bar one, bore moustaches; their striped jerseys were woollen and heavy while their shorts reached their knees. The goalkeeper in the front row was enormously fat and held a ball so solid it appeared to have been fired from a cannon.

'That's the Sheffield United side from 1905,' Nigel said.

'You follow them?'

'No, I hate football. I just love the fact the goalie is so fat. "Fatty Foulkes", they called him. Can you imagine him fitting into modern football?'

'He'd struggle to fit in the dressing room.'

Heather continued browsing while he carried on the search.

Nigel was glad of having something to do. It took his mind off the trauma of the previous night's events. He knew at some stage tiredness would engulf him but, at that moment, the adrenalin, the disbelief at what he had experienced served to heighten his senses.

'I'll make a brew,' Heather said. She weaved her way through to the kitchen, a small space to one side of the sitting room.

'Sorry about the mess,' Nigel said, wondering when it had last been cleaned.

'I'm a murder detective,' she said, popping her head around the door. 'I'm used to dealing with scenes of carnage.' She winked and disappeared back inside.

Nigel smiled. 'The kettle's on the hob. It's not

electric, I'm afraid. The tea is in a metal tin next to the oven. The pot should be around there somewhere. I can't remember where the strainer is.'

Heather's face appeared around the door once more.

'The tea cosy?'

'I don't have one.'

'I was winding you up.'

'Oh,' he said, feeling foolish.

'I'm not au fait with making tea with leaves,' she admitted.

'I thought you were northern,' he said.

'Funnily enough, we have tea bags up there now. Electricity too.'

He smiled, realizing he was being teased once more. It felt good. Heather returned to the kitchen.

'You might find a box of some in a cupboard somewhere,' he shouted.

'Welcome to the twenty-first century.'

He smiled again and went back to his shelves. Finally he found the book he wanted, lurking in an alcove under a treble volume detailing the development of land enclosure. A book he still intended to get around to reading, but which suddenly lost its lustre whenever he picked it up.

It was one of his newer books, a simple dictionary of first names. He flicked through to Eleanor and saw his hunch was correct. Good, he thought. He made a note of the other derivations of the name – Ellie, Nell, Nella, Nellie – and variant spellings so that they could be passed on to Foster.

Heather emerged with two cups of tea. 'You might want to do the genealogy of the contents of your sink,' she said, smiling. 'Some of it looks like it goes back centuries.'

She stopped, trying to find a free space to put the cups down. Nigel quickly swept a pile of books and magazines off the table in the middle of the room and on to the floor. Heather sat down on the sofa and took a wincing sip of hot tea.

'I've made a note of the derivations of Eleanor,' Nigel told her. 'I was right: it means "shining light".'

She took the piece of paper from him, looked at it and then put it in her jacket pocket. 'I'll phone it through to him,' she said, sighing. 'God, I'm knackered. How you doing?'

Nigel didn't know. He felt shaken, frayed, as if he needed to keep occupied, to have a task. He stood, cradling his tea, in preference to sitting down.

'OK.'

'Sure? Because we have people you can talk to about this. Good people. I've used them before.'

'I'll live,' he said, immediately regretting his choice of words.

Heather nodded and took another sip of her tea.

The details of the night before were still hazy – it seemed a different age, not a matter of hours – but one episode seeped back into his mind. He needed to mention it. 'At the newspaper library, when I was waiting for some files, I did a search on DCI Foster on the computer.'

'Oh, yeah,' Heather said. 'Why?'

He shrugged. He didn't know. It was just something he did with people he'd met, whether on the Net or in the archives.

'Don't know. Something to do. I don't know anyone else who might have appeared in the national press during the last decade.'

'You found out about his dad, didn't you?'

'You know about it?'

'We all do. I wasn't on the team at the time, but I heard all about it. They didn't charge him, so he kept his job. It's that simple.'

Nigel was not convinced but saw no profit in prying further. Heather was looking at him.

'He makes no secret about it: he knew his father was going to kill himself and he didn't try to stop it. That's not the same as killing him yourself. His dad wanted to die. Foster let him. For some people that's what any loving son would do; for others, it's tantamount to assisting suicide. Someone at the top took the former view. I think they were right.' She took another swig of tea then looked at him, her brow furrowed. 'So if I poked around in your past, what would I find, Nigel?' she asked, sitting back on the sofa.

'Nothing much,' he muttered.

'Well, you had a job at a university, then the next minute you're back in your old job as a genealogist. Sounds interesting to me.'

This was the one subject he wanted to avoid. He felt that after Heather had been open about Foster, he could not clam up. But how much to tell?

'I met someone. It didn't work out,' he said.

'"Didn't work out" so badly that you left your job? That's some "didn't work out".'

'Let's just say, all of a sudden, the past seemed a more inviting place,' he said.

She scanned the room, the teeming shelves, the old cases and chests on the floor, the sepia-tinted photographs, the array of vintage clocks and watches, none of which told the right time.

'Seems like it always has,' she said.

14

Foster was back at the morgue. I should get myself a bed here, he thought. A visit to the Gents and a quick glance in the mirror showed it to be an appropriate place to be – his skin was the colour of ashes, deep gashes of black under his eyes. Some of those on the slab looked better than he did.

He got there as Carlisle was finishing the autopsy on the tramp.

'Anything new?' he asked.

'He wasn't hanged to death, that's for sure,' Carlisle said. He pointed to the neck. 'There's no fracture of the vertebrae. But then, if a drunken tramp were to commit suicide, one would hardly expect an expert job. But there is no mark from the rope around his neck, which there would have been if the noose had been applied before death, and no sign of bruising either. No signs of any capillary damage in the heart, lungs or eyes – or anything else that indicates asphyxiation. The only visible marks on the body are quite severe pressure sores on his buttocks and shoulder blades, congruent with spending a lot of time on his back.'

'Bed sores?'

'Yes.'

Foster knew that a lot of those who slept rough, and fell ill and became more immobile, suffered these sores. Pavements, cardboard boxes, tended to do that to damaged bodies. Though this guy did not look like the sort who'd been outstaying his welcome at death's door.

'So what killed him?'

'Heart failure.'

'You sure?'

'Almost certain. What caused it is less clear. All the internal organs were in good condition, including the heart. It seems as if it just failed. We've sent some specimens out to toxicology. That may give us more of a clue.'

Foster looked at the body, the well-tended hands and feet, the clear skin. 'Doesn't that strike you as odd? A derelict from the street in good working condition? No enlarged heart, no cirrhosis of the liver, no blood thicker than porridge? What did he drink on the streets? Wheatgrass juice?'

Carlisle pulled a face. 'I can only tell you based on what I see: his body is in good condition, exactly what you would expect of a healthy man in his forties. Though there are signs of drug use, specifically a few marks on the arm. He could be diabetic, of course . . .' His voice tailed off; he moved to the arm and picked it up. 'The reference was scratched on with a smaller implement than the one used on Darbyshire.'

'Like a Stanley knife?'

'It's consistent with the use of that, yes.'

'So there was a reference, but no stab wound and no mutilation?'

Carlisle shook his head. 'I've checked the entire body. He possesses every fingernail, eyelash and tooth he should.'

Why stage the hanging, Foster thought? There was no reason to cover the murder up, not when you've carved a message on one part of the body. Had something gone wrong?

Carlisle removed his gloves with an urgent snap. 'I need a cup of coffee,' he said. 'Then I have another body to look at. Care to join me?'

'Yes to the coffee, no to the body. Not until you've finished, anyway.'

The two men turned to walk to the door. Foster stopped.

'You've done with this guy?'

'Not sure there's much more I can do. Not until we get the results from toxicology.'

'Good. If it's all right with you, I've got someone outside who's here to clean him up.'

Carlisle bristled. 'He's been washed thoroughly,' he said, defensively.

Foster shook his head. 'No, I mean a different kind of clean-up.'

The embalmer worked with great care and gentleness. She was a dowdy, motherly woman with a round, cheerful face that seemed at odds with her profession.

'Sometimes I like to speak to them as I work,' she had warned Foster when she arrived.

'Feel free,' he replied. 'Not sure you'll get much conversation.'

She stroked the dead man's tangled, bedraggled hair. 'Let yourself get in a bit of state, didn't you?' she said in a sing-song voice.

She brought over the tap used to hose down the tables. Shielding the dead man's face with her hand, she carefully wet the hair with a few gentle squirts. Then she applied shampoo, working it into the scalp with her fingers in circular motions, rinsing it off with the tap. She produced a comb from her bag and straightened the hair, breaking up knots with a few stern strokes. With a pair of barber's scissors she started to trim away.

'Can't say I've ever had to just cut someone's hair

and give them a shave before,' she said, without looking at Foster. 'Usually the last thing I do after they've been prepped. If they need it, of course.'

'Sorry,' he said.

'No, it's quite nice, to be honest. I used to do this a lot back in the days when it was common to have an open casket or viewings and you had to make the deceased look the best you could. But less and less now. People don't want to see their relatives or friends once they've passed over. They cut themselves off from death.'

For a fleeting second, Foster recalled standing over the body of his dead father. In his professional life he had seen countless dead bodies, hundreds, but nothing had prepared him for the effect of seeing the lifeless body of the man he had loved and idolized.

'Who is he?' the embalmer asked, stepping back to admire her work between snips.

'We don't know,' Foster said, back in the present. 'That's why I asked you to come and do this. We hope it'll help.'

In less than five minutes the hair was neatly cut. Then she produced a bar of shaving soap and a brush and with some hot water lathered up the man's beard. With a few gentle strokes of a razor, she began to remove it.

'Why not just use an electric shaver?' Foster asked,

marvelling at the almost tender way she cupped the man's chin in her hand as she shaved him, a world away from the clinical way that bodies were usually dealt with in the morgue.

'Never shaves as close,' she added, the serene smile still on her face. Soon the beard was gone. 'There you go,' she said.

Foster said goodbye, showing her out.

He returned and stood at the end of the table, by the man's feet. He looked at his face. The jawline was firm, the cheekbones prominent, not sunken. He was looking at the face of a dark-haired man in his mid-forties. The state of the hands and feet, his teeth – yellow-tinged but well-maintained – the shape of his face, all indicated a man who had taken care of himself before he fell into disrepair. Foster guessed a white-collar worker of some sort – a man who, until recently, lived in comfort.

At the incident room Foster pinned two pictures of the tramp – one unkempt, one groomed – and one of the unknown dead woman to the whiteboard. The room was quiet, most of the team out pounding the streets around the previous night's crime scene in search of a break. The morning had brought nothing new: no witnesses, though Drinkwater had brought in the garage owner and Foster was waiting for news on his interview.

After fetching a coffee, he went to his desk and sat down at his computer. He called up the missing persons database. Beside his keyboard he laid out a freshly printed picture of the groomed corpse. He narrowed the search by entering what he knew of the body: male, Caucasian, aged between forty and fifty, black-grey hair, five feet ten inches in height, brown eyes, average build. Under distinguishing features he mentioned the birthmark on his back, thankful for the latter detail because it would take thousands off the search results.

There were fifteen hits.

He called them up. All but one carried photos. Each time the image loaded on the screen, Foster enlarged it and held up the picture of the tramp to one side, eyes flicking between the two. Most were palpably different men, but the two he thought might possibly match up were put aside for closer inspection.

Then he saw him. Graham Ellis. A passport picture. The similarities between the two men were striking. The shape of the face, the thin lips . . .

There was a knock on his open door: DS Jenkins. She nodded a wordless greeting.

'How's Barnes?' he asked.

She shrugged. 'Pretending he's fine. He needs time to digest it all. I offered him counselling . . .' Her voice tailed away, sensing his distraction.

'Look at this,' he said, turning his screen to face her.

She came forwards and leaned on the desk.

'Now look at this.'

Foster held up the photograph of the unknown corpse. Heather's eyes flicked between the two for some time. She stood up.

'They look alike,' she said. 'Who's the dead man?'

'That dead man is the same tramp we found swinging in the playground in Avondale Park.'

'He scrubbed up well.'

'Well, he's no tramp, that's for sure. Or if he was, not for very long.' He looked at the screen once more. 'And if he's the same guy as the one here, then two months ago he was working at a firm of solicitors in Altrincham.' He continued to look at the screen. 'What I don't understand is why he was hanging in the first place. Post-mortem says he was dead fifteen hours before we found him, so he was killed a fair few hours before he was strung up. In which case, why do it?'

'To make it look like it was suicide, not murder?'

'But where does that fit in with everything else we

know about the killer? He carves references into his victims for us to see. Why be shy about actually killing someone?'

'It was his first. Perhaps he wanted to put us off the scent for a few days. It worked.'

It was a pertinent point, delivered with no sense of self-justification, though he would not have blamed her if she had. But he did not agree.

'No, he wasn't trying to cover anything up. The opposite, I reckon: the hanging tells us something.'

'What was the cause of death?'

'Heart failure. Cause unknown. Tox might tell us more.'

He made a mental note to chase up the toxicology report on Darbyshire. They had had long enough; it was time to start shouting at them to get their arses in gear.

'Do we have any ID yet on last night's victim?' Heather asked.

Foster shook his head slowly. 'Carlisle's doing her as we speak. There's a whole pile of missing person reports out there. Start with the most recent. Call Khan back in to give you a hand.'

Soon after Heather left, his phone rang. It was Drinkwater calling in from Acton. The garage owner was proving of little use. He had an alibi that stood up.

'Get a list of everyone who's ever rented the place,' Foster said.

They were still looking for the way in. Something had to give somewhere, he thought, if they kept pressing.

He looked once more at the details of the missing solicitor on screen: 'There is great concern for Graham Ellis, who has been missing since 25th January. He was last seen drinking in a pub near his home in Altrincham, Cheshire.'

His firm was Nicklin Ellis & Co; he was a partner. Foster rang directory enquiries and was put through to their offices. It was Sunday, but he thought it was worth a try.

The message kicked in. The office was closed, as Foster expected. However, as he hoped, there was a number to ring in case of emergency. He dialled it.

'Tony Penberthy.'

The voice was eager, young.

'Hello, sorry to trouble you on a Sunday.'

'No worries,' Penberthy replied, with a hint of an Australian accent. 'How can I help?'

'I was hoping to have a word with my usual solicitor, Graham Ellis.'

'He's not on duty at the moment, sir. But I'm sure I can be of service. What's the problem, Mr . . . ?'

'Foster,' he answered, seeing no reason to lie. 'It's

a bit delicate. Without sounding rude, I'd rather chat to Graham about it. Should I call back tomorrow?'

There was a pause at the other end.

'Look, Mr Foster, there's a problem here. You see, Graham Ellis has gone missing.'

'God. When?' Foster winced at his poor acting skills.

'A little over two months ago. Came as a real shock.'

'I bet it did. He just vanished?'

'He was drinking in the pub across the road after work with a few of us. Seemed fine. Left to go home. Never seen since.'

'We were friends in the past. Lost touch. No one's heard anything?'

'Nothing.'

'I hope he's OK,' Foster added, remembering he was posing as a concerned member of the public, not a detective.

'Yeah,' the Australian said.

'You don't sound too convinced.'

There was a pause. Foster wondered how far to push it. The Australian seemed garrulous and he knew that, as a breed, solicitors weren't allergic to the sound of their own voices.

'Well, the word here is that he's taken his own life.'

'He didn't strike me as the suicidal type,' Foster

added, wondering what the 'suicidal type' actually was. It didn't matter. It kept the conversation going. Better this than being passed around the local nick in search of whichever copper took the report and filed it in the bottom drawer.

'Yeah.'

He sensed the solicitor's unease; he changed tack. 'I'd like to send his wife a card, share her concern. Do you have an address?'

'He was divorced.'

'Really?'

'Last year. Very messy.'

Foster scribbled a note. 'Poor bloke,' he muttered.

'He had a tough time of it,' the Aussie replied.

'He was always a big drinker.'

'He was still putting it away. Especially during the last year or so. We reckon after leaving us he went back to his local and sank a few more, then decided he'd had enough and got a train somewhere.'

Foster knew that if the man downstairs was Graham Ellis, then whatever problems he'd found in the bottom of his glass that evening, he'd been going home to bed when he left that pub. But he never made it. Foster badly needed an ID of the body.

He ended the call and set about contacting West Midlands Police. But just as he was about to dial, the phone burst into life. It was the desk sergeant at Notting Hill police station. They'd had a walk-in, a man claiming to know about a possible murder. He was insisting on speaking to someone senior.

'The man has a package with him, sir,' the sergeant said, quietly yet forcefully.

When Foster arrived with DS Jenkins at Notting Hill, the man was sitting in an interview room nursing a cup of tea. He was dressed casually, yet still appeared smart: brown cords, navy-blue jumper over an open-necked shirt, a mane of dark hair that flopped occasionally over his brow. His face, shapeless yet with skin so clear it was hard to determine his age, eyes watery-blue, seemed familiar to Foster.

On the table was a shoebox.

'Sorry to keep you,' Foster said, introducing Heather.

The man nodded, smiled briefly. His eyes were vacant, the face white. He seemed in a daze.

'Simon Perry,' he said slowly, mechanically in a clear voice that indicated a wealthy upbringing.

The name was vaguely familiar, too, but Foster's eyes were drawn to the container on the table.

'What's in the box, sir?' Foster asked.

Each word he said took time to penetrate the field

of shock and bewilderment that seemed to envelop Simon Perry. Eventually he spoke without emotion or expression.

'My sister's eyes.'

'Are you the only person who's handled this?'

'That I'm aware of, yes.'

'We'll need to take your prints,' Foster said. 'Rule out which are yours.'

'Of course.'

Foster pulled on a pair of latex gloves, and lifted the lid.

The bottom of the box had been padded with a bed of cotton wool. Resting on it were a pair of eyes. Foster could not believe the size: the whites were the size of golf balls, part of the optic nerve trailing behind them pathetically. He realized just how much of the eye was out of sight. They seemed intact, which indicated great care had been taken during their removal. There was little colour to them, a blue tint to the iris perhaps: presumably whatever pigment had been there had vanished in the hours since their removal.

He replaced the lid. 'What makes you think they're your sister's?'

'The colour.'

'I couldn't make out much colour, to be honest . . .'

'She suffers from albinism.'

'She's an albino?'

Perry's vacant eyes just continued to stare as if he had failed to hear.

Heather spoke. 'What does her albinism involve?'

The change of voice appeared to reawaken him from his stupor.

'Fair skin, fair hair, but mainly her eyes; they are the lightest blue. She's the first one in generations. It's a recessive gene. Dammy is a throwback.'

'Dammy?'

'As in Damson.'

'That's her name?'

'No. Her name is Nella. Damson is her nickname because our elder sister is known as Plum, though her real name is Victoria. Family joke.'

The joyous wit of the English upper classes, thought Foster. Nella was one of the names Barnes had suggested might tally.

'Does your sister have any tattoos that you are aware of?' he asked.

Again the pause while the words penetrated. 'Not that I recall. Can't say I've ever studied her that closely. But it wouldn't surprise me if she had.'

'Sorry to be as bold as this, Mr Perry, but does your sister have breast implants?'

Perry looked at him; Foster could see he was only just managing to hold it together.

'Yes, she does. Her unusual looks get her a lot of attention. She doesn't exactly run away from that attention. Makes the most of it, in fact. Hence the implants. She has a newspaper column, dates men in the public eye.'

Great, thought Foster. If the body in the morgue was hers, every reptile in London would be crawling all over the case within hours of this getting out. Serial killer, socialite and journalist, police missing the chance to catch her murderer: he could see the fall-out already.

'Are you a journalist, too?' he asked.

'No. An MP.'

As if the story was not sensational enough. He wondered whether the Perrys had risen to the top of the social and professional tree through hard work or a network of old school pals and family friends. Smart money was on the latter.

'Can I ask when was the last time you heard from Nella?'

He couldn't bring himself to use her nickname.

'Friday afternoon. She and her latest boyfriend, a painter, were due to come to dinner last night. She rang to say it would be only her; they'd had a tiff. She never arrived. I thought perhaps they'd made up, that sort of thing. I called her mobile, but it was off. Assumed she'd get in touch with one of her apologies at some point. She's very good at them; she'll make you forgive her anything.'

Foster was making notes. It was only when he looked up that he saw tears streaming down the man's face.

'Sorry,' Perry said, pulling a handkerchief from his trouser pocket.

'No need to be. Don't bottle it up on our behalf.'

Heather left the room and returned with a glass of water. She put it on the table and Perry gave her a thankful grimace.

'Do you have her boyfriend's details?'

Perry passed on what he knew. 'You think he might be responsible?'

Foster shrugged. 'We can't say.'

'I've never thought much of him,' Perry added, face reddening. 'Bit of a poseur, but never thought he was violent.'

'When did you notice the package?' Foster asked.

'Not until this lunchtime. It was on our back door-step. I took the rubbish out and there it was.'

'We need to take this box and the eyes for further examination. We'll also need to go and have a look around your garden, speak to some of your neigh-bours, see if they saw anyone or anything last night or this morning.' There was only one more question Foster needed to raise. 'If you feel up to it, we'll need you to identify the body of a young woman we found murdered last night.'

Perry nodded slowly, as if in a trance, pulling absent-mindedly at the loose skin under his chin.

'Of course,' he said faintly. 'Look, I need to make a phone call. Could you leave me alone for a few minutes?'

Foster and Heather left the room.

'The killer's getting more elaborate,' Foster hissed. 'More and more confident. Maybe too confident; they always make a mistake when they start to play too many games.'

Heather nodded. 'I know Dammy Perry,' she whispered. 'Well, not personally, but I've seen her column. It's in the *Telegraph*.'

'Really?' Foster said. He got whatever news he needed online. He despised newspapers, their spin, lies and wilful deceit. 'I never had you down as the broadsheet type.'

She flashed back a sardonic smile. 'It's one of those diary columns. Except, rather than pop stars and footballers, it gossips about wealthy families, particularly the misbehaviour of their scions.'

'Serious stuff, then.'

Inside they could hear Perry murmuring on the phone.

'Don't suppose he's a member of the Socialist Workers' Party either,' Foster said.

Heather ignored him. 'It sounds like it's her. Bit of a new departure, if it is; sending the body parts to another member of the family.'

Foster sighed. 'The pattern is all over the place. First victim looks like he was kidnapped two months before he was killed; the second barely two hours before he was killed. The second and third have had body parts removed, the first didn't. The second's hands are still missing, the third's eyes turn up the same morning as the body. The only thing that's constant is the reference and the fact that the place and time accord with the murders of 1879.'

The door handle turned. Perry emerged from the room. 'Let's get on with this,' he said.

15

Nigel had done all he could do to occupy himself that day, but no matter what he did – opened a book, retreated into the past as his usual method of escape – he was unable to expunge the image of the dead woman, her sightless eye sockets, her alabaster skin punctured with holes like black moons.

Towards the end of the afternoon, as he lay wide awake in bed seeking sleep he would never get, he heard the sound of his telephone. Thinking, hoping, it might be Foster and Jenkins, he scrambled out from the tangle of sheets and found it. The voice on the other end was familiar but unwelcome.

'Hello, Nigel.'

Gary Kent.

'What do you want?' he snapped. Knowing exactly what.

'Dammy Perry.'

'What?'

'The young woman whose body you stumbled across, if that's the right phrase, this morning. Was wondering if there's anything more you can tell me?'

'I'm not saying anything,' Nigel said, preparing to put the receiver back in its cradle.

'What, got another student in your bed, have you?'

Nigel froze. Unable to react.

'Two hours on a university campus can teach you many things. Hardly national news, but I'm sure I could get it placed somewhere.'

'Are you blackmailing me?'

Kent ignored his question. 'What's this about the cops getting the wrong tube station?'

How did he know *that*?

'Goodbye, Gary.'

He put the phone down, then picked it up and laid it off the hook. His hand trembled; Kent had shaken him. Dammy Perry, he had said the name was. At least Nigel now had a name to go with the face. He did not know what to think about Kent's revelation that he knew what had happened at the university. Should he tell Foster and Jenkins? He decided against it.

He dressed. He needed to go out, to walk and expend some energy. In the back of his mind he knew where he was going, but didn't yet want to ask himself why. Something was drawing him back there.

The early-evening air was fresh; it was still light and the streets around the Bush were crowded. He headed straight past the Green towards Holland Park, under the roundabout gridlocked by traffic even at the weekend. From there he headed up Holland Park Avenue, turning left into Princedale Road, past the silent garden squares overlooked by enormous stucco townhouses. Soon he was in the warren-like streets of Notting Dale. It was as if the air was different, less clear. He passed the old brick kiln on Walmer Road, the only relic of the time when the Dale was famous for three things: remorseless poverty, brick-making and pigs. Once, when the police came in to settle an altercation, the locals rose up against them, forming bricks out of the dried pig shit that covered the ground and hurling them at the cops. Dickens had written about this area, describing it as one of the most deprived in London, amazed that such squalor existed in the middle of such elegance.

The brick kiln was now a converted flat. Worth half a million pounds.

At the top of Walmer Road he cut through the corner of a council estate, arriving at Lancaster Road. He could feel his throat tighten as he neared the scene. What he expected to find when he got there, he didn't know. He walked to Ladbroke Grove, past the tube station, following the same route as the previous night. There were fewer people but still the same throb of energy and life; it felt strange to him, as if the whole area should be in shock and mourning.

At the opening to the alleyway a solitary police-man stood sentinel. Behind him Nigel could see tape flapping in the wind; the scene was still closed. There was no way through. He walked up Ladbroke Grove, taking the first left down Cambridge Gardens, then a left on to St Mark's Road. As he turned he saw a police car blocking the entry, behind it more tape fluttering forlornly. Part of him was relieved; he wasn't sure what his reaction would have been if he'd been able to visit the scene.

He looked around: it was an anonymous part of town, nestling in the lea of the overhead motorway and a raised railway line. A light under the Westway glowed in the half-light, illuminating three recycling bins with broken glass scattered on the floor around one bin. He decided to make his way back home, perhaps stop off for a recuperative pint.

He passed under both the Westway and the tube line. A train rattled overhead, shaking the structure. He crossed over, past a newly built close of houses. And stopped.

He walked a few steps back. He read the name of the street once more: Bartle Road. It was not much of a street; on one side were beige-bricked bungalows, on the other were private parking spaces bordered by an old stone wall that backed on to the arches of the railway, where a garage had made its home. Nigel felt his heartbeat quicken. So this is where it was.

He walked down the street, counting off the houses. One, two, each of them identical. After number nine he stopped: between it and the next building was an incongruous gap. Visible over the top of the wall was a tangled bush, little else. The next house after the gap was number 11. It was true, he thought; there is no number 10. When Rillington Place was bulldozed in the 1970s, it was rebuilt and renamed Bartle Road. But, obviously, the developers had decided to take no chances and had left a hole where number 10 should have been.

These sordid stories of London's past delighted him; dark secrets that offered a glimpse behind the city's net curtains. Ten Rillington Place was the home of John Christie, a post-war serial killer who strangled a string of young women he had lured back to his rotting, soot-soaked little Victorian terraced house. He had sex with their lifeless corpses before either burying them in the garden or, as he did with his wife's remains, stowing them in a cupboard. He was hanged for his crimes, though only after Timothy Evans, a barely literate neighbour of Christie's, had been wrongly executed for murdering his wife and child. The real culprit, Christie, had been chief prosecution witness at Evans's trial.

Nigel stood staring at the gap. He had come to revisit one murder scene, only to encounter another. Little more than a hundred yards away from this scene of horror, another serial killer was writing his name into London legend. When he was eventually brought to justice, would they bulldoze any of the buildings in which this killer had struck? Nigel knew such efforts were futile. The past cannot be erased so easily. You can knock something down; you can change names; you can try all you want to wipe these acts from history, he thought. But the past seeps back through the soil, like blood through sand. Or lingers in the air. Always there.

He pulled his brick of a mobile from his pocket and dialled Foster.

Seeing his sister's mutilated corpse had broken Simon Perry. After nodding to indicate it was her, his legs had crumpled beneath him. Foster helped him to a side room and summoned a doctor. He was sedated and taken home. After making sure he was all right, Foster returned to the corpse. The cleaned, livid wounds across her breasts spelled out the reference. Closer inspection of the body also revealed several track marks in her arm that suggested drug use. Her internal organs displayed no sign of damage from heavy use.

He and Heather returned to the incident room in Kensington. Waiting for them was Nella Perry's boyfriend, Jed Garvey. He turned out to be the sort of Trustafarian fool for whom Foster had nothing but disdain. With no need to make a living between dates, dealers and dinner parties, these people, he imagined, flitted from one job to another, alighting on something that would fill their time, give them a cachet, until it became financially unviable and they were either bailed out or moved on to a horse of a different colour.

Jed Garvey was a painter, so he said. Foster guessed that Picasso and Pollock needn't worry about their place in history just yet. He was beanpole skinny, over six feet in height. His face was long and cloaked in at least a week's growth of stubble. His hair looked like it had fallen out of a tree and landed on his head. He was wearing a battered suit jacket over a V-neck jumper, faded jeans and baseball boots.

His face was gaunt, drawn from hearing of his girlfriend's death. They got him a coffee and let him stew for a few seconds.

'That is one good-looking bloke,' Heather said.

'You don't mean you think that lanky streak of piss is attractive, do you?' Foster said, appalled.

'There's something about him.'

'Yeah, a bundle in the bank courtesy of Daddy.'

'Cynical or jealous – difficult to guess which.'

'Jealous? Of him? The Bumfluff Kid?'

'Word has it he's dated some of the most beautiful young models, actresses and society beauties in London.'

'He's welcome to them. You spend a lot of time reading those gossip columns, then?'

'Light relief,' she said. 'Funny, Dammy Perry used to mention him a lot in her diary.'

'Bet she did. That's how it works for these people, isn't it? There's probably a thousand artists out there better than him, but they aren't shagging society journalists.' Foster sighed. 'You handle this one. I'm worried there might be more severed parts by the end of the interview if I do it.'

They went back into the room. Garvey was seated, his arms wrapped around his chest, staring at the desk in front of him. Heather put the coffee down and gave him a comforting smile.

'I realize this has come as a bit of a shock,' she said.

Garvey just nodded, eyes vacant.

'We need to go through a few things. Just routine. It will help us catch whoever did this.'

Garvey nodded once more. 'The last thing I said to her was "Fuck off",' he said, then shook his head. 'Do you know how awful that feels? To know that was the last thing you said to someone you loved?'

Heather nodded sympathetically. Foster felt an unexpected twang of sympathy. The last thing he got to say to his father was that he loved him and respected him.

'I can't imagine,' Heather said softly. 'Tell us about the last time you saw her.'

He took a deep breath. 'It was Friday lunchtime. Dammy was in good spirits because her agent had got her a deal for a book idea she had. We went to the Electric on Portobello Road to celebrate. A few friends joined us; we ate, drank champagne, they left. Then, well you know what it's like, you've been in high spirits, you drink too much, you say the wrong thing.'

'What did you say?'

'She thought I was jealous. I've been struggling a bit lately, not showing or selling much. It was getting me down. After a few drinks I suppose I got a bit peeved that she'd got a deal for an idea she'd scribbled on the back of a fag packet, yet here was I, with a studio full of pictures that nobody wanted. I said something about good fortune smiling on her and she laid into me.'

'What did she say?'

'She called me a waster, a loser, said that I was lazy

and expected the world to come to me. That's when I told her to fuck off. She got her bag, got up and walked out. Didn't say a word; didn't even look at me.'

'You didn't try to follow her?' Heather asked.

To Foster, this sounded suspiciously like criticism, but Garvey took it in his stride.

'No. We rowed a bit but always made up. She's feisty . . . *was* feisty. Best thing to do in those circumstances was call it a day, and apologize later.'

The fact that he would never get that chance was left hanging in the air.

'Do you know where she went afterwards?'

'I assumed she'd gone home. We'd just started living together. When I got back and she wasn't there, I just thought she was at some friend's. It had happened before. She'd put me in the cooler for a day or two.'

'Surely, on Saturday, when she hadn't come home, you got worried?'

'To be honest, I got so wasted on Friday night that Saturday just drifted by. I tried to call her a million times on her mobile, but it was off. We were supposed to be going round to her brother's on Saturday night, but she just didn't come back. I went out and got wasted again.'

'Let me get this straight,' Foster interjected. 'You

have a row, she walks out and you don't see her for two days and you don't do anything other than leave a few messages on her mobile? You don't try her friends, her brother or anyone else?'

Garvey flicked his eyes from Heather to Foster. 'With respect, you didn't know Dammy; she was an independent spirit. She wouldn't have appreciated me stalking her.'

She might have done, given that she had been kidnapped and was then killed, thought Foster, but he said nothing.

'Sorry, but I need to ask you some difficult questions,' Heather said, stepping back in, waiting for Garvey to indicate that would be OK. 'When you'd rowed before, did Dammy ever go off with someone else? I'm thinking specifically of another man.'

'Never. No way. She'd had her fair share of boyfriends but, as far as I know, she was faithful. She once told me she'd cut my balls off if she ever found out I'd cheated on her. I know where she went. She'd have gone to the Prince of Wales in Holland Park; it was her favourite pub. She knew people in there, the staff, the regulars. It was why I didn't go there; didn't fancy venturing into enemy territory during a state of conflict.' He smiled weakly, though it vanished immediately. 'Of course, now I wish I had done.'

Garvey's head bowed and his eyes looked to the floor.

And you always will, Foster thought.

He remembered the Prince of Wales on Princedale Road as an old man's local boozer, all stained carpets and garish lights; now it was stripped wood bars, Belgian beers, and candles on each table. There were few traditional pubs left in the area. Foster wondered what happened to the regulars of gentrified pubs. Did the brewery round them up and shoot them?

Checks had been made on Dammy Perry's movements. Garvey had been the last of her family and close friends to see her; a scan of her credit card and bank-account history showed no activity since Friday morning.

It was early evening and the pub was still full from the Sunday-lunch trade, the bright young things of Holland Park and Notting Hill taking the edge off their weekend hangovers. Heather asked to see the manager, a fat, amiable-looking Geordie. He had not been at work on Friday, but called one of his bar staff across. Karl was a wiry, dark-eyed man in his thirties with a long face that wore the leathery imprint of a life lived in front of a bar.

Foster asked if there was somewhere quiet to speak and Karl led them out to the beer garden, which was empty save for two smokers gathered under an overhead burner. The familiar scent drifted under Foster's nostrils and reminded him how much he missed the habit.

Foster asked if he knew Dammy Perry. He did.

'Was she in here on Friday afternoon?' he asked.

'She came in about three or four o'clock, I reckon.'

'On her own?'

'Don't remember anyone else with her. A couple of people she knew were here having a drink, so she sat with them. They left after about half an hour and she came out here.'

'On her own?'

'No. There was a bloke, too.'

'Where did he come from?'

'Can't remember. Think he came in for a drink after her. All I remember is coming out here to collect a few glasses and seeing him and her sat at that table. They were both smoking. I remember that because she didn't smoke unless she was well gone. Is she all right?'

Heather was scribbling furiously.

'We found her body last night. She'd been murdered. We think she was last seen here on Friday.'

'Christ,' he said, wind knocked from him. 'Murdered? Who'd want to murder a gorgeous woman like that?'

'That's what we're trying to find out,' Foster said. 'Did you know the man she was sitting with?'

'Never seen him before.'

'When did they leave?'

'I don't know. I came out about an hour later to collect more glasses, about five o'clock, and they'd gone.'

'Would anyone else have seen them?'

'Sonia was on, but she was working the bar mainly.' He scratched absent-mindedly at the back of his head. 'Still can't believe she was murdered, like. That's horrible.'

'Was there anything about him you remember?'

He spent some time in thought, stifled a yawn, then spoke. 'Nothing springs to mind. He was wearing shades and he had a round face, pudding-basin sort of dark hair. He was thickset, too, but he was sat down so . . . He was drinking Virgin Marys, I know that. Can't remember the face, but I never forget an order.'

'Is there anyone in the pub now who was in then?'

'Don't think so. Sunday's a different crowd to the rest of the week.'

'We need you to come and help us do a photofit as soon as possible.'

'Sure, if it's OK with the boss.'

He went inside to check.

'Darbyshire disappeared after going out of a pub for a smoke,' Foster said to Heather. 'Ellis and Perry were last seen in a pub. Think we're getting closer to knowing how he picks his victims up.'

'Pretty public place to operate.'

'Look at it this way: it's an easy way to lace a drink.'

'Rohypnol?'

'Something like that. Next thing you know, they're out of it.'

'Park your vehicle nearby. Help them in. Nothing untoward about helping someone the worse for wear outside a pub,' Heather added.

The barman returned. 'I'm ready when you are,' he said.

'We'll also need to get in touch with whoever was serving the bar that night. Sonia, was it?' Foster said.

'The boss says he'll give her a call.'

'What was Dammy drinking, do you remember?'

'Same as always. Vodka, lime and soda.'

Ruled out Rohypnol. The makers put a blue dye in it to guard against spiking. She would have noticed. Though it could have been a counterfeit. And there were any number of other 'date rape' drugs it could be. Toxicology would tell them more.

A few hours later, they called it a night. Foster was looking forward to getting home, climbing into a few glasses of red then seeking sanctuary in sleep. His whole body ached and creaked from weariness; a headache had settled behind his tired eyes.

They had a sketch of the suspect. Tomorrow they would show it to everyone in the lives of their three victims, as well as to everyone who might have seen them in the final hours before their disappearances. They had also lifted a print from the box containing Nella Perry's eyes. It had been put through the database, but there had been no matches. Still, together with the description, it was a start.

He would wait until Detective Superintendent Harris, his boss, was in tomorrow before he released the sketch to the media. Harris had been summoned back from his holiday in Spain, so Foster knew he would not be in the best of moods. The press bureau had been briefed after sinking under an avalanche of calls when Nella Perry's demise circulated around Fleet Street. There was to be a briefing at eight the following morning for the whole team, a chance to sift all the facts and see what emerged.

Then there had been Barnes's phone call, about Rillington Place. It fascinated him. Was there any significance to it?

He found Heather preparing to leave.

'Ever heard of psychogeography?' Foster asked her.

She made a face. 'Teach it at universities now, do they?'

'Don't start me,' he said. 'No, it was Barnes's phone call. For some reason he found himself back in North Kensington, near the murder scene. Apparently, just around the corner is the site of 10 Rillington Place.'

'The Christie–Evans murders,' exclaimed Heather.

'I remember a mate of my old man, a gnarled old-school detective,' Foster said. 'You know, the sort you'd want on the job if your daughter had been killed. He was talking about that case once. He knew one of the coppers who was given the job of removing the bodies. Someone asked him a few years later whether he received any counselling. He said, "Well, the district inspector bought me a pint."'

Despite his exhaustion, Foster rumbled with laughter.

Heather looked heavenwards. 'So what did Nigel want?'

'He just thought I should know that Rillington Place was near, in case it was important.'

'Do you think it is?'

'Could be. Anything could be. At the moment this case is like moulding milk; it's spilling out everywhere.' He paused. 'I told him we'll need him tomorrow. I can't help feeling that if we're going to get anywhere near to solving the present, we're going to have to know everything we can about the past. Only then will things make sense.'

'And what is psychogeography?'

'According to Barnes, it's the theory that some places always carry the stain or stigma of the past; these places can then have an effect on people's emotions, behaviour and actions.'

'Sounds interesting,' Heather said.

'Sounds like he's lost his marbles,' Foster said. 'You're quite taken with his barmy little theories and interests. You like him, don't you?'

'He's good at his job,' she replied, flicking a stray hair from her brow.

'Not that sort of like, the other sort.'

'Do I fancy him, you mean?'

Foster smiled. Heather often did that: confronted the subject head-on, rather than skirt around it. She claimed it was her northern upbringing, where people called a spade a bloody shovel. In the south of England, so her theory went, people euphemized and pussyfooted around. Whatever the reasons, Foster liked it and he knew she admired him for the same quality. Unlike some other junior officers, she had never been intimidated by his presence or nature.

'He's all right,' she said. 'Quite dishy.'

'Really?' he replied; Foster had him down as a bit geeky.

'That's because the last three blokes I've seen have been coppers. He's about as far removed from that world as can be. For a start, he's intelligent.' Foster ignored the slight; she wasn't finished listing his qualities. 'Yes, he's a bit shy and reserved but he has lots of energy. He's a good listener, too, which is hardly a trait you meet in most modern men. And he's enthusiastic and passionate about what he does for a living, not world-weary and cynical. God, I'm so bored with world-weary and cynical.'

Foster knew both adjectives could well be applied to him. He could not remember ever having been innocent and idealistic. Those attributes tended not to flourish in murder squads.

'He also has a gorgeous pair of blue eyes that you want to dive into,' she added, then gave him a victorious smile. 'You did ask.'

'Well, can you lead him astray after the case is closed?' he said, putting on his jacket.

16

Detective Superintendent Harris was sitting in Foster's chair when he arrived the next morning. He was waiting, leaning forwards, a frown on his tanned face. Foster's head was heavy; three pints in the pub, then half a bottle of claret before turning in hadn't helped. But he needed it to get to sleep – an alcohol-induced coma was preferable to a restless night.

Harris said nothing, no greeting. Merely tossed a copy of a morning tabloid on to the desk. Foster picked it up.

There was a picture of Dammy Perry on the front page, dressed in a full-length gown, straw hair, broad smile, bleached eyes peering from the page. She looked ethereal, otherworldly. Above the picture, in bold type, the headline read: 'Could She Have Been Saved?'

No, thought Foster. He turned, as directed by the story, to page three.

'There are six pages in total,' Harris said.

'Jesus!'

'And there's a leader on the comment page. It says we should hold an investigation into how our forces came to be at the wrong tube station and missed the chance to catch the killer.'

Foster was only half listening as he leafed through the pages. The headlines were a succession of lurid questions: 'When Will Fiend Strike Again?' 'What Are Cops Doing?' There was a picture of Simon Perry, 'Slain Dammy's Brother', managing to look both bereaved and self-regarding.

'Fish-and-chip paper,' Foster said, tossing it back on to the desk.

A thin, joyless smile spread across the superintendent's face. 'To you, Grant, it may be. But this is exactly what we don't need. Do you know how bad this looks?'

Foster was in no mood to get into an argument about media perception. 'I can see how, reported like this, it looks bad. But the fact is, we discovered he was going to dump a body only a few hours before he actually did. The genealogist found out it was to be Notting Hill. There wasn't time to research the whole history of the London underground. It was a genuine, honest mistake. In any case, she was dead before her body was dumped.'

'Her brother will cause us no end of problems.'

'Her brother's a chinless fool.'

'Who sits on the Home Affairs Select Committee.'

Foster said nothing; he was prepared to weather Harris's public relations paranoia.

'What about the first victim? How come nobody realized he'd been murdered until almost a week after his body had been found?'

Foster explained the story of the tramp who wasn't. The severity of Harris's expression did not alter. He had been in the army in his younger years and, with his ramrod straight back, salt-and-pepper hair and overweening pomposity, Foster guessed he might have made a good officer.

'We need more manpower,' he said, when Foster had finished.

'I agree.'

'I'm bringing Williams's team in from South.'

That wasn't what Foster had in mind. They needed more infantry, not another general. He started to protest. The room, lit only by the thin sunlight of the early morning, darkened perceptibly as two masses of grey cloud met and became one.

'I'm taking charge,' Harris said. 'And you won't like my first decision.'

Foster said nothing; he could feel the tension bulging in the back of his arms.

'DCI Williams's team, and most of yours, are going back out on the streets, finding witnesses, digging up all they can on the victims – their lives, their enemies, every single thing they can find. They will show the sketch you've got to everyone who's ever known these victims. I'm also releasing it to the media. We're going to shake down every single ex-con in London who's ever picked up a knife. Williams will coordinate the investigation on the ground and report back to me. You will concentrate on the past. Find out what the hell happened in 1879.'

'Sir . . .'

'Grant, there is a man out there murdering at will,' he said, his finger jabbing towards the window. 'The press are all over it. They're saying it's the biggest manhunt since the Yorkshire Ripper.'

'So you're going to turn it into one?'

'Yes, if it means we catch the murderer,' he barked back.

'We've been behind the eight ball all the way through this investigation and now when, if we haven't yet got a foothold, at least we've got a bit of purchase, you're standing me down?'

'Not standing you down, Grant. Asking you to oversee a different part of the investigation.'

The one that involves being shut away in dark rooms poring over documents, books and maps, Foster thought.

'We need to understand everything that happened back then. What is it someone once said, "The past is another country"?'

'So is France. Never wanted to go there either.'

Harris simply shook his head. 'My mind is made up.'

In one respect Foster knew Harris was right; to solve the present they needed to solve the past. But the killer was to be apprehended in the present, and that was the task he wanted to see through himself. Instead, he would be stuck in some archive with Barnes when they finally caught this creep.

'The ex-wife of Graham Ellis is coming down today to identify the body. I fixed it up.'

'I'll handle it,' Harris said immediately, rising from Foster's seat. He picked his papers up from the desk, uncurled his wiry frame and walked out without another glance.

Foster picked up a pen and hurled it against the wall.

Nigel was standing outside the newspaper library, puffing on a roll-up, when Foster screeched to a halt in his car, then reversed at speed into a space. He and Heather got out, Foster striding three yards ahead of her. As he reached the door, he did not meet Nigel's eye, muttered no greeting, merely brushed past and went into the small reception area.

'Don't ask,' Heather murmured to Nigel, who flicked his cigarette stub to one side with forefinger and thumb, then followed her in.

The security guard on reception was waiting to take them to their room. They went through a set of double doors into the small 'café' area, which was nothing more than a collection of chairs, tables and vending machines. They headed left through more double doors into an area that Nigel knew was for staff only, then straight across the staff canteen into a small room that smelled as if it had lain unused for some time. The walls bore the shadows of long-gone pictures and calendars. It was windowless and, when Nigel absent-mindedly ran his finger along the only table, it was thickly coated with dust. Two swivel chairs and a battered wooden chair had been put in there for their use.

Foster shut the door behind them. 'We're working here,' he barked.

Nigel didn't understand why, but sensed it would be unwise to ask. Foster detected his bemusement.

'If we work upstairs, or wherever the main bit is, what's to say Joe Public doesn't have a look at what we're doing? Or your mate Gary Kent, or some other enterprising hack, doesn't slip a few quid to one of the staff in exchange for having a glance at the same papers we've been looking at? Here we know we can get some privacy.'

'But that doesn't solve the problem of the staff being bought off,' Heather interjected.

'No, but I've asked for copies of every single national newspaper that was published in the 1870s to be brought here.'

'Every one?' Nigel asked incredulously.

'Yeah. So if they want to work their way through that lot, they can. By the time they reach 1879 ... Well, they won't. They're too lazy,' he said.

There was a knock on the door. Foster opened it, mumbled a few words and then closed it. In his right hand Nigel recognized the 1879 volume of the *Kensington News and West London Times* from which he had located details of the third murder on Saturday night.

'I asked the duty manager to personally bring me the *Kensington News* for 1879 and mentioned that, if word got out, I would know exactly where it came from.'

He tossed the book on to the table. Dust billowed from between the pages as it landed with a thumping slap.

'We look in here first,' Foster said. 'When the other stuff arrives, we look through that. We build up as much information about these murders as we possibly can.'

'Most of the national newspapers will be on microfilm,' Nigel said. 'We need . . .'

'A microfilm reader is on its way down, Mr Barnes,' Foster said.

Nigel could see that when Foster got his teeth into something, it came away in chunks.

Foster took the job of scouring through the newspaper volume. He turned over the pages until he reached the next edition, dated Friday April 11th.

'Here we go,' he said.

Heather came and looked over his shoulder. Nigel stayed where he was, staring at the microfilm reader he'd just been brought.

THE KENSINGTON HORRORS:
YET MORE OUTRAGES

Once more, last Saturday morning in Notting Dale, came another of those sadly terrible scenes with which the area has become only too accustomed during the past two weeks.

To describe the event as clearly and succinctly as possible, it is necessary to describe the location which has been the scene of this latest crime. Saunders Road, an incomplete terrace under construction in the heart of the new Norland Town, stands directly west of the West London Junction railway line, in what was until recently deserted commons and farmland.

Last Friday night the occupants of Saunders Road knew little of the horror that took place only yards from where they sought repose, and the throw of a stone from the Norland Castle, where Reverend Booth and his Salvationists are seeking to win hearts and mend the ways of the local poor. As the residents of that quiet street slept soundly abed, the butchered body of poor John Allman, an Irish-born commercial traveller, aged 38, of nearby Stebbing Street, a devoted father of three, was hidden on a small patch of waste-land at the western corner of the terraced street. The next day, around midday, one of the occupants seeking air on a constitutional was met with the awful sight of Mr Allman's corpse face down beneath the detritus!

Reports suggest Allman, a man of repute and good standing among neighbours despite a known liking for drink, had been making his way home from the Queen's Arms tavern at the junctions of Queen's and Norland Road when he was attacked by the ghoul. Like his poor three fellow victims, a stab wound to the abdomen was enough to ensure his demise.

Despite the police's unwillingness to confirm the atrocity, the news spread that the Kensington murderer had been at his ghastly work again, and within an hour, the environs surrounding Saunders Road were closed to the public by cordons of police. Bedlam then ensued. As night fell, a gang of roughs wielding torches waded across the boundary into Shepherd's Bush Common, upon hearing of a mendicant smeared with blood in that vicinity. Assuming him to be the culprit, they went in search, terrorizing the filthy scores of unwashed who live their pitiful lives upon the patch of land known as the Green. Encountering a terrified gypsy, the bloodthirst of the mob caused them to beat him almost senseless. The poor soul, believed to be innocent, perished of his injuries.

Foster paused in his reading. 'Here he goes again,' he said, a sadness in his voice.

Heather whispered her disbelief behind him.

Alas, it is with great sadness yet increasing anger that we report that the Kensington Killer struck once again, bringing yet more fear and hysteria to our small part of the world. Fewer than 72 hours after the body of poor Allman was found, the lifeless figure of William Kelby, a draper in his fortieth year, was found in Powis Square by a passer-by as the bell of All Saints Church tolled for the first time after midnight on the 8th. His throat had been cut. That damned, demented spirit had been at his evil work once more before slipping back into the safety of the shadows.

The police have failed utterly in their attempts to prevent this ghoul butchering almost at will, the total now being five poor unfortunates slain by a single stab to the heart. Outsiders are beginning to regard North Kensington, Notting Hill and the Dale as dens of infamy so deep as to be impenetrable. We are one and all, so to speak, branded on our brows with the mark of Cain. That this stain has been fixed on the locality by reason of the crimes committed with such impunity in its area, who can doubt? And the police have had five crimes in which to obtain clues and catch the fiend, but have failed without question.

We request the culprit be caught. Nay, we, on behalf of our terrified readers, demand it.

Three victims in eight days, Foster thought. Five in two weeks. Even if there was little doubt, this confirmed his view that this was personal. A mere copy-cat would surely have selected a killer with a less hectic schedule.

The following week's edition announced that three days after the fifth victim was found, the police arrested a thirty-year-old crofter named Eke Fair-bairn. Barnes told him the meaning of the name was 'handsome child', which seemed cruel given the newspaper's description of Fairbairn as a 'giant', whose 'aspect was gruesome to behold'. A mob had gathered at the station in Notting Dale, hundreds of people baying for the suspect's life. A set of makeshift gallows had been erected.

The police made confident noises to the press about the arrest. The suspect's neighbours queued up to confirm that they had always known he was a bad one, that there had always been something shifty about him. He was single, but his mother and father, who shared his house, had been forced to flee the area, though whether as a result of shame or mob rule was not elucidated. Then the suspect was charged. The newspaper, previously incredulous at the police's incompetence, had reversed its position: the division and its senior detective in charge of the case were now being celebrated, albeit with one caveat. 'We trust a conviction will be secured,' a leader thundered ominously.

Foster's mobile rang, sucking him back into the twenty-first century. It was Drinkwater.

'Andy,' Foster said.

'How's it going, sir?'

'He killed five times.'

Drinkwater let out a whistle. 'Two more to go, then.'

'What you after?'

'Just wanted to let you know that the first victim has been officially identified as Graham Ellis.'

'The ex-wife come up with anything interesting?'

'Not really. She had nothing to do with him over the last year of his life. Not an amicable divorce, apparently.'

'I presume someone's going through the firm's files to find out whether there's anything that links Ellis with Darbyshire and Perry?'

'A team's on its way to Cheshire as we speak. There's one other thing: we've finally got the tox report on Darbyshire.'

'And?'

'Traces of GHB in his blood. PCP too.'

Foster knew 'liquid Ecstasy' – or 'Grievous Bodily Harm', as it was quirkily known on the street. Its original use was as a surgical anaesthetic, before word spread and people started to use it for weight loss. Then it was picked up by clubbers sated by Ecstasy and seeking a different high. Widespread use had led to another, more sinister purpose: as a 'date rape' drug that rendered victims incapable, coma-like. It was easy to get hold of these days, so this discovery hardly heralded a breakthrough. Though at least it shed light on the killer's MO.

'Enough to kill him?' he asked.

'No. Just enough to make him lose consciousness for a few hours. Williams and his team are at the pub now, and they seem intent on tracking down every GHB user in London.'

There would be a few of those. GHB was not just the drug of choice for those too ugly, shy or perverted to attract members of the opposite sex without knocking the object of their lust out, but also clubbers who wanted to shed their inhibitions.

'Makes sense,' he said eventually. 'Anything on the other two?'

'They reckon first thing tomorrow for Ellis, the day after for Perry, but Harris is telling everyone he's put a rocket up their arse to get the reports later today.'

'Tomorrow morning it'll be, then. Call me if anything else turns up.'

Foster snapped his phone shut.

'What's going on?' Heather asked.

'The ex-wife confirmed the tramp was Ellis. Which means, if the last sighting was correct, the killer held him for two months. Darbyshire tested positive for GHB. Which explains why he was able to hold Ellis for that length of time. That's a truckload of GHB, though.'

It also explained the bed sores. He had been on his back for the whole time.

'He kept him drugged and sedated for all that time? But he held Perry for little more than a day, and Darbyshire for only a couple of hours.'

Foster shrugged. 'Perhaps the day he kidnapped him was the only day he could get to Cheshire. Maybe his job, or something else, keeps him in London most of the time.' Foster knew he was getting somewhere. 'Or his job took him to Cheshire on that day and he thought he'd take his chance.'

Nigel was silent, staring at the giant screen of his microfilm reader as if hypnotized.

'What have you got so far?' Foster asked him.

Nigel, still looking at the reader, scrunched up his face in response.

'Nothing much different to what we know. Not about the killings, at least.'

Foster felt a flicker of anger. Nigel had told him that *The Times* would prove to be the best source of a reliable day-by-day narrative of the killings and their aftermath.

'There is one thing, though. *The Times*, which usually kept itself above the fray, wrote three leaders castigating the police, including one on the day of

Fairbairn's arrest. These killings were big news. Questions were even asked in the House of Commons about the police investigation. Also, the man they arrested is described in one report here as a "lunatic".'

Foster couldn't see the significance. The guy had slaughtered five people in two weeks. That was hardly the behaviour of the sane.

'They had a very different way of classifying mental illness back then,' Nigel continued. 'From 1871 onwards, census returns recorded if someone was a lunatic, an imbecile or an idiot. The latter meant someone was classed as congenitally mad. An imbecile was someone who was judged to have been sane once but had become insane. A lunatic was prone to losing his or her reason but had moments of clarity. That covered a multitude of conditions. New mothers, for example. Back then, post-natal depression was considered a sign of lunacy.'

'So what you're saying, Nigel, is that this guy might have been mentally unstable, but it doesn't mean he was psychotic, or schizophrenic?' Heather said.

'No, he could just have been a bit odd. An eccentric.'

'Did they let lunatics stand trial back then?' Foster asked.

'Certainly. You'd have to be well and truly off your rocker to be declared too insane to stand trial. The

Victorians believed in crime and punishment with few exceptions.'

'Find out whether this guy stood trial. If he did, what happened to him, everything. I also need to find out where Saunders Road is. If it still exists . . .'

Heather interrupted to get his attention. 'I looked it up on Streetmap on the Internet. There is no Saunders Road in wio or wii.'

'Shit,' Foster said.

'The local library should know,' Nigel suggested.

'The newspaper report mentioned that the road was being built,' Foster added. 'It also said it was in Notting Dale, by the railway track. That means it must have been on the border of Kensington and Chelsea with Hammersmith and Fulham. You know what runs through there now, don't you? The Westway – a motorway. You telling me he's going to throw a body out of a car on one of London's busiest roads?'

'An underpass runs beneath it,' Heather volunteered.

A darkened underpass. That would be too obvious, Foster thought. Nothing this guy did was obvious.

He needed to be out there, moving the investigation on, not stuck in a room reading, flicking through old newspapers.

'Heather and I are going to the library, then. We'll

see where this road was exactly. Nigel, you stay here and find out whether Eke Fairbairn was tried,' he said.

17

Nigel enjoyed the sense of being alone with the information. Foster and Heather had barely spoken over the past couple of hours, but the sighing detective was a large, distracting presence; he made a simple act such as turning a page sound symphonic. Now the room was empty, and the only noise was the buzz of the strip light above his head. Nigel felt he could roll back the years and build a complete picture of the events that followed the 'Kensington Horrors'. He had asked for the *News of the World* reel to be brought to him, so that he could soak up every nuance and detail, the more salacious the better, and immerse himself in the case.

The picture swiftly became clear. The accused was a simple giant, 'nearer seven feet than six'. Nigel knew this would have marked him out as extraordinary in a time when the average size was about a foot shorter than the present day. The man was itinerant, travelling the country in search of work, as many of his class did, transported by the booming railways. The press had used this common fact to imply shiftiness, as if there were sinister reasons behind Fairbairn's many travels. One interview with a Liverpudlian, a native of the city where Fairbairn had worked on the docks for less than a year, said that he had been hounded from his job by colleagues.

'He weren't right,' was the damning verdict.

There was no shortage of neighbours to echo that view. Fairbairn kept himself to himself, he didn't mix, he barely spoke. Each character quirk was taken and finessed to insinuate a loner, a crank, a nut. Even more damning was the fact he was known to frequent local pubs, an insignificant nugget the *News of the World* regarded as important enough to mention in every update on the investigation.

On 5th May Fairbairn, now almost universally known as 'The Giant', appeared at the Old Bailey. He loped to the dock and spent the whole proceedings fixing his focus on the floor. 'Not once did he raise his baleful gaze from his boots,' *The Times* reporter noted. 'Not even when his name was called, nor even when his fateful plea of Not Guilty was recorded.'

Two weeks later, on 19th May – the wheels of justice were not slow to turn in the nineteenth century – the trial began. The court was teeming, the best seats bought by the upper classes in search of low-class thrills. When Fairbairn took his place in court, high-pitched gasps broke the expectant hush. Most of them emanated from wealthy women in the ringside seats. This being the judicial equivalent of opening night, they were dressed in their best – hats and all. One reporter noted the rustle as one after the other they produced fans to cool themselves: 'Such was the crush around the venerable court that gathering breath was a trial.' The same reporter noticed the mixture of distasteful and admiring looks directed towards the defendant, which accompanied the furious fanning.

Those in the cheap seats were less demure. Cries of 'Hang, you bastard!' and 'Let him dangle!' led to at least four men being ejected, a scene described by the man from *The Times* as 'a sordid kerfuffle'. Through it it all Fairbairn's gaze never once lifted from his feet. Instead of the giant man who had appeared at the arraignment, Fairbairn seemed to have been physically altered by his ordeal. His shoulders slumped, he had lost weight, he winced when he moved, and one arm remained seemingly immobile at his side. 'Never has a sorrier, more pathetic creature answered such a grave charge,' *The Times* opined.

Nigel noted with interest the fact that Fairbairn was being charged with only two of the Kensington killings, presumably for lack of evidence regarding the other three. He recorded this in his notepad, knowing that it might be something to pursue later. The two he was answering were the first and third killings, just over a week apart.

The case was prosecuted by Mr John J. Dart, QC, MP who, from the transcript provided by one of the newspapers, was not going to allow the opportunities afforded by such a stage to be squandered. There was no physical description of the barrister, but Nigel pictured a portly, pompous politico, florid features glowing under his white wig as he preened on the floor of the packed courthouse. He opened by asking the jury to strike from their minds all that had been written about the case, which would be decided on the known facts.

Here Dart turned and slowly raised his finger in the direction of the accused. *The Times* recorded how the eyes of the courtroom followed the direction of the digit.

It is the Crown's case that that man stood there, Eke Fairbairn, did with malice and in cold blood murder Samuel Roebuck and Leonard Childe.

Dart held his pose, allowing the impact of his gesture and words to settle on the audience. Once again, from the public gallery, came the cry 'Let him dangle!' followed by a brief halt in proceedings while the judge called for order. When they reconvened, Dart outlined the prosecution case.

On the evening of March 24th, Mr Roebuck, as he was in the habit of doing, was seeking refreshment in the Clarendon public house on Clarendon Road. According to witnesses, Mr Roebuck had taken a considerable amount of porter during the evening hours. He was a working man and this was nearing the end of a working week. It is not for us here to judge his behaviour. No, Mr Roebuck has met our maker and judgement has already been passed by a higher authority. Late in the evening he was described as drunk yet not incapable. For reasons unknown, you will hear how Roebuck became embroiled in a quarrel with the prisoner at the bar, which culminated in the ejection from the premises of both men, the expectation being that the quarrel would be settled there and not within sight of womenfolk. The two men departed . . .

The Times noted here how Dart walked the length of the jury rail before returning to his original spot without saying another word, until:

Roebuck was not to be seen alive again!

Once again he allowed his words time to imprint on the consciousness of those present. Next he outlined the details of the second murder charge, relating to Leonard Childe, a 38-year-old blacksmith. Again, the night before he was found stabbed, Childe had been drinking at a local pub. Fairbairn had been drinking in the same pub and, as with the previous charge, was seen to row with the victim. Both were evicted from the premises. Dart said the prosecution would also produce a knife found at the lodgings of the accused, and an expert witness who would testify it was the same knife that had caused the fatal wounds.

The *News of the World* reported how, as the prosecution's opening speech came to its close, Dart lowered his voice to a hoarse whisper.

It is the prosecution's case that the accused is a man incapable of handling strong drink. A man who, rather than settling his quarrels with his fists or turning the other cheek, did brutally pull a knife and slay both unfortunates. Good Christian men know evil lurks in the bottom of a glass. We contend there is an even bigger evil lurking in the heart of the accused. Together they have forged a combustible and repellent concoction that has been midwife to these obscene and ungodly acts.

18

'If this map is right, then it should be somewhere around here,' Heather said, turning a photocopy of a map one way and then the other in the hope its mysteries would become clearer.

The bray of a car horn from their rear made them both jump.

'The bastard,' Foster said, checking the rear-view mirror and seeing, from the neck down at least, the male driver of a white van, slapping his steering wheel in frustration at their pedestrian pace.

'Sir, don't,' Heather cautioned.

Foster bit his lip. He wanted to stop the car, climb out and, as the white-van Neanderthal bristled, produce his badge, administer a bollocking and tell him to watch out. The roads of London, where men and women developed the patience of toddlers at being held up in the choked streets, agitation growing at their role as insignificant cogs in the great city's grinding daily machine, had long since been a bugbear for Foster. The resentment caused by the morning's meeting with Harris, the ignominy of being sidelined, had not yet dissipated. Venting his spleen on a gormless van driver might prove cathartic.

Instead, aware from the corner of his eye of Heather's concern, he merely continued to dawdle, gaining solace from the knowledge that he was adding a few increments to the rising blood pressure of the bottom-feeder behind him. Sure enough, there came another blare of frustration, just after Heather indicated that he should turn left on to Queensdale Road.

The street was empty. They parked outside a Sikh temple at the end of the road and got out of the car.

'That's where the Salvation Army mission was,' Heather said, poring over the map once more. They had gone straight to the local studies section of the library at Kensington Town Hall. Within seconds of asking for a map they had obtained one, printed only a few years after the killings of 1879. Saunders Road was on there, at the end of what was then Queen's Road, now Queensdale. They made a photocopy and drove straight to this spot.

Foster stood and looked at the map with Heather. He saw the angle of Saunders Road on the map, then gazed up at the point where it would have stood in the present day.

'Jesus,' he said.

Heather was as quick to work out where the road

had been. It was a road no longer; instead, twin tower blocks, brown, beige and monstrous, two plinths of sixties functionalism, soared above them into the steel-grey sky. To their left was a terrace of handsome Victorian townhouses, costing well over a million each, Volkswagens and Beamers sitting patiently outside. Across the road was a different world: high-rise living with its neighbours from hell and claustrophobic menace. Despite spending all his life in the capital, it still took his breath away to see how these two quintessential styles of London existed side by side, rubbing away at each other like silk and sandpaper.

They worked out from the map that it was the nearest of the two tower blocks that covered the ground where Saunders Road had been.

'This guy's having a laugh,' Foster said.

The pair reached the entrance of the grubby building. A young black woman leaving with a crusty-nosed child gave them a suspicious look, rumbling them as police immediately. The local force were probably seen and heard on a nightly basis, Foster thought. Inside the lobby, the smell of piss, neglect and bleach was heady rather than overpowering.

'Twenty-four floors,' Heather said, looking at the lift. She did not press the button to summon it, for which Foster was thankful. He dare not contemplate the evils it may contain. However, at that moment it opened. An acned youth in a white tracksuit, and blessed with the furtive face of a rat, stepped out.

'How many flats in this building?' Heather asked.

He stopped, looked at both, a vacant worry spreading across his face. Foster caught the unmistakable sweet whiff of marijuana.

'Dunno,' he said. 'Maybe a hundred or summink.'

'Thanks,' Foster said and let him pass, though not without a long withering stare to worsen the youth's stoned paranoia.

'So, a hundred-plus flats, any of which could be the one our killer uses to dump the next victim. He could be in there now.' He swiftly corrected himself. '*They* could be in there now.'

Heather nodded. 'Nothing for it but to go door-to-door and keep an eye on every scroat who comes and goes.'

Foster plunged his hands deep into his coat pockets.

'No point checking on who in this place has a record,' he dead-panned. 'Bet only the cleaning lady and the lift engineer don't.' He gave his colleague a grim smile. 'Come on. Let's make a quick phone call before we start.'

They went back to the car, where he switched on the heater and the radio. Together they formed a background murmur.

Andy Drinkwater's phone seemed to ring for an age. Eventually he answered, sounding breathless.

'It's Foster.'

'Sir,' Drinkwater exclaimed. 'You heard the news?'

'What news?'

'We've pulled in a suspect. Happened about twenty minutes ago.'

'Who?' He could already sense conflicting emotions: joy that the killer might have been caught before he could strike again; frustration that it was someone else who made the nick.

'Details are still a bit fuzzy. He's called Terry Cable. He fits the description on the sketch. Apparently, he's previously served time for manslaughter and has a record of using GHB, including once for a date rape, though the charge was withdrawn.'

Bang to rights, then, thought Foster.

'What was your news?' Drinkwater asked.

'We've found the place where the next killing will be. Or, at least, where the next body will be found. A tower block beside the Westway. Was hoping I could round up some help.'

Drinkwater paused. 'It's all hands to the pump here, sir.'

'Don't worry, Andy. I understand. Keep me updated.'

'Will do.'

The line went dead.

'What?' Heather said, desperate to be in the loop.

'They've pulled someone in. Sounds promising.'

'Yes,' she said, and clapped her hands together once as she spoke.

Foster didn't share her sense of triumph, and he could see she'd noticed.

'You're not certain, are you?' she queried.

Foster shrugged. 'We have a suspect, at least. At *last*.' But no, he thought, I'm not certain. 'Come on,' he added, turning the engine over. 'Let's get a coffee. We need all the energy we can get if we're going door-to-door in a tower block.'

19

The hours had fallen away. A member of staff put his head around the door to ask Nigel politely if he needed anything, and mutter apologetically that the library closed in half an hour. Nigel first had to shake his head to bring himself back into the present, and then checked his watch to make sure the librarian was not joking. He wasn't; it was four thirty exactly.

'Did the detective make any provision for me staying after hours?' he asked.

The assistant shook his head dolefully.

'Don't suppose I can without his arrangement, can I?'

The assistant affirmed that was the case.

Nigel found his phone and called Foster. He told him that the library was to close in thirty minutes.

'How much more have you got to look at?' came the reply.

'I'm on the final day of the trial; they're about to reach a verdict, I think.'

'Well, find that out. But there may be no need

to dwell on it too long. Between me, you and the gatepost they've got someone in custody.'

Like Foster, Nigel could not decide whether he felt elated or disappointed.

'But we still need to plough on and dig out what we can,' Foster continued. He paused. 'Tell you what, I'll ask them to let you stay there longer. But they won't have anyone to bring you what you need, so you'll have to make do with what you have. Send me photocopies of anything significant you find out about the trial. But don't pull an all-nighter or anything like that. Chances are, we'll need you tomorrow.'

That was fine with Nigel. He just wanted to reach the end of this newspaper narrative. The thought of leaving it now, albeit only overnight, was agonizing.

The trial had lasted just three days: two for the prosecution to open and present their case, half a day for the defence – defendants were not allowed to give evidence on their own behalf – and a further half a day for the judge's summation. While the first two days had been given acres of coverage in the two newspapers Nigel was relying on, the third was not; the defence case amounted to little more than a half-hearted plea for innocence from a barrister and a former employer of the accused, who said he was a man of simple yet good character. It merited a few paragraphs only. These were set against a litany of prosecution witnesses, who attested to the accused's drunken, violent nature, and the pages their testimony garnered. If the newspaper was to be believed, there could be only one verdict.

On the evening of the third day the jury retired, reaching a verdict within twenty minutes. The judge, one eye no doubt on the fact that the edition dead-lines of the newspapers had passed, delayed until the next morning. Nigel could only wonder what that night was like for the condemned man – the dragging agony.

The next morning the courtroom was awash with people. Of the two reporters, the *News of the World*'s intoxicated, excitable representative best conveyed the exquisite tension of what happened next.

Every pair of eyes were on the dock. No event took place for what appeared to be an eternity, until the sound of a door opening below and the shuffle of feet on wooden steps indicated Fairbairn was on the way to his assignation with fate. The collective breath of the crowd was audible as the prisoner loped into the view of the galleries. This time, the first occasion during this trial, there were no cries, no declamations. Only silence unbroken. As always his gaze was to his feet, but once did Fairbairn raise his head and look towards the gentlemen of the press crushed into a single gallery. For all the world he looked as if he would speak to us, that the mute would break his silence and offer a sign of the obvious turmoil which raged within that gigantic cold heart. Yet there came only a heavy, baleful stare that communicated little, until his eyes settled back on his boots once more.

The clerk of the court appeared and all attentions were focused on the bench where Mr Justice MacDougall would take his seat for this final act. Breathless silence continued to reign, so much so that a pin could have been heard to drop, but it was broken with a gasp of such volume one would think that it had been rehearsed by the company present. The act that had brought forth this collective sound of wonder was the clerk's placing of the black cap on the bench in front of where the judge would sit. My eyes went to the accused, to gauge his reaction at the sight of that awesome piece of apparel that indicated his terrible end. He was still peering down in front of his body, perhaps contemplating the abyss into which his mortal body would soon be launched.

The judge entered the court, resumed his place and asked the foreman of the jury if a verdict had been reached. The foreman answered in the affirmative and, when asked what that verdict was, replied 'We have agreed that the accused is guilty'.

The clerk asked the customary question whether the man had anything to say before the sentence of death was passed. At last that huge face lifted from its earthly gaze and another gasp issued forth from those around. In a voice low and doleful, barely audible, Fairbairn at last loosed his tongue.

'I never done the thing,' he murmured, and that was all the pitiable creature could muster.

As was usually the case, the execution was fixed three clear Sundays after the sentence had been passed. But there was no sign of interest waning in the story: the next day *The Times* in a leader pronounced itself pleased with the verdict, and congratulated the prosecution for offering such a compelling case.

Nigel's eye was also caught by another report of a gruesome killing in North Kensington. Under the headline 'Man Slays Family' was a short report of a man named Segar Kellogg, who had slit the throat of his wife, stabbed his son and then smothered his two daughters before turning the knife on himself. The son, the story said, was still alive though in a grave condition. The surname delighted Nigel: he came across it rarely. It was an occupational surname given to slaughtermen in Essex. John killed hogs. When the time came for a name to differentiate him from other Johns, he was named John Killhog. Over the centuries this had become Kellogg. How appropriate,

Nigel thought grimly, that a man bearing that name had slaughtered most of his family.

Subsequent articles in the *News of the World* concentrated on the daily comings and goings of the condemned man. There appeared to be incredulity at the lack of a confession – Nigel knew it was customary for newspapers and periodicals to print special editions with the repentant ramblings of condemned men and women – and the view appeared to be that Fairbairn was harbouring secrets so dark that he was afraid to unburden himself. Others noted that he insisted on his innocence to whoever visited his cell. His mood was described as 'serene', yet elsewhere as 'dark and morbid'. The Sunday before his execution the *News of the World* appeared to have grown weary of his reluctance to confess all, and carried barely a paragraph about him. It did note that an application had been made by the Royal College of Surgeons for Fairbairn's body to be submitted to them for dissection and study, a matter which was under the consideration of the Home Secretary.

Fairbairn was led to the gallows, only once faltering in his step. The executioner, Norwood, and his subject then shook hands. Fairbairn was asked whether he wished to say any final words. He turned to the selected reporters and said: 'I never done the thing.' Fairbairn died instantaneously, so the reports suggested, though, as was customary, his body was left on the scaffold for one hour before being taken down and transported to the Royal College of Surgeons.

Nigel stumbled out into the approaching twilight, after faxing what he'd found over to the incident room, and made his way to the tube, the details and events of the trial and execution replaying in his mind over and over. For some reason he felt immense sorrow for the dumb, child-like mute who had received the ultimate punishment. He thirsted to know more, to immerse himself in greater detail. A glance at his watch told him no archive would still be open. Instead, that evening, he would have to throw himself on the mercy of the Internet. Surely such a momentous set of murders, the trial and its aftermath would still ripple down the years?

This hunger for more knowledge grew keener during the hour it took him to reach his flat in Shepherd's Bush. He was puzzled by Foster's silence, but figured the detective had been detained by other business. Perhaps they *had* caught the killer. Nigel did not actually care; his interest had been pricked by the events of 1879. He wanted to discover as much as he could to satisfy his own curiosity. He booted up his computer before he had even removed his jacket or put his bag on the floor. As soon as it came to life, the luminescent screen providing the only source of light in his flat, other than the remains of the day shining weakly through his window, he sat down and opened his Internet connection, typing the name 'Eke Fairbairn' into his search engine.

Two pages. Twenty-seven results. Is that all, he thought? He had expected more. It was as if what he had read and learned that day had vanished, airbrushed out of history.

He checked the results. Nearly all were linked to sites connected to the Hunterian Museum, housed within the Royal College of Surgeons. According to the first link he followed, the museum's collection of anatomical exhibits included the skeletons of several criminals who had been dissected following execution. Among them was that of 'murderer Eke Fairbairn'. So Fairbairn's body was on actual display? Another link confirmed it was. He checked the museum's opening times: nine the following morning. He sat back and rested his hands behind his head. Tomorrow he was going to meet the Kensington Killer.

Foster threw his jacket on the kitchen table and filled a glass of wine to the brim. It had taken him and Heather the entire evening to doorstep the first five floors of the tower block, twenty flats of surly men and women with a reflexive suspicion of the police. They had not seen anything out of the ordinary in the past few days, nor anyone new moving in. Even if they had, Foster sensed he'd be the last to know. He had had to co-opt DC Khan for the next day, but it still meant another forty-eight hours going door-to-door. The exact time they had before the killer was due to deliver his fourth victim.

It had taken five killings for the police in 1879 to bring the murderer to justice. This time he wanted it to stop at three.

He went to his jacket pocket and pulled out a folded envelope. Inside were copies faxed by Barnes of newspaper reports of the 1879 trial. Foster sat down at the table and began to read. Soon, tiredness crept in. He grew weary of having the trial filtered through the lens of a Victorian hack. He wanted to learn the details first-hand, assess the evidence himself. He called Barnes and left a message, asking if the original court transcripts were available and to contact him first thing in the morning. Some clue as to why this was happening would be in there.

He stood up and stretched. He walked through to the lounge and wondered what to do with himself. This house had long since stopped being a home; it was more a place in which he rested and refuelled. It had always been like that, ever since his father's death. Eight years in which he had shut down every part of his life apart from work.

He wondered what his dad would make of this case. When he first became a detective, shortly after his father had retired, Foster would go through current cases with him, get his opinion, his hunches, ideas on where to look next. His dad would give examples of tough cases he'd cracked, but would always warn against making assumptions: 'Nearly every mistake that I know of has been made when people start seeing what they want to see, not what's actually there.' Foster always emerged from those conversations with a sense of purpose, a plan of action.

For the first year or so following his father's death, he still heard his voice. He held conversations in his head, outlining the problem, the sticking point, his father's voice responding in its usual economical way. But it faded, began to wane. He could conjure up images of his father, and occasionally he would hear him speak. But, when he sat and consciously tried to bring him to mind, he was out of reach. The voice merged into others, those of colleagues, friends. The past had slipped away.

But if he ever needed the sage words of his father, it was now. Could he get it back? Rebuild his father's memory? Can you summon a voice back from the void?

He went to the bureau, unlocked it and lifted the lid. There it still all was, exactly as it had been left. He had done this countless times, picked up the paperweight, stared at the pictures, then closed the bureau again. But this time he decided to go further. He looked at the picture of himself as a boy, with his mum on Camber Sands. It brought back no memory; he had been only two. These people were strangers. Neither of his parents was interested in photography, and few pictures existed of him and his sister. Yvonne, he thought, a memory stirring. Not a pleasant one either. She lived on the other side of the world with her family; he hadn't seen or spoken to her since the funeral. She blamed him, not only because of what he did, but for not including her, consulting her. He remembered the last words she had flung at him before she walked away from the church, as the rain slanted down in sheets.

'One day I will forgive you. But right now that day seems a long, long way away.'

He knew it was down to him to re-establish some sort of contact, to bring that day forward, but the longer he left it the more difficult it became. He winced and cast the image and the anger in her voice to one side, returning to the photo of his younger self at the seaside. Still, no memory came.

There was always one memory he could not erase. His father, frail and pale, lying on his bed, a monumental weariness seeping from every pore. It had overridden the figure of his youth. The tall, rigid man, not an ounce of fat on him – unlike Foster, whose excesses and indiscipline had bestowed a tyre of fat around his middle. His father did everything with economy: drank, ate, slept. His emotions too; all was confined and controlled.

Foster put the picture back down and rooted through some papers. A few paid bills, an invitation to a Met dinner, other trivial day-to-day correspondence, none of which bore his father's imprint or any semblance of his soul.

His mobile, bursting to life, broke this bout of introspection.

'It's Drinkwater.'

'How's it going?'

Drinkwater paused. 'Well, it's going. Where are you?'

Foster noted his young colleague's hesitancy. 'At home. You get a starring part in the Terry Cable interview?'

'I sat in for a bit.'

'What's your gut feeling?'

Again, Drinkwater paused. 'He fits the profile; he's got previous for violence, including sexual assault, which fits in with the Dammy Perry killing.'

'There was no sign of sexual assault there.'

'He carved her breasts up, sir.'

'That wasn't motivated by sex,' he said. 'But go on.'

'Well, the clincher seems to be his use of GHB. They found traces in Ellis's blood. Loads of it. Seems you're right: the killer kept him topped up with it for the whole time he held him. In the end his heart gave way.'

Before he could be murdered, Foster thought.

'This guy's a user himself, and has used it on other people. Mainly women. Also, his car was seen on Ladbroke Grove on the night Darbyshire was dumped.'

'Sounds like they're sniffing the right lamp post,' Foster said.

But he was puzzled; if this guy did spike all three victims with GHB, then a more damning sighting would have placed him in one of the pubs in which they had last been seen. Surely Williams and his team were parading him in front of drinkers, showing his photo to bar staff?

'But,' Drinkwater said.

'But what? Come on, Andy. I know something's bugging you.'

Drinkwater took a deep breath. 'OK, he fits the profile, he uses GHB and, yeah, we have an eyewitness who places him near the scene of one murder. But everyone here is acting as if it's open and shut. They're spraying this bastard with hot shit. They've dug up every bit of sleaze on him – and that's a lot, believe me – and are giving him it with both barrels. He hasn't been allowed to sleep, his brief seems next to useless, and the bloke is petrified. Doesn't know what's hit him. You just know they're going to keep coming at him until he crumbles.'

'So, what's the problem? If he killed three people then they should do everything except take his fingernails off with pliers.'

'Thing is, sir, you've seen the crime scenes, you've seen how little's been left at them. You've said yourself how calm and calculated this killer is. Does a bag of sleaze with a GHB problem – who gets flustered the first time a copper asks his fucking name – seem like the killer to you?'

He didn't. And Foster trusted Drinkwater's judgement.

'Anyone else got their doubts?' he asked.

'No one,' Drinkwater said emphatically. 'They're all but breaking open the champagne. They've got the go-ahead to raid his place today and they think, even if that doesn't turn up enough, he might crack.

One of them said they might have enough already, if they sprinkle it with stardust and the CPS are willing to give it some topspin.'

Foster knew he had no basis to go to Harris; to do so would compromise Drinkwater. And the suspect was only being questioned. While that remained the case, it made no sense to cause a scene.

Except that the killer was due to strike in the next forty-eight hours.

20

Nigel had not seen anything like it. Rows upon rows of organs and other, well, 'specimens' was the best word he could muster, preserved in formaldehyde. His eyes were drawn – half through fascination, half through revulsion – to a jar in which a perfectly formed, tiny human foot floated free in its sea of liquid. The severed left foot of a small child killed by smallpox, whose body was dissected by the surgeon to try to understand that awful disease. Nigel wondered darkly if the parents were aware their little one's corpse had been carved up so the world could better understand the viruses that threatened it.

Next he was enthralled by a set of jars in which the dead fetuses and offspring of what seemed to be every mammal and creature known to man were suspended in their formaldehyde baths. There was something clinical, yet hauntingly beautiful, too, about all these samples, lit and stacked on shelves in their thick glass containers, like some nightmarish pharmacy. He knew now where notorious British artists – charlatans and poseurs, to his jaundiced eye

– gained their inspiration. Carving up and preserving cows was not a new pursuit.

Nigel enjoyed new discoveries like this, secret places where London's past had been preserved. Literally, in this case. Once again the years fell away, the atmosphere of the time rose up from the murk. A world of disease, crude surgery, experimentation, discovery. A world on the cusp of change.

It heartened him that a place such as this existed. A centuries-old collection of anatomical and surgical artefacts that told the story of modern surgery in the most graphic way possible. Only in London, he thought. Only in this benighted, storied city would there be a room where pickled wombs, babies' limbs and infant sloths were lined up for the inspection of the general public. Looking around, he guessed that most of those doing the inspecting were medical students, though a few art students were among them, sketching away, brows furrowed in concentration.

He had already dwelled for more minutes than he had intended at a section of the museum displaying early surgical instruments, aghast at their nightmarish design, his imagination conjuring macabre pictures of the agony they would cause an unanaesthetized patient aware of every incision and slice. Nigel had been expecting to see a few rusty scalpels and fake skeletons. Instead, he had stepped into a few quiet, plushly decorated rooms that resembled a cross between an horrific art installation and the set of a Cronenberg film.

He wondered who the people were whose organs had been pickled, their livers, hearts, kidneys immortalized. Perhaps they had been donated to John Hunter, the pioneering eighteenth-century surgeon whose collection this was, by grave robbers. Nigel knew these men made a living from selling corpses to medical schools for dissection and study, the fresher the better.

He checked the pamphlet he'd picked up on the way in. Fairbairn's body was on the mezzanine.

There were yet more exhibits upstairs, where it was less crowded. Here the story of modern surgery was told in greater detail. Nigel cast his eye around the room until it alighted on a glass case featuring a skeleton.

As he got nearer, he could see the dirty, yellowed skeleton was that of a large man. Probably around the same height as Foster, perhaps a few inches taller. The eye sockets were vast black caverns; the ribcage was wider than any other part of the body, save the shoulders, and the rictus grin was sinister.

Nigel scoured the display case for some form of identification. Falling to his haunches, he saw a small inscription beside the skeletal feet.

'Eke Fairbairn. Murderer,' he read. 'The dissection of executed criminals was abolished by law in 1832. However, in exceptional circumstances, the Home Secretary and the family of the executed convict gave permission for his body to be released to the College for further study. His skeleton has stood in the museum ever since.'

Nigel stood and peered more closely at the giant man's bones. He was no medical expert but he could make out what appeared to be breaks or cracks to parts of the body, to the right tibia and collarbone, while the enormous skull appeared misshapen. But was this any surprise, given that it had stood for more than a century and a quarter inside a glass case, presumably being taken out and moved several times? Probably a case of wear and tear. He remembered references in the newspaper reports he had read the previous day to a limp. The defendant stood awkwardly, and there had been something wrong with his arm, which suggested a deforming Victorian malady such as rickets.

Nigel checked his watch and cursed under his breath. It was ten thirty and he had not yet called Foster.

By ten thirty Foster and Heather had covered a further two floors, more flats of the surly and unresponsive. One woman complained of her neighbour playing music at four a.m., waking up her small child. The neighbour explained he worked nights and was just unwinding when he got back in, claiming the woman next door was twitchy and neurotic. They nodded and smiled, not wanting to get drawn into petty conflicts. Each flat they visited was duly checked against the electoral roll; flats where they obtained no response would be visited later in case the inhabitants were at work. Any new tenants would have their backgrounds checked. Foster hoped their presence at the scene would flush out the killer, force him to do something that would draw their attention to him.

At the very moment when he was wondering whether he would ever get the smell of urine in the communal hallways out of his nostrils, his mobile rang. It was Nigel.

'Where have you been?' he asked, without greeting.

He could tell Nigel was taken aback, stuttering his response.

'Look, I asked you to get in touch with me first thing,' said Foster. 'It's ten thirty now.'

'Sorry,' the genealogist managed to mutter. 'I was at a museum,' he added.

'What for?'

'I've found the killer, the 1879 killer.'

'Have you been drinking?'

'I mean that the museum I went to this morning had Eke Fairbairn's skeleton in a glass case on exhibition.'

'Why?'

'His body was given to medical science after his execution. There was a plaque on the case he's kept in. All it said was that he was a murderer, nothing we didn't know.'

'Can anyone see this?'

It occurred to Foster that if the killer was copying Fairbairn's spree, then he may well have gone to pay respects to his predecessor himself. Maybe even more than once. He would give this museum a call, see if they'd noticed anyone suspicious hanging around or, even better, whether they had CCTV footage of the displays.

'Listen, Nigel, I read the newspaper reports you faxed over. Very interesting. But what I want to see are the original records of the trial: transcripts, descriptions of evidence, the judge's summing up. Is there anywhere I could find that sort of information?'

'The National Archives. We know he was tried at the Old Bailey, and the Proceedings of the Old Bailey give a verbatim report of everything that happened in court. But the newspapers were pretty exhaustive . . .'

'I just want to see it myself, how it happened, how it unfolded, without any interpretation whatsoever.'

They arranged to meet in a few hours at the National Archives. In the interim, Barnes said there was something he wanted to check out at the British Library.

'Whatever,' Foster said wearily. 'Just don't be late.'

Three hours later Foster arrived at the National Archives in Kew, half airy modern glasshouse, half monstrous pebble-dashed carbuncle. It reminded Foster of a modern university campus, though once inside he saw the student body was more mature. There was an atmosphere of determination, of people purposefully going about serious research, congregating in small groups to whisper their findings, dead ends described, problems shared and solutions suggested.

Nigel met him at reception. They went to the café, the tables overflowing with people. Barnes told him he had ordered the Criminal Proceedings of the Old Bailey covering the session in which Fairbairn's trial had been held, and that it would take up to an hour for it to be ready. In the meantime, he had something for Foster to read.

From his case he produced three photocopied sheets. Not more newspaper reports, Foster thought.

When Nigel handed them over, he could see they were copies of pages from a book.

'What is it?'

'It's the memoir written by Norwood, Fairbairn's executioner. They all did it; people lapped up their experiences. Anyway, it turns out that Fairbairn was his first execution. There's a lengthy account of it in the book; here's an extract from that. You might find it useful.'

Foster began to read.

On my arrival at the prison, I was met by a warder, dressed in ordinary prison garb. He took my name and pulled on a large string, which rang the Governor's bell. In a few seconds I was met by the Governor himself, a very nice gentleman, of military bearing, and very well dressed. We passed time with the usual niceties. He said that I should make sure of taking a substantial tea this evening, what with all that was to follow the next day.

He passed me on to the Chief Warden, who kindly showed me to my quarters, a snug lodging at the back of the gaol. We shared a smoke together and I could see this gentleman was agitated by what was to happen. He said he felt quite upset about the fate of Fairbairn, that he hoped the man would get a reprieve. I asked why.

'Because, sir, I feel he is not guilty of the crimes for which you will hang him.'

I said nothing. It was not my position to question the workings of justice, merely carry out my work in the most expeditious manner possible. I admit now, as this was my first hanging, that I started to experience some unease at the prospect.

The next day I rose at 5 a.m. and, not being able to stomach the prospect of breakfast, I made my way to the scaffold, where I ensured it was clean and ready. Then, at 7.45 a.m., I returned with the group to play out the last scenes of the drama. We went to the doctor's room, to which the prisoner was brought. He was a man of enormous height, though the stoop of his body tried to cover for it. He said not a word. He was taken to an adjoining room, where he and the minister conducted prayers. When they returned, I was called to do my duty. I approached Fairbairn. His mournful brown eyes looked up at me, a sight I will see in my mind's eye until the day I leave the earth. I still don't know why, but I patted his gigantic shoulder.

'Keep your pluck up,' I heard myself say, for my own benefit.

Fairbairn walked without assistance to the scaffold. For his last words he proclaimed only his innocence in a slow, sonorous voice. I placed the hood over his head, my hands only then showing signs of trembling. The noose was placed around his neck, and I made certain he was placed under the beam of the drop. Everything was in place and, as quick as lightning, the culprit was plunged into the hereafter.

Afterwards, once he was confirmed dead and left to hang for the necessary hour, I stepped out for some air. The Chief Warden was having a smoke.

'Is it done?' he said softly.

I nodded.

'God have mercy on us,' he said, tears brimming his eyes. 'God have mercy.'

Foster finished reading and looked at Nigel. It was becoming paramount for him to examine the trial testimonies. What had happened to so disturb the Chief Warden? No mention was made of any doubts harboured by the other officials.

Nigel checked a computer terminal by the side of the café. The material had been delivered to the reading room. Foster followed him upstairs to the collection area, through a room of silent reading and thought. From the counter they picked up a large cardboard box file and found an unoccupied table. Nigel opened the box and Foster could see an enormous bound book, of more than a thousand pages in length. Nigel lifted it out and carefully placed it on the table. The writing on the front said 'Proceedings of the Old Bailey'.

Nigel leafed through quickly. 'Just one word of warning,' he said, turning to Foster. 'The pages are dry, but don't be tempted to lick your fingers to help turn them, not unless you want a security guard humiliating you in front of everyone.' Nigel went back to flicking through the volume. Eventually, he stopped. 'Here we go,' he said, and pushed it towards Foster.

At the top of the page was the number of the trial and the date. Below it were the words 'Eke Fairbairn, indicted for the wilful murders of Samuel Roebuck and Leonard Childe'. The judge was Justice Mac-Dougall, while Mr John J. Dart, QC, MP conducted the prosecution, a revealing and apt choice of phrase, Foster decided as he read through his melodramatic opening statement. Good to see barristers have always sought to promote themselves as well as their cases. But it was not Dart's interpretation of events he was seeking.

The first witness was Mary Hesketh, the barmaid at the Clarendon Arms, who testified to the defendant being drunk and having a row with Roebuck before being thrown out of the pub.

The next witness was described as a local businessman and ombudsman of good standing; his name was Stafford Pearcey. On the night of 24th March he was taking a late-evening constitutional. As he passed the Clarendon Arms he saw a man dressed in work clothes leaving the pub, lighting a cigarette. He set off towards Holland Park. A few seconds later, he passed a man he now knew to be Eke Fairbairn, wearing a 'look of fury' as he watched the other man depart. Despite the best efforts of the defence during cross-examination, the witness maintained that despite the lateness of the hour, and the lack of light, he was absolutely sure that the man he saw in the shadows was Fairbairn. Furthermore, he claimed to have seen Fairbairn set off in pursuit of the man he had earlier seen leaving the pub. The defence brief then began to question the witness about his relationship with several members of the police force, not least the senior investigating officer, Detective Henry Pfizer, but the prosecution objected, sustained by the judge.

A similar template was followed for the second killing on the indictment, staff and fellow drinkers confirming that, after an afternoon and evening spent drinking in solitude, Fairbairn had been involved in a row with the deceased. This time there was no passing businessman to see him tracking his victim. More damningly, the next witness was the aforementioned Detective Henry Pfizer, who confirmed that the knife produced in court was one they had found in the digs of the defendant.

The defence brief's response intrigued Foster.

'Detective Pfizer, would it be true to say that these killings attracted the full attention of newspapers, both local and national?'

The detective agreed it had.

'And not all of that attention, none of it in fact, was complimentary. Indeed, it would be fair to say that most of the criticism of the police's handling of the case was trenchant, was it not?'

The prosecution objected, for reasons not given. The judge urged the defence to ask its questions.

'My point is this, my lord. The date on which this knife was found was, somewhat conveniently one might say, the day after a fifth victim had been found and one newspaper was calling for the police to solve the case without delay.'

The prosecution objected; this time it was sustained. The defence barrister's next comment was struck from the record and the jury dismissed while the judge spoke to the court. No reason or explanation was given.

The prosecution rested. The defence's case was meagre. The only witness was one who spoke of Fairbairn's good character. There was no attempt to try and support the previous inference that their client had been framed.

The judge, Justice MacDougall, summed up.

'When you come to consider your verdict I want you to forget the imputations by the defence concerning the conduct of the police investigation, in particular the wicked slur against the name of Stafford Pearcey, a man of high standing and repute within the local community. If you believe his testimony then that would be a major point in proving the prosecution's assertion.

'Likewise, I would ask you to discount the defence's inference that the police in some way planted the knife at the lodgings of Mr Fairbairn. We heard from the detective in charge of the case that the knife was found in the belongings of the prisoner at the bar, and there is no reason I can see to indicate that Detective Pfizer is guilty of fabrication. I have known him stand in this court for nigh on a decade and not once can I remember him being anything other than an honest and dedicated officer of the law.'

With directions like that, the verdict was a formality. After sentencing, the defence made a quick plea, asking for leniency, claiming their client had a mental age of only ten, therefore did not have full comprehension of his actions, or their consequences, and was unfit for the gallows. The judge dismissed it at a stroke.

Foster finished reading. He was so engrossed, he had failed to notice Nigel leave and return with a bundle of documents. When he looked up, Nigel pushed a worn piece of stiff paper in front him – Eke Fairbairn's post-mortem.

At the top was Fairbairn's name and his age. The examination had taken place at Newgate Prison and revealed that the deceased was 'well nourished', 6 feet 9 inches, 197 pounds. He had been dead one hour, and there was a deep impression around the neck from the rope, as well as signs of constriction in the surrounding area. There had also been frothing and bloodstaining around the mouth, the tongue forced outwards. The lips, ears and fingernails had turned blue. Foster had seen it in strangulation victims. He checked the internal examination: there was no fractured vertebra.

'How good were they at hanging people in 1879?' he asked Nigel.

'Hit and miss,' he said. 'The long drop had only just been introduced. They broke the neck on some occasions but, on others, they didn't. One guy, called John "Babbacombe" Lee, survived three judicial hangings in 1885.'

Foster scanned down to the bottom of the page. The cause of death was asphyxiation.

Foster rubbed his face with his hands, almost overwhelmed by the exhaustion that was clinging to him like a mist. A potentially innocent man had been hanged. The poor bastard had not even suffered an instant death. His spine had remained intact; instead, he was strangled by the rope and his own bulk. Foster knew that could have taken minutes, not seconds. He supposed that was the way justice worked back then. Few convinced of his guilt would have cared about Fairbairn's suffering.

Yet what he discovered next was even more disturbing. The pathologist noted the presence of a number of fractures, six in total: his right tibia and fibula, right wrist, collarbone, right ankle, a rib and the jaw. You didn't get injuries like that falling down the courtroom stairs. The injuries were estimated to have been inflicted approximately seven or eight weeks earlier; around the time he was awaiting trial. Foster knew, there and then, they had tried to beat a confession from him. To cause that amount of damage, they must have used him as a trampoline. How had Fairbairn even made it into the dock? He must have been strong as a bear not to collapse under the weight of agony. And they made this broken man stand trial.

History came to life: Foster conjured up an image of a towering mute with the brain of a child, bovine and silent as policemen rained down blow after sickening blow upon his body for a crime he knew he did not commit. Then, when the same man came to end his life, they left him to dangle and choke, legs kicking futilely in the air, seeking ground they would never touch. He felt his fists clench with anger, tempered by a sense of professional shame.

He knew then, they had their motive.

'I've seen this before,' Nigel said.

It took some time for Foster to return to the present and realize what he had said. 'What do you mean?'

'Not *this*, not an exact replica of these events.'

'Then what?' Foster said, screwing up his face in bewilderment.

Nigel's eyes did not blink. There was a zeal to him, hands dancing as he spoke. 'The past is a living thing: it's always present. Most of us are not aware of it, most of us ignore it, but it's *there*. You can't just sweep it away, forget about it. Look at this case. It's clear to me and, from what I can see, to you, too, that in 1879 a grave misjustice took place. The world then forgot about it, or tried to. Pretended justice had been done. But you can bet that anyone who seeks to forget the past has a corpse in the basement.'

The memory of his father, that once giant man rendered broken and brittle in the weeks before his death, flashed across Foster's mind.

Nigel went on. 'But the past isn't like that; you can't just bury it, mark it down as history. When someone is drowned at sea, it can take an age for the body to be washed up. No one knows where, no one knows when. The only thing that is certain is that the sea will eventually give up its dead.

'It's taken more than a hundred and twenty-five years, but the events of 1879 have finally washed up.'

Nigel watched Foster stride away, off to rejoin the effort at the tower block. He had appeared troubled by what Nigel had said about the ever-present past. He had gone silent, looked down, before knocking the table with the flat of his hand and getting up to leave. Before he went, he asked Nigel to see if he could trace the descendants of Eke Fairbairn. The man had been beaten, convicted on scant evidence and then hanged. Was there anyone who might seek to take revenge for their ancestor's maltreatment?

Nigel left the reading room. Throughout the afternoon, at intervals, he had spotted Dave Duckworth. Each time he looked over, Duckworth turned away, though it was clear he was watching their movements.

He headed for a bank of computers that held the

online census returns. As he sat down, there was a light tap on his shoulder.

'Who was your friend?'

He turned around. It was Duckworth.

'I'm just doing a bit of work, Dave.'

'Private client?'

'Something like that.'

'Just that he looked like a detective, that's all.'

Nigel stared back, saying nothing.

'Perhaps you've got police protection now.'

What was he on about?

'Maybe someone has taken a contract out on your life.' A smile played on his greasy lips. 'Perhaps the family of a nubile history student.'

Nigel kicked back his chair and stood up. 'You've been speaking to Gary Kent, haven't you?'

Duckworth backed up theatrically, eyes flicking right and left, hands up. 'Calm down. Kent told me about your woman trouble at the university. Never had you down as that sort.'

'What sort is that, Dave? She was a mature student, twenty-nine years old, two years younger than me. An adult. Don't make me out to be some sort of predator who stalks young women. Now leave it. And tell your mate Kent to fuck off, too.'

He was shocked to hear the venom in his voice, and an expletive he rarely used. Those seated around them had stopped peering at their screens and had turned their gaze on him. A security guard appeared at his shoulder.

'Could I ask you to lower your voice, sir, and mind your language?' he said. 'Otherwise I will have to ask you to leave.'

Nigel continued to stare at Duckworth, but nodded to acknowledge the security guard, then unballed his fists and sat back down. Duckworth took the seat next to him.

'Dave, I have never ever been thrown out of an archive. But, at the moment, it seems worth it – if only to have the satisfaction of punching you in the face,' he hissed. He had never hit anyone in his life either, but his threat was genuine.

'I'm sorry,' Duckworth said. 'One wasn't very tactful. It has never been my forte, as you are well aware. It's just that I sense an opportunity here for you and, yes, me too, to make ourselves a few pounds at the expense of the fourth estate. Kent was telling me they have a man in custody. I am helping him out with his researches into Terry Cable's background, and helping him locate a few relatives. He's already compiling a piece about his troubled life, what made him a killer. He's been informed by a reliable source that Cable is guilty and will be charged.'

'That's what I've heard, too,' Nigel lied.

'The thing is, Kent is also desperate to find out what the historical background actually is. Why were you involved? What was the family history angle? It would be an exclusive – and, let's just say, the remuneration would not be insignificant.'

Nigel shook his head slowly.

'If you were reluctant to use Kent – after all, he is not everyone's cup of lapsang souchong – there are several other reporters I can name who would sell their own daughters for this tale.'

Nigel just wanted to get on with his search. If he threatened Duckworth again, he would be thrown out. He could always go to the FRC but, by the time he had rattled across London on the tube, he would barely have time to get under way.

'I've made it clear that I'm not interested, Dave. Now, please, leave me alone. Surely you have some dirt to uncover about the ancestors of some second-rate celebrity.'

Duckworth shook his head, as if rueing Nigel's lack of commercial nous.

'Actually,' he sniffed, 'as well as the Cable stuff, I have a very lucrative private client. Doing a bit of bounceback for him; been doing it for several months. Currently working my way through some Metropolitan Police records. Without much luck.'

'Good for you,' Nigel said, staring at the screen.

'You know, Nigel,' Dave said, standing up, 'there's no point returning to this job if you're not willing to adapt to the times. Private clients are all well and good when they pay well, but there's a fortune to be made from the press and media. I've got three jobs for TV companies at the moment: I'm hiring people to help me out. I can put a lot of work your way, if you're interested.'

Nigel ignored him.

'Suit yourself,' Duckworth said and shuffled away.

Much as it pained him, Nigel knew Duckworth was right. Private clients alone did not pay the bills and well-paid jobs involving serious research, losing yourself for weeks in another world, were rare. The best-paid jobs came from the press, either wanting you to trace the ancestry of the newsworthy and famous, or tracing descendants and relatives of someone in the public eye they could doorstep, and from TV companies seeking to satisfy their thirst for new formats. Working for the police might be thrilling, but it would soon end and was unlikely to lead to anything else. Given his paucity of clients, the time may well come when he would be forced to take a long spoon and sup with Duckworth.

That was for another time. Here was a job in which he could lose himself; and it was unfinished. The future could wait.

He entered Eke Fairbairn's name into the 1871 search field, typed London and hit enter. Two results. One fitted the bill. He was sixteen years old, living on Treadgold Street, North Kensington with his father, Ernest, and mother, Mary Jane. There were no other siblings in the home at that time. Nigel went back to 1861: the family were at the same address, Eke was six, and there was a girl, Hannah, aged nine, and a boy of four, Augustus. What had happened to Augustus in the intervening ten years? Perhaps he had died, which may have explained why the Fairbairns did not have any more children. Hannah was different; she would have been nineteen by 1871 and may well have married. He made a note in his notebook to search out a death certificate for Augustus and a marriage, or death, certificate for Hannah.

The Fairbairns left Notting Dale, probably to escape the shame and opprobrium Eke's conviction had brought upon them. But where did they go? He scoured records for London, then widened out to the whole country, but found no trace of an Ernest and Mary Jane Fairbairn living together, or who were single, and the right age. He scoured online death certificates and found his answer: Ernest died aged forty-six in 1881; Mary Jane's demise came two years later at the age of forty-five. In the same records he found confirmation of the death of their son, Augustus.

The National Archives were about to close. There was no more to be done here. He knew Hannah was the only survivor of the Fairbairn family. Had she managed to continue the bloodline?

It was late and Foster's suit wore the ammonia smell of the tower block when he arrived home. Without even pausing to take his jacket off, he booted up his sleek chrome laptop that lived on the kitchen table. It was the only time he used that piece of furniture; most of his food was eaten standing up, late at night or early in the morning.

He charged a large glass of wine and sat back down as the computer chuntered and whirred. The top of his head felt as if it was in a vice, pressure pulsating both sides. Each time he raised his eyes to focus, he felt a dull ache behind them.

The killer, if he was still at large – and something told Foster he was – was due to strike the next night. The very next night, they would discover if Terry Cable was the right man: if no body was found, it meant Harris's confidence was justified. If not, well, they had a fourth murder on their hands. Foster wanted to do all he could to prevent that happening.

By nine that evening he, Heather and Khan had knocked on the door of every single flat in the block. They had a list of everyone: who lived where, which flats were vacant, which had new tenants, all cross-referenced with the electoral roll. There was little they could do about the empty flats, or those where they had received no reply, other than to watch while the hours counted down. He was meeting Heather at six the following morning to do just that.

He wanted help: the whole area under surveillance, ART if possible. He'd spoken to Drinkwater. The suspect still hadn't been charged and they were going before the court the next morning to ask for another forty-eight hours. They were convinced of Cable's guilt; he had no alibis for any of the nights when the victims had disappeared, nor when their bodies were dumped. But they had not found any physical evidence, and Cable was not confessing.

Foster rang Harris to ask for help watching the tower block, but was knocked back; they were all employed trying to produce something with which to charge Cable.

'He's our man,' Harris kept repeating.

Forest gave up. He asked to interview Cable, to look into his eyes and see him speak.

Harris was adamant he should take a few days off.

'You look exhausted, Grant,' he said.

Foster knew Harris didn't want his doubtful, brooding presence undermining the certainty of his men.

He checked his watch. If he went to bed now he could get seven hours' sleep, perhaps ease the ache in his head. But Nigel's words at the National Archives kept ricocheting around his brain. 'Anyone who seeks to forget the past has a corpse in the basement,' he had said, words that carried a gruesome resonance for him. Foster had done all he could to forget his past and its terrible events, devoting himself to work, surrounding himself with gadgets and shiny things, medicating himself with alcohol, in effect shutting down his life. Yet this case had brought forth a torrent of memories and images of his father and his final hours.

He forced himself to think of the case – was there anything he and Heather had neglected to do? – but Nigel's words haunted him still. Perhaps Harris was right. Cable's arrest could have laid the events of 1879 to rest. Time would tell.

In little more than twenty-four hours they would know if the past was about to give up more of its dead.

He was sinking further. Tumbling head over paw into his own private Hades. His state of mind matched the squalor and filth and degradation of the stinking Dale in which he now plied God's work. Jemima and the little ones kept well out of his way. For days he had not seen them, and when young Esau had crossed him that morning following his ablutions, he had whimpered and cried and sought sanctuary in his mother's skirts. Her look was one of horror and bewilderment, no recognition for the creature he had become. But this was the Lord's work he was doing, he could not rebel, nor ignore his calling. God had total authority. He remembered Saul and knew he could not deviate from this chosen path. 'It is hard for thee to kick against the pricks.' It was for someone to show these pitiable creatures the foolhardiness of their ways, to show them the consequences of their alcoholic servitude. By walking the streets of that benighted Dale, those London avenues, gateway to the infernal regions, he could see his actions were justified; there were few souls staggering to and fro in their drunkenness, few women of loose virtue to allow those same fools to claw and paw at their soiled flesh. His mission would soon be over, he knew that; but these streets would be cleaner and less putrid for his actions.

Then he would meet his judgement.

The Dale was deserted, he noted with satisfaction. His fingers sought and held the hilt of his blade in his pocket, twitching against the cold steel. In this moment of distraction he inhaled through his nose, and at once almost retched at the sulphurous, rancid stink. He was not but a short walk from that mephitic swamp the local folk called the Ocean. A collection of clay pits in an ignored brick field, great holes where stagnant water, pig effluent and human excrement and waste had gathered to create one noxious pond with an unholy stink that stayed in the nostrils for days. Swiftly, from the pocket of his woollen coat, he brought a handkerchief doused with scent and clasped it to his gagging mouth. The nausea passed. He stood up, chastised. Until the deed was done, or the Ocean's miasma was downwind, he could take air only through his mouth.

He walked down the new Walmer Road, past those streets of shame. Nowhere in London was more degraded and abandoned than life in those wretched places. He shuddered when he thought of what passed for life in that acre of sin surrounding William Street and the disgusting habits of the deluded fools who inhabited them. Yes, these people were poor; but what little money they had they squandered. Dissolute half-clad girls smoking in lice-ridden rooms, plying their awful trade with the steady inflow of certain submerged and criminal types.

They needed to learn the error of their ways. Once again his hand clasped the hilt of his dagger as he felt his gorge rise.

He managed to pass the despicable swamp without retching, then turned right on to St James Square, the air becoming cleaner, breathing easier among the respectable class whose dwellings sat around that glorious church. It made his heart swell to see its awe, silhouetted against the mild night sky. Passing it put purpose in his step, not that it had been waning.

He followed the road until it joined Saint Ann's Villas, where he turned left towards the Royal Crescent on the edge of the Dale. A quick right took him down Queen's Road. There were more people present here, the terror not as strong. He would soon change that . . .

He stood by the chapel on Queen's Road, hidden in the shadows, watching that place. The Queen's Arms. The stench of ale, wafting towards him on the breeze, was overpowering, almost as unbearable as the stink from that stagnant pit he had passed earlier. Again he breathed only through his mouth. He twisted his neck to one side, hearing it crack and feeling the relief from the pressure. He was calm, prepared, ready.

The door of the pub swung open; two men stumbled out. They squared up to each other, as if fixing for combat. But another emerged to intervene and one was pushed away, turning to leave. A huge man. He let him pass by, not wanting to risk such a mighty foe. Seconds later the other protagonist in the brawl that never was staggered from the public house, muttering obscenities and oaths at no one in particular. Much more like it, he thought.

The smaller man hawked phlegm into his throat and expectorated copiously into the street. Then he adjusted his cap and set off walking, veering slightly to his left before righting himself. Once more he brought phlegm into his throat and cleared it.

He shook his head, as if to rid it of the fug, and increased his speed. 'Bastards,' he muttered to himself.

In the shadows he waited to see which way his victim would go. Praise God, the man went straight on, towards him. The man crossed the road, expectorating once more. He felt the knife in his hand and stepped from the shadow, falling in behind. The man turned instinctively, saw him and stopped.

'Aye, what's this business?' the man slurred, his face puzzled, addled.

Without breaking stride he continued walking to him, pulled the knife from his pocket and drove it home, twisting sharply when it was sunk to the hilt.

The victim's eyes turned glassy, rolled heavenwards — he would find no comfort there — and a gasp of air hissed from below, accompanied by the gurgle of his death. When he pulled the knife clear, the man collapsed to the floor. Immediately he picked up his quarry, carried it ten yards to a patch of ground upon which it seemed they were building yet more dwellings. Like a doll, he tossed it to the ground, not even bothering to hide the fruits of his labour. Only then did he look around: he saw no one. He was truly blessed. He replaced the knife in his pocket and hurried away from the scene, yet another night's work complete.

21

Nigel reached the Family Records Centre as dawn approached after yet another night of fitful sleep, studded with dark, half-remembered dreams. Foster had arranged for the centre to be open at Nigel's request. Phil on the desk was there waiting to let him in. It was barely six a.m., but he was still whistling. A tune Nigel could not make out. It was only as he returned from locking up his bag and coat that he realized it was 'Where Do You Go To My Lovely?' by Peter Sarstedt.

'You whistling that for my benefit, Phil?' he asked.

Phil looked bemused. 'Didn't realize I was,' he said, vaguely hurt.

Nigel moved on. As he drifted towards the indexes, he heard Phil start up once more. This time he couldn't make out the tune at all.

He went straight to the marriage indexes and hunted down the reference for Hannah Fairbairn, to a carpenter named Maurice Hardie. Thank God it wasn't John Smith, he thought. At a terminal upstairs he tracked them via the census. In 1881 they were living in Bermondsey with three children; a nine-year-old girl and two boys, aged seven and three.

Next he was faced with a familiar problem. They simply vanished from the census. The death indexes told him that Maurice and Hannah died a day apart in 1889. A call to the General Register Office revealed influenza had claimed them both. They had been reduced to poverty, clinging on to the bottom rung of Victorian existence inside Bermondsey Workhouse. Two days later, their younger son, David, succumbed to the disease in the same desperate place.

That left two children: Clara, who would now be almost seventeen, and Michael, two years her junior. There was no record of their deaths so Nigel presumed they must have survived, but subsequent census returns proved fruitless. Neither was there a record of either getting married before the turn of the century.

He left the FRC, walked down Myddelton Street, through Exmouth Market, taking a left down Rosoman Street until he reached the London Metropolitan Archives on the corner of Northampton Road. Here were seventy-two kilometres of records, dating back to 1607, about the capital, its inhabitants and their lives. More pertinently, it held the records for the city's Poor Law unions, who oversaw the running of the individual workhouses, in this case the St Olave Poor Law Union.

He ordered the admission and discharge register. In 1886 all five of the Hardie family were admitted. They had come voluntarily. The two young boys were malnourished, Michael awarded the stark description 'imbecile'. Nigel knew exactly what had happened. Like many of the poor, they had chosen institutionalized grind and servility in order to survive. Maurice and Hannah would have slept in separate dormitories, the children too. There would have been minimal contact with each other. Wearing a uniform, woken at six, a day of menial work, in bed by eight; only the lack of bars and locks distinguished these places from prisons. People were free to leave at three hours' notice, but to what? To starve, to freeze on the streets? They were imprisoned by circumstance.

Nigel wondered what events had led Maurice to abandon any hope of providing for his family and to seek the charity of the authorities. An injury perhaps? The boys were not yet old enough to support the family, and there was not enough work for young women like Clara to provide for them. In 1888 she had discharged herself, to try and lead a life beyond the workhouse walls. Maybe she believed she might even be able to reverse her family's fortunes. Yet a year later, her parents and elder brother were dead, probably interred in the cheapest coffins possible and buried in the same unmarked grave. The day after David's death, Clara came to collect her surviving brother, 7th September 1889.

Where had they gone? Nigel spent two hours searching through the registers of every asylum in London. Michael did not show up; he must have gone to live with Clara. But then the pair had slipped through a crack in time.

Outside he blinked against the late-afternoon spring sunshine. Time had spun away, hours lost as he buried himself in the past.

Then it struck him. An idea. He did not know what prompted it, but he had learned in his career as a genealogist always to follow a hunch. He returned to the FRC and went straight to the 1891 census. He typed in Clara Fairbairn and her date of birth.

There she was: same age. She had taken her mother's maiden name. Why? He could only guess. To shake off the stigma of the poorhouse perhaps? He clicked the link to reveal other members of the household. Michael Fairbairn. He was living with her in a house in Bow, east London. All the other occupants of the house, Michael aside, were young women: all between the ages of thirteen and eighteen.

Clara was the eldest. Nigel guessed it was some sort of boarding house. Her occupation was given as matchworker. That and the location explained everything: she was working at the Bryant and May factory. She had found work, albeit of the most arduous and dangerous kind: working fourteen hours a day, prohibited from talking, punished for dropping matches, and at risk of contracting disfiguring and fatal cancer from the ever-present yellow phosphorus used to make the matches.

On the 1901 census Clara, aged twenty-nine, was listed working as a domestic servant at an address on Holland Park. Michael was not at the same address. Instead, he was living and working as a groom at stables on Holland Park Mews. It seemed a reasonable assumption that Clara had somehow inveigled Michael into the job when she got hers. A year later, Michael was dead of heart failure. A year after that, Clara was married, to a clerk named Sidney Chesterton, three years her junior. Nigel felt sure the two events were related; only now that her brother was dead was she able to forge a life of her own.

She and Sidney had four children, two of each sex. The first-born, a boy, had been named Michael. They settled in Hammersmith, at that time a semi-rural London satellite. On each birth certificate Sidney's occupation grew grander so that, by the birth of his fourth child, he was a manager. What he managed wasn't clear, but the Chestertons were middle class. Clara had come a long way from the workhouse steps. She eventually died in 1951. She was seventy-nine, an amazing age given the deprivations of her early life. He shook his head at her indomitability, wondering whether her descendants knew of her sacrifice; did they realize how this woman, who probably appeared to them only in sepia-tinted photographs at the bottom of a drawer or a box, had altered the path of their family, hauled it from the shadows and preserved a bloodline?

The centre was empty, the last remaining member of staff alternately glancing at Nigel and the clock on the wall, closing on seven o'clock. There was no way Nigel could complete the job that night, and his eyes ached. He called Foster and told him how far he'd reached. The detective was barely lucid, distracted by the looming deadline and the awful, impending prospect of a fourth victim.

Foster gazed up at the tower block, like a climber contemplating an unconquerable face. In the dusk light it seemed less ugly, yet still inscrutable. People had come and gone throughout the day, and he and Heather had watched them all: every delivery was checked, each workman questioned, each resident who left and arrived cross-referenced against the list they had. Nothing appeared different, or out of the ordinary.

At intervals Foster went and checked each and every bin, alley and scrap of wasteland around the block. Each time there was nothing to see; but while he could tell himself that he had been watching, and no one had slipped in without his knowing, he still expected to lift a lid or peer around a corner and see the sight he dreaded most of all.

As night fell there seemed little option but to sit in the car with Heather and wait. The lights of the flats flicked on one by one and the stream of people in and out became an intermittent drip. Gangs of youths congregated on a street corner, drinkers weaved their way to the pubs and late stragglers made their way back from work. Shouts, pounding bass and the feed-me screams of babies wafted through the air, mingling occasionally with the irregular sound of sirens hurtling along the Westway. He got out only once, to shoo away a mongrel threatening to piss on his offside rear tyre.

Foster had never felt so helpless. He ticked off the hours as they passed: ten, then eleven, midnight. The anniversary of finding the fourth victim in 1879 had begun. The first three had been found in the hours between the middle of the night and dawn. He saw no reason why this might be different.

The city noise abated, the streets cleared, though the sirens never stilled. One by one the lights of the block vanished, a few remaining illuminated as the wee small hours came and went, insomniacs staring numbly at screens. He and Heather barely spoke. There was nothing for it but to see how this would play out.

Dawn came. He let Heather doze. Foster had passed the point of tiredness, when sleep could come easily, and lapsed into a wired, restless exhaustion, unable to stop his leg from bouncing manically as he sat still. His mum used to call it St Vitus's dance, he remembered through the fog in his brain. He had not done it in years.

As the sun rose, the tower block woke from slumber. The first workers left, the sybarites returned. Heather came round and poured two cups of stewed coffee from a flask.

'What do we do?' she asked.

'We wait,' he said. 'There is nothing more we can do.'

His phone rang. Andy Drinkwater.

'You're up early,' Foster said.

'I never went to bed. Big development last night.

About three it came through that they'd found a knife similar to the one that may have stabbed two of the three vics in Terry Cable's garden, beneath the rosebushes or something. It's with forensics now.'

For a second, Foster was speechless. 'That's bullshit,' he blurted out.

'What do you mean? I'm only telling you what I know.'

'I know, Andy,' Foster said. 'It's just that I'll bet you all the blow in Amsterdam that the knife they found did not stab James Darbyshire or Nella Perry. And if it did, then it was planted in the garden to fit him up.'

'Everyone here thinks it's a breakthrough,' Drinkwater muttered. 'No sign of any action your end?'

'None,' Foster grunted. He knew that every minute that passed without a fourth victim would harden Harris and his cronies' conviction that the right man was in custody. He ended the call, still shaking his head in disbelief.

'What's up with you?' Heather asked.

'The past does repeat itself.'

'That's a bit cryptic. What you on about?'

'In 1879, as you know, there was a series of murders in Kensington. The newspapers went ballistic, the natives got restless and the cops panicked; they arrested a guy to stop bucket after bucket of shit being tipped over their heads. Then they realized they'd better get a case against the man they'd chosen to be their suspect. So, lo and behold, a knife turns up in his lodgings.'

'You've told me all of this.'

'Yes, but what I haven't told you is that, lo and behold, a knife has turned up in Terry Cable's garden, just when the press were beginning to get a bit restless about the lack of any charges.'

He could see Heather take this in. Ready to play devil's advocate.

'Have you considered the idea he might actually be guilty?'

'Considered it. Dismissed it. Come on, Heather, you can see what's happening here as clearly as I can. They're so desperate they've convinced themselves that he's guilty. It doesn't follow that, because he's the only suspect, he's the right suspect. No one has given me any indication of a possible motive.'

'What about the GHB?'

'That's coincidence: detail, not motive. Why did he kill these people? Why did he remove parts of their body? Why did he leave them in those exact same places on those exact same days? They have no answers to those questions. We know why – the killer's following a pattern. And because of what happened during and after the trial in 1879, we may even know the motive.'

'So they have a suspect and no motive; you have a motive and no suspect.'

'I know in which position I'd rather be,' he muttered.

'You hope we find a body, don't you?' Heather said, turning to face him, a smile on the corner of her lips. 'Proves you right if we do.'

'No,' he maintained. 'I *think* we'll find a body – different from *wanting* to. And we might find the killer. But we would have had a damn sight better chance if we had more manpower and if everyone had not been scattered to the four winds trying to fit up some sleazeball to deter a shitstorm in the press.'

His gaze returned to the tower block. Inside, the lights were coming back on.

Noon came. Foster was still there, spent by lack of sleep. He was beginning to doubt whether it was worth it. Cable seemed certain to be charged; a fourth body had not turned up, after all. Had he been wrong? Heather might have been right: Cable could be their man. He shook his head to clear it. However blurred his thinking had become, he still refused to accept Cable's guilt. Of course, if Barnes called and told him that Terry Cable was a descendant of Eke Fairbairn, that would change everything; until then he would not move.

He had sent Heather home to grab a couple of hours' sleep. She was reluctant, but he needed someone with energy at his side when the names came through from Barnes. He sat there, window open, a cool breeze helping keep him awake, blowing in more sounds from the street. For the past half-hour loud music had been blaring from a window high up in the tower block, indistinguishable white noise save for the thump of a bass and what sounded like handclaps. There was something familiar about it, Foster thought, but from a hundred feet below it was impossible to assign any tune to the rhythm. Whoever lived in the flat obviously loved the song because each time it ended, it would start again.

His arm was out of the window, absent-mindedly tapping on the car door, beating time along with the percussion and bass. After a few repeat hearings he thought he'd found the rhythm, and it was possible to make out the melody carried by the singer. Foster started to whistle a tune. A disco song, he was sure. Not his favourite genre; he was more a loud guitar and sneering, disenchanted vocals man, but there were a few disco tunes he'd admit to liking. What was this one, though? It was bugging him so much he felt like climbing out of his car, jumping in the lift and asking whoever was playing it to death.

Each time the rhythm changed to indicate the chorus, he started to whistle the hook. The singers were a group of women, though a hazy recollection suggested there might have been a bloke with them. It rhymed with 'boots', the only word of the chorus he remembered. Then it came: 'Going Back To My Roots', by Odyssey. Got it, he thought, content to have scratched that itch.

Then he stopped, sitting forwards, as if an ice cube had been put down his back.

He sprang from the car, jogged to the tower-block entrance, through the doors and punched the lift button. It clanked into action, but he couldn't stand the wait. He took the stairs, striding up two at a time, adrenalin overriding fatigue. By the time he reached the tenth floor he could feel his heart pumping in his ears. Through a door he reached a dim corridor, lit only by grubby windows at each end. There was no need for him to follow the numbers on the door; he could follow the noise. As he strode down the corridor it got louder and louder, more and more distorted. A straw-haired woman in a worn red dressing gown over jeans and a T-shirt, her face creased by smoking, stepped out of her door into the corridor. She saw Foster, clocking his suit.

'Are you here about whoever's making that bloody noise?'

'Who lives there?'

She shrugged. 'Bert died six weeks ago. I thought it had been empty since. Council's probably given it to some fucking kids who're gonna make my life a misery.'

'Go back inside,' Foster said. 'I'll sort it out.'

'You better,' she said and disappeared, though Foster noticed she left the door slightly ajar.

He stopped at number 65; the bass was making the door hinges rattle, as if they might blow. He knocked loudly. No response. He tried once more. No answer again.

He took a step back, lifted his foot and crashed his heel against the door. It failed to budge, but he sensed another attempt might break the lock. It didn't, but on his third kick he heard a splinter, and with his fourth attempt it flew open.

He walked in to be faced with three doors. The noise was coming from the one in front of him. He opened it and was almost floored by the wall of sound. In the middle of the room on the floor was a small, round chrome CD clock radio. The LCD display showed 12.15. Save for the clock, the room was unadorned. A grubby net curtain barely covered the window, through which he could see the outline of central London. He made for the stereo and, covering his hand with the sleeve of his shirt, he bumped the off switch. At last, silence.

Now that one of his senses had been restored, he looked around. The place stank. The flocked white wallpaper was stained and grey, bearing the shadows of old furniture. To one side was a kitchen. He walked in; nothing except a few battered, obsolescent white goods.

He returned to the small entrance hall. Opened one door and was hit by the smell of pervasive damp. The bathroom. Nothing except the drip from a scaled bath tap. Closed the door, tried the next one.

The smell hit him first. One he knew well. It emanated from the only thing in the room. The body of a woman. From the stench, he knew she had been here longer than twenty-four hours. She was on her back in the middle of the floor, dressed in a pair of jeans and a brown sweater. A few flies buzzed around her. He pulled a handkerchief from his pocket and put it over his nose, then leaned down for a closer look. It was the hair he noticed. There was none. From the brow to beyond the crown was only a fleshy mass and the white dome of her skull.

She had been scalped.

22

Edward Carlisle shook his head.

'This is like something from the Wild West,' he said, peering at the exposed scalp. 'I think what he's done is lifted up the hair – from what's left at the back it was brown, about shoulder-length. Then twisted, used the point of the knife to slice around the parting, and then pulled the whole thing off. Must have taken some doing. I'll tell you one thing, though.' He looked up grimly. 'From what I see here, I believe she was alive when he scalped her.'

Foster couldn't imagine what that was like. Didn't want to. 'How long she been dead?' he asked.

'Around sixty hours or so.'

Monday, he thought.

'And from the lividity on her back I'd guess she's been lying here all that time, maybe a few hours less,' Carlisle added. 'Again, she did not die here, she was moved post-mortem. Again, there's a single stab wound to the heart that probably killed her. You can survive being scalped, particularly when as much care has been taken as this.'

The killer knew they might be hanging around, Foster thought. So he got her up here before the place was surrounded. One step ahead again.

Detective Superintendent Harris walked into the room, his long face leached of colour and rigid with concern. 'What's the preliminary verdict?' he said, hands on hips.

'She was stabbed and scalped,' Foster said.

'Scalped? Jesus Christ.'

'She's been here since Monday night. She was probably killed then.'

Harris stared down at the floor. 'You sure about those timings?' he said to Carlisle.

'About as sure as I can be.'

'Cable's innocent, Brian,' Foster said. 'You pulled him in Monday afternoon. He couldn't have done this.'

Harris nodded slowly. Foster knew he would be playing this out in his mind, how it would go down with the press and the upper echelons of the Yard.

'Of course, you've got the knife,' Foster added.

Harris rubbed his chin ruefully. 'Not the knife involved in the killings. Forensics confirmed that this morning.' He let out an enormous sigh. 'OK, he's still out there. I accept that. I should have given you more cover here. I accept that, too.'

Foster held his hands up. 'Would have been too

late, Brian. He was ahead of us. We may have found the body sooner, that's all. But the fact remains that we have one person to try and save, one last chance. The fifth victim will be killed before one a.m. Sunday morning.' It passed through his mind that they might already be dead. 'The body will be found in Powis Square. We have two days, perhaps less.'

'How do you want to play it, Grant?'

He was back in favour. Back in charge.

'I'm waiting on a phone call that will help me decide,' he said.

Carlisle interrupted. 'There appears to be no identification on her, but the killer missed this in her back pocket.'

He held a tightly balled piece of paper in between forefinger and thumb. Foster took it and peeled it open carefully. It was a receipt.

'Supermarket. Monday morning. She paid by credit card.'

Harris summoned a detective and asked him to get an ID as soon as possible. Heather entered the bedroom, her hair still wet from a shower. Through the open door, Foster could see forensics working the clock radio. She glanced at the victim, then looked at him.

'Nigel's been on the phone. He's been at it since first thing this morning. He's already traced a number of Fairbairn's living descendants and hopes to have them all by the end of the day.'

'Someone going to fill me in?' Harris asked impatiently.

'In 1879 the police arrested a man in connection with the murders in Notting Dale and North Kensington. He was charged with two of them, tried at the Old Bailey, found guilty and hanged.'

'I see.'

'Except for one thing: he almost certainly didn't do it. He was convicted on the evidence of a single witness, who claimed to have seen him following one of the victims.' He wasn't sure how Harris would react to the next detail. 'But the police also conveniently found a knife at his lodging house, although the suspicion was that it was planted.'

Harris flinched. 'We didn't plant that knife in Cable's garden, Grant.'

'I didn't say you did. But the similarities are there. My guess is the killer planted it. Maybe he wanted to make a point.'

'What point?'

'Fairbairn was treated like a punchbag. The investigating team beat the shit out of him, broke almost every major bone in his body to try and get him to confess. He had the mental age of a child, barely able to finish a sentence, but they still hanged him. For a crime he didn't commit. And then they ballsed up the hanging and he choked to death at the end of a rope.'

He paused.

'The killer is seeking to avenge that injustice. And they were seeking to frame an innocent man to make the point that the police never change. Our family historian is tracing every living descendant of Eke Fairbairn, the wrongly accused. We need to feed all their names through the computer and see if any of them set alarm bells ringing. Then we still need to track down each and every one of them in the next twenty-four hours and see if they can explain their actions during the last few weeks.'

Harris's expression changed from interest to incredulity. 'You're telling me that a descendant of this man has copied the killing spree his ancestor *didn't* do in order to prove his innocence?'

Foster nodded. 'It's the best theory I have. Whoever did this knows their way around the world of family history. What's to say they weren't researching their genealogy and found this dark secret? For someone already on the edge, that's the sort of thing that could tip you over. What I can't answer is why he chose these victims. Perhaps they were just selected at random: wrong place, wrong time.'

Harris did not look convinced.

'Where are these names Nigel's compiling?' Foster asked Heather.

'Nigel's faxing them through to the office,' she said. 'So far, they're scattered all over the country, as you'd expect. We can arm everyone who goes out on the doorstep with the sketch of the man seen drinking with Nella Perry at the Prince of Wales, see if anybody we track down matches it.'

'I'll get back to the incident room and get on to it, make a few calls,' Harris said. Cable's name went unmentioned. Foster knew he would be let go, perhaps charged with possession. The press would be told that no charges related to the case would be made. When they discovered there had been a fourth victim, put two and two together and realized she was killed when Cable was in custody, the bad press of a few days ago would seem like *Hello!* magazine.

Foster said he would follow him back soon. Harris could make sure other forces spared the men needed to interview those outside of London. It would have to be handled carefully. Turning up unannounced at people's homes, informing them someone had been delving into their family history without their knowledge, that their ancestor was wrongly executed for murder, and they were now suspects in a current murder inquiry, was not a common approach.

He was glad to be back in the thick of it, yet

unwilling to leave the past behind. There was still more to be learned there.

He and Heather left the room. They were met by the detective who Harris had tasked with identifying the victim from the supermarket receipt. A few simple calls had turned up the name of the credit-card holder. A 41-year-old woman, Patricia MacDougall. Divorced, single. They had an address. Foster jotted it down.

As he wrote her surname it hit him in the gut like a punch.

Nigel pulled fiercely on a roll-up outside the FRC. Heather had told him of the fourth victim. Foster had been right, he mused; the man in custody had been innocent. She did not elaborate further, other than saying the victim was a woman. The image of Nella Perry's corpse flashed across his mind. Nigel puffed away. Since that night he'd been able to busy himself with the case. Once he'd faxed through the complete list of Fairbairn's descendants, his work for the police would be done. He'd be alone, time on his hands, the events of the past few days hard to deal with.

He felt his phone buzz in his pocket. It was Foster. His voice was excitable, higher in pitch.

'What was the name of the judge?' he said.

'In the 1879 case?'

'No, in the trial of O. J. fucking Simpson. Of course I mean the 1879 case.'

Nigel scoured his memory.

'Justice MacDougall.'

Foster muttered some form of expletive.

'He wore a black cap, didn't he?'

'They always did when they passed a sentence of death. Why?'

'It's not confirmed but we think the fourth victim was called Patricia MacDougall.'

Could be a coincidence, Nigel thought.

'And she was scalped. Her hair was removed from the top of her head. The exact place where a black cap would have been. Do you follow what I'm saying?'

Nigel did.

'She was born on 15th May 1965. Don't know where. Can you trace her genealogy and see if there's a link? I need it quick. Quicker than beer turns to piss.'

'What about the Fairbairn list?' He'd been working quickly. He guessed there were only a few more to trace.

'Forget about that. Come back to it,' Foster urged.

Nigel went to birth indexes for that year and found three women of that name born in that quarter. He went back outside and called Foster. They had some more information; her middle names were Jane Webster. Patricia Jane Webster MacDougall.

He identified the right one. The certificate gave the names of her parents, which allowed him to trace their wedding certificate and, from that, Patricia's grandfather. He worked quickly, skipping back three generations in no time, the calls to the General Register Office starting to stack up as he unearthed references more quickly than they could locate the corresponding certificates. Eventually the information he could glean from the era of modern civil registration came to an end and he was left with the name of the dead woman's great-great-great-grandfather, Montgomery MacDougall.

Nigel felt his pulse quicken: this was their man. He died in 1898 at the age of eighty-four, his occupation high court judge. Nigel was shocked to discover he was still sitting at his death, growing ever more senile. Nigel wondered how many other innocent men his incompetence condemned to the gallows.

He phoned Foster, who was already on his way to the FRC with Heather. Two minutes later they'd arrived and found an empty corner of the main room.

'She's a direct descendant,' Nigel said.

A look of certainty appeared on Foster's face. 'That does it. Patricia MacDougall was killed because of who her ancestor was. The mutilations have been telling us this all along. He cut off her hair to let us know why he's doing this.' He started to nod his head. 'Forget about the Fairbairn list for now. I'll get you some help to finish it off. Let's look at the other victims. Ellis wasn't mutilated, but he was found with a noose around his neck. I bet if we check his ancestry it will lead us straight back to our old friend Norwood, the executioner.'

Nigel made a note in his book. 'I'll need Ellis's date and place of birth.'

'We'll get you it. Darbyshire's hands were cut off. Who might have used their hands in the case?'

'Someone handling evidence,' Heather suggested.

Foster screwed up his face. 'Don't think so. I'll get you his date and place of birth and you can work out if there's any link to 1879 in there. The same with Nella Perry. Her eyes were missing. Her ancestor saw something. See if there's any link to Stafford Pearcey, the main prosecution witness. Once we've confirmed all four are related to the case, let's go back to the trial and work out who's left: who hasn't had a descendant butchered.

'Then we can find out who might be next.'

23

That evening Foster, frayed by exhaustion and intermittent bursts of adrenalin, was parked outside the house of John Fairbairn in Barnes. He was the second name on the list that Khan had completed under Nigel's tutelage. It was shorter than he thought. Only thirty-two people. The first on the list had been eighty-three, lived in a nursing home, and ate her lunch through a straw.

More evidence had been found at the scene of Patricia MacDougall's murder. A fingerprint left on the back of the CD in the clock radio player matched the unidentified print they had lifted off the box containing Nella Perry's eyes. Foster had decided to ask each descendant for a print to rule them out.

He and Drinkwater knocked on the door. It was opened by a brown-haired man in his forties, a mug of tea in his hand. Foster noticed he was wearing slippers.

He looked at both Drinkwater and Foster.

'Yes,' he said warily.

Foster flashed his ID. 'Mr Fairbairn?'

The man nodded, eyes narrowing.

'Sorry to bother you at home. I was wondering if we could grab a few moments of your time.'

'What's happened?' he asked.

'Can we explain?' Foster said, gesturing inside, not wanting to have this exchange on the doorstep.

They followed Fairbairn in. The house was warm, the smell of baking billowing from the kitchen. A woman stepped out, rubbing her hands on a tea towel. Foster nodded in greeting.

'Something smells good,' he said.

She smiled but looked immediately at her husband for reassurance.

'These two detectives say they want a word with us.'

'You actually, Mr Fairbairn,' Foster said. 'But your wife is welcome to join us; it's not an interview.'

They went into the lounge. The TV was muted. Fairbairn turned it off.

'Tea or coffee?' he asked.

'No thanks,' Foster said. 'I've been mainlining coffee all day.'

Drinkwater asked for fruit juice. Mrs Fairbairn scurried off and came back with a jugful rattling with ice.

'So what's this about?' Fairbairn said.

Foster drew a deep breath. 'Can I ask if either of you are at all interested in family history?'

Fairbairn stared at him as if he had just propositioned his wife. 'Are you being serious?'

'I am, yes.'

The couple exchanged bewildered glances. 'As a matter of fact, I am. It's been a hobby of mine for several years now.'

'So you're aware of your own family history?'

'Yes. Well, only until the 1740s. My inability to read Latin prevented me going any further back. Can I ask where this is leading?'

'To Eke Fairbairn.'

Mr Fairbairn stared at Foster for a few seconds without speaking. 'How the heavens do you know about Eke?' he asked.

'Long story,' Foster said. 'Let me ask you a few questions first, then I'll explain. Do you know what he did?'

'He was a murderer. He killed two people and was executed at Newgate Prison in 1879.'

'When did you find out about him?'

He looked at his wife. 'About five years ago?' he said to her.

She nodded. 'About five years ago,' she repeated.

'And how did it make you feel, discovering there was a murderer in your family?'

Fairbairn shrugged. 'To be honest, I thought it was fascinating. I don't go in for ancestor worship.'

'Ancestor worship?'

'Yes, I see it all the time in the family history group I'm part of. People venerating one particular person, usually the most successful, or the most hardy, to the exclusion of the others. Conveniently ignoring the black sheep. Some people welcome the failures and misfits; others turn away and pretend it never happened, go into denial.'

'Have you researched your ancestor's trial?'

'I've read some of the newspaper reports,' Fairbairn said, becoming impatient. 'Sorry, I really have to ask why you're so interested in this. Is the case being reopened?'

'You could say that,' Foster replied, then decided to cut to the chase. 'There's been a series of murders in West London over the past few weeks. Whoever's doing it has been copying the murders of 1879, for which your ancestor was hanged. It's our belief that Eke was an innocent man, that he was fitted up by the police in order to deflect public and press criticism.'

Fairbairn was speechless, his mouth opening and closing without making a sound.

'We also think that the person who is committing these murders is aware of the miscarriage of justice and is avenging what happened back then. First, we want to rule out descendants of Eke Fairbairn.'

Fairbairn's expression turned to disbelief. 'I'm a suspect?'

'In a tenuous sort of way, yes, you are,' Foster said.

'I can categorically deny murdering anyone,' he replied bluntly. He shook his head.

'I can believe that,' Foster said. 'But it'd help if we could rule you out of our inquiries. A fingerprint would be one way.'

He agreed. Drinkwater took his print, then asked him where he had been on the nights the bodies were dumped. He was at home, a story verified by his wife. Foster believed him, but decided to keep an eye on his movements for the next twenty-four hours or so. When Drinkwater had completed the routine, Foster asked a few more questions.

'Have you shared the story of Eke Fairbairn with any other family, friends?'

'My immediate family know. My son, who's at university, and my daughter, who's at a friend's tonight. My brother and his wife. They live in Oxford. And, of course, my family history group.'

'All of them?'

'Yes, I gave a small talk about it.'

'When was that?'

'A year or so ago. They were fascinated. As I said,

most people who become interested in family history embrace all their ancestors, not just the ones who happened to make the most money and give birth to the most children.'

'Did you notice anyone giving what you said undue attention, asking a lot of questions?'

Fairbairn smiled rather condescendingly. Had he not been so tired, it would have pissed Foster off.

'Detective, I'm forty-nine years old. With the odd exception, in comparison to the rest of the group I am a mere whippersnapper. No one in that group is physically capable of murder. But tomorrow evening is our monthly meeting. You could come along and see if you can spot any likely killers.'

Foster smiled thinly and took the name of the group and its secretary. The circle of those who might know about the injustice had just widened, he thought ruefully, when he could do with it shrinking.

Foster got up to leave.

'What makes you think Eke wasn't guilty?' Fairbairn asked.

'I know a bad case when I see one,' was all Foster replied. He did not mention anything about Fairbairn's ancestor having been beaten and broken before he was hanged. He sensed John Fairbairn would discover that for himself now.

'It's funny,' he said, as he showed Foster and

Drinkwater to his front door. 'I was only talking about this with my brother recently. When I started to research our family, my mother, who died four years ago, became very distressed. She told me I mustn't get involved because there was a murderer in the family. That was the first I heard of it. She died not wanting to know. To her, it was shameful. It had been a dark family secret for years, rarely spoken about. Now it turns out there was nothing to be ashamed of; he was innocent.'

They said goodbye. Foster was puzzled. The family was ashamed of Eke? This probably meant Clara had not passed down the story of her brother's innocence. Perhaps she had assumed her brother's guilt.

'Interesting that he's researched the history, isn't it?' Drinkwater said. 'He might have been lying when he said he didn't know about the miscarriage of justice.'

Foster shook his head. 'I doubt it.'

He thought about what Fairbairn said regarding his mother's attitude to her ancestor, and it saddened him. Eke Fairbairn had not only been condemned to die but, for more than a century, his name had been a source of shame for those who shared it.

Nigel called it a night at ten, index blindness causing his head to ache. His aim was to go home, grab a few hours' sleep and return to the FRC refreshed. He anticipated spending the next day there; probably the night, too.

Back at his flat he flopped on his sofa. I might just pass out here, he thought, rubbing his hands down his face again and again, names, dates and references pulsing through his brain. He turned on BBC Radio Four, the backdrop to his life. He even kept it on while sleeping, a low background murmur through the night. He joked to visitors that he was trying to soak up as much knowledge as possible, even at rest, when in fact he was seeking comfort. A man with a high, lisping voice was reading extracts from a book, some sort of travelogue. He settled back on the sofa and closed his eyes.

The front door buzzer startled him. Who the hell was that, at this time of night? He went to the intercom.

'Hello,' he said irritably, expecting some drunken fool who'd chosen the wrong flat number.

'It's Heather.'

'Oh,' he said.

'Sorry, did I wake you up?'

'No. Not at all. I just got back, actually. Just had the radio on and . . .'

'Can I come in? Very nice, Shepherd's Bush, but I don't want to stand here all night.'

'Of course,' he said. 'Sorry. Bit dazed.'

He pressed the release button. He heard the entrance door slam and her feet shuffling up the stone steps. He opened the door to his flat. As Heather came towards his landing, he could see she was carrying something in her right hand. Looked like a bottle of wine.

He let her in and she walked through to the sitting room. Nigel caught a waft of her perfume as she passed. She took her jacket off and laid it over the arm of the sofa.

'Be a sweetheart and open that up,' she said, handing him the bottle of wine wrapped in white paper. 'Barely had a glass all week and, given the week it's been, I need one. Just been round to the house of one of the Fairbairns from your list. Nothing doing. It was only down the road so I thought I'd drop by, see how you were.'

Nigel smiled. Despite his exhaustion and the fact he had only come home to snatch a few hours' sleep before heading back, he was delighted to see her and the wine. Before, on the morning after Nella Perry's murder, her visit seemed routine – more out of professional concern. This was different. Or, at least, it felt so. For a second he cursed the circumstances – in a few hours both of them would be back at work – and wished it was a normal Friday night and their time was their own. He went through to the kitchen, rattled around in a drawer teeming with loose cutlery, tin openers and other appliances until he found a corkscrew that worked.

'How did the research go?' Heather asked, appearing at the door behind him.

'Good,' he said, cursing as the blunt corkscrew gouged the cork to shards. He forced it back in and slowly pulled it out without losing too much of the cork in the wine. From the back of the cupboard he selected two wine glasses, part of the best set he had, infrequently aired. He handed her the glass.

'Here's to catching the killer in the next twenty-four hours,' she said, clinking glasses.

She gave him a smile. Nigel loved the way it animated her whole face. She took a sip then pushed a wisp of hair from her forehead.

'How good is good?' she said, walking to the armchair. She sat kneeling, curling her legs underneath her.

Nigel sat on the sofa. 'Well, Ellis is going to be difficult to trace, given how common the surname is. So I've put that to one side. I did Darbyshire first. Bit tricky due to the possible variations in the spelling of his name, either with an "a" or an "e". But I managed to get back to around 1879. His direct ancestor of that time, his great-great-grandfather, was a guy named Ivor Darbyshire, newspaper editor.'

'Which newspaper?'

'Don't know yet. He's not listed in the old copies of *Who's Who*, so it's unlikely to be a national. He lived in Kensington. I thought perhaps he might have edited the *Kensington News*; they were the ones who piled a lot of pressure on the police back then.'

Heather nodded. 'Darbyshire's hands were cut off. Journalists write or type with their hands, even if they talk out of their arse. Makes sense.'

'I got a much better hit with Nella Perry's ancestry.'

Heather pulled out a notebook from her bag.

'Her direct ancestor was Stafford Pearcey, the main witness at Fairbairn's trial.'

'Bingo.'

'It wasn't easy. There was no sign of anyone named Pearcey being involved with the family. But I did find that, in 1892, Seamus Perry was born a bastard. His mother was Irish; her name was on the birth certificate but the father's wasn't. In 1891 I found her on the census. Niamh Perry. She was Stafford Pearcey's housekeeper.'

'Was he married?'

He nodded.

'Dirty old sod.'

'At least he didn't cut her off without a penny,'

Nigel said. 'Looks like he paid for Seamus to go to Harrow.'

'And as a result we have the Perrys of Notting Hill. Wonder if they're aware they only exist because their ancestor shacked up with someone below stairs.'

'I think I know why Stafford Pearcey gave evidence that implicated Eke,' Nigel added. 'In 1893, he died. In prison. He'd been sentenced for embezzlement. He was probably at it for years, but he either paid the cops off or did favours for them, like the one at Fairbairn's trial.'

Heather shook her head sadly. They sat in silence, the radio chuntering away in the background. Nigel usually leapt in to fill moments like these, feeling awkward. Not now.

'At least we now know his motivation,' Heather said eventually. 'If you want revenge for something that happened more than a hundred and twenty-five years ago and don't have access to a time machine, then the best you can do is torture and kill those who carry the guilty men's genes.'

'Make them pay for the sins of their forefathers,' Nigel added. 'I said this to Foster earlier. The past is with us all the time, buried and hidden, yet it always comes to the surface. It refuses to be ignored.'

Her glass was empty. Nigel took it to the kitchen and filled it. His tiredness had lifted, the wine having a galvanizing effect. Heather's company, too. When he returned she was staring at him, a look of curiosity on her face.

'Do you wonder when your past will surface?'

'What do you mean?' he said, warily.

'Your family past. When Foster and I first met you, in that café, you mentioned you were adopted. You didn't know your own family history.'

'Yes, occasionally I do think it will surface.'

That was half the truth. The secrecy of his past was a constant, lurking thought at the back of his mind. As hired historical help, he had performed thousands of successful searches of people's family history. Yet the fact remained that he knew nothing of his own. One day, he knew, that would change.

'I thought when you were adopted, you could access the records and find out your natural parents,' Heather said.

'You can.'

'But you haven't?'

'Yes, I did.'

'So what happened? Sorry, I'm a bit nosy.'

He smiled. 'That's OK,' he said. 'Not much to report. It gave me the address of a woman, who turned out to be dead. No record of a father and no one else around to speak to about it. I left it there. Not knowing your past doesn't stop you living your life. Actually, it can help you sometimes; no successes to live up to, mistakes to avoid. That can be liberating. But there's always an absence, a sense that something's missing. Just a void and a lot of unanswered questions.'

Nigel took a large sip of his wine. Heather was looking at him, twining a strand of hair around her index finger. He sensed more questions. He didn't mind. He welcomed her attention.

'Do you have any music?' she asked suddenly.

'I have a record player,' he replied, looking around at his room, piled with books and magazines, space at a premium. 'Somewhere.'

'What, vinyl? Jesus, Nigel, you're a walking anachronism.'

'I just like old things. Everything now has built-in obsolescence; it goes out of fashion, or they bring out a new model, make you think you have to have it. Mass-produced crap that promotes dissatisfaction. I like a thing well made. An object that, when you hold it, enables you to actually picture the man or woman who made it standing back and admiring their work.'

He got up out of his chair, wandered over to the bookshelf, shifting a pile of weathered periodicals to one side to reveal a dust-strewn record player. He lifted the lid; the arm had become detached.

'The arm is broken,' he said, waving the severed limb.

'Funny, you don't get that with a CD player,' Heather said.

She got out of her chair and went over to the radio, turning the dial slowly. Finally, she found a station playing music, an old soul song Nigel didn't recognize. His tastes stretched to the work of Bob Dylan, Neil Young, Leonard Cohen and a few other ageing singer-songwriters of the early seventies. The collection stopped at about 1974, the year he was born. Given how she smiled when the sax-laden chorus of the radio song kicked in, that might not have been the late-night listening she was seeking.

She sauntered back to the chair, and drained the remnants of her wine. He went to give her a refill but Heather placed her hand over the top of the glass.

'I'm driving,' she said.

He poured himself another and they sat listening. Heather had closed her eyes. Nigel wondered if she might fall asleep. When the song finished, she opened them again.

She sighed deeply. 'It's so good to be able to relax in the middle of all this,' she said. 'Foster can't do it, can't switch off. I think it's vital.'

Nigel could sympathize with Foster. Since

stumbling across Nella Perry's body on Sunday morning, he could think of nothing but doing all he could to catch her killer. Sleep came in fitful spurts; only by chasing the killer through the past could he cope.

Heather seemed to sense his thoughts. 'I know how you're feeling,' she said. 'It gets obsessive.' She spread her hands out wide. 'Welcome to my world.'

'How did you get into detective work, if you don't mind me asking?'

She shook her head. 'Not at all. I did a criminology degree at university. When I finished, I wondered what I would do with it. The way I saw it, there were two options. I could continue to study, live in the world of theory and make bugger-all difference, or I could join the police force. I took the unfashionable option.'

'Why London?'

'I'd like to say all human life is here and, therefore, there is no more interesting and challenging place to do a job like mine. Which is true. But the fact is, I followed a bloke down here. It didn't work out; me and London did.'

More silence. The song ended.

'So who was it who broke your heart at the university?' Heather asked.

Nigel was startled at first, but the wine emboldened him.

'Who said she broke my heart?' he replied, smiling.

'You did. When I was here Sunday morning. Well, you didn't say that explicitly. But it was clear from the look in your eyes that it was painful. You do the vulnerable look very well. It's those blue eyes.'

He didn't know what to say.

'A combination of the eyes, the thick square-rimmed glasses, and the shy smile. Bet you went down a storm with the student body.'

His face must have betrayed a hint of panic.

She reacted immediately. 'She was a student?' voice rising with surprise.

He nodded. He felt it right to tell the whole story. If this wasn't to be the only time he was to share a drink with Heather, and he genuinely hoped it wasn't, then it made sense to furnish her with the truth.

'She was twenty-nine. A PhD student. Not one of mine. I was hired to try and set up a family history degree, but, while I was planning that, they asked me to take some history modules. Lily was chasing a job at the uni and, because she was doing a PhD and had a bit of time on her hands, she was assigned to help build, plan and research the family history course with me. We became close and eventually we . . .' He tried to search for the right word.

'Got it on?' Heather offered, eyes twinkling.

'You could say that, yes.'

'So, what went wrong?'

'She was married.'

'Oh.'

'She was separated when we started seeing each other. I didn't know there was a husband. Anyway, she told me about him one day. Then she said he had got back in touch, wanted to give it another go.'

'She told you that on the same day she told you that her husband existed?' Heather said with disdain. 'The cow.'

'Yes, well. Obviously, she didn't choose me. They offered her a job at the university and, frankly, the idea of working with her every day after all that had happened was pretty unpalatable. Plus, there was a funding problem and so the family history course was being put on the back burner. So I walked away.'

'You did the right thing.'

He shrugged. 'I'm over it, by the way.'

She raised her eyebrows at him. 'Why are you telling me that?'

He felt the burn of embarrassment in his cheeks.

Heather smiled, then glanced sideways in search of her bag. 'Listen, you look knackered,' she said. 'I'll let you go. Don't want you to fall asleep in the birth indexes.'

She stood up, Nigel too.

'You're the first person I've ever told that to,' he said.

'Anything you say might be taken down and used in evidence against you,' she replied.

He was tired, but he did not want her to go. Her presence was like a balm. He knew when he closed the door and went to his bed, the image of Nella Perry would be back and he would lie in the dark, unable to sleep, listening to the blood pumping around his body.

'Thanks for coming round,' he said.

Again she gave him one of her smiles.

'I mean that,' he added.

She stood by the door, lingering a few seconds. Nigel felt the urge to say or do something.

'No problem,' she said. She walked towards him, put her hand on his shoulder and kissed his cheek. Her lips were soft and brushed against him lightly. She went back to the door.

'Maybe we can do this again. Obviously, when the case is done.'

'I'd like that,' she said, putting her bag over her shoulder. 'Though next time, try and get the cork out of the bottle properly.'

24

Nigel allowed himself four hours' sleep and was back at the FRC within five, after being scooted across early-morning London by a cab driver eager to make use of the empty roads. With no one around he took the liberty of smoking a string of roll-ups in the canteen, to give him the energy rush the scalding machine-dispensed coffee failed to do.

From his notes on the investigation and trial, he worked out there were three other key figures whose descendants remained untouched: the ham prosecution barrister John J. Dart, QC, MP; Joseph Garrett, who conducted Fairbairn's defence; and Detective Henry Pfizer of Scotland Yard.

Dart first. Nigel wondered darkly if one of his descendants was about to lose their tongue as well as their life in retribution for his verbosity. He found him immediately on the census of 1881, his age forty-seven, living in Bexley Heath, his constituency.

Heather joined him; her smile was warm. Silently, he sighed with relief. He was not sure what the previous evening had meant, if anything, but the thought of seeing her again made him anxious. Would she act as if nothing had happened? Her smile had indicated she would not, though the tense look on her face betrayed the fact that time was running out and it was paramount they work fast. His mind returned to the task.

Dart's prominence made tracing him and his family straightforward. The entire clan shared their time between houses in the country and central London. It took the whole morning, but he had soon drawn up a list of descendants. Heather faxed it through to the incident room so the names could be checked and their whereabouts noted.

Nigel took a break. Heather went off to make a phone call. In the canteen he was accosted by Dave Duckworth.

'So, Mr Cable was innocent,' he said, plunging his hands into his pockets and rocking back and forth on his heels.

'Seems so.'

Duckworth stared at him. 'A pain in the proverbial, because the background research was shaping up to be a well-paid little piece of work.' Duckworth put his hands in his pockets and sighed, then looked back at Nigel. 'I saw your female amanuensis was back at your side this morning.'

Nigel took a sip of his coffee. 'You should be the detective with those levels of observation.'

'Interesting work, is it?' Duckworth said, ignoring the sarcasm.

'Just doing some bounceback.'

'Ah, like I did. It keeps body and soul together,' Duckworth replied.

Nigel looked at him. 'Not as much as lifting your skirt for the tabloids, though?'

Duckworth ignored the slight. 'Sometimes one can have enough of finding the ancestral skeletons in the closets of the rich and famous. The work was a pleasant piece of research. And surprisingly lucrative, too. In fact, I'm hoping to make more money out of it. Not that the client, an intriguing fellow named Kellogg, knows that yet.'

Nigel nodded absent-mindedly – he'd switched off, wanting to be left alone to plan the rest of his research. He looked up and saw Heather weaving her way through the lunch crowds. Duckworth spotted her, too, and scuttled away. She watched him leave, lip curled.

'What did that creep want?' she asked.

'Just poking his nose in,' Nigel replied. 'Goes with the job.'

'He's an oil slick,' she shuddered. 'The team have

the Dart list. They've started working down it one by one.'

'What about the Fairbairn list?'

'Nothing so far. Couldn't get much sense out of Foster. He sounds knackered. Told me he managed to grab a few hours' sleep at his desk last night, first he's had in three days. I told him to go home and get some rest, but he blustered. At this rate he'll probably end up keeling over.'

Back at the indexes, Nigel turned his attention to Detective Henry Pfizer. The surname was soon explained: he was born in Berlin, then part of Prussia. It seemed he left the country of his birth as a young man, escaping the turmoil and upheaval that permeated many parts of Europe in 1848. England was a safe haven. Henry had met and married a London girl, Maria, and they had a son, Stanley. Much of this he gleaned simply from the 1881 census. He turned next to the 1891 census, but there was no sign of the family. A glance at the death indexes yielded no explanation either.

Nigel pulled a battered address book from his bag and found a number for a German genealogist he'd asked to carry out research for him in the past, usually tracing the roots of those who had emigrated from what was now Germany. He made the call, asked him to check records from 1881 onwards for Henry or Heinrich Pfizer and his English wife and child, making it clear that he would pay well for a prompt response.

The dead end frustrated him. They always did. The challenge came in overcoming such obstacles. You needed to think laterally, follow a hunch. He would return to Pfizer later; first there was Joseph Garrett. This one was straightforward. He managed to tear through the generations. The two World Wars took their toll on the males in the Garrett line, and the name almost died out in the 1960s. But he managed to locate five living descendants.

He was listing their names when the call came through from Germany with results of a preliminary census search. No records of any Pfizer of that age, or any with an English wife, on German censuses. He had not returned to the land of his birth.

Foster was dying on his feet as the day wore on. He stalked up and down the incident room, manically running his hand back and forth over his head. Coffee no longer had a galvanizing effect. All it did was make his head and eyes ache. He felt the old craving for nicotine. During times like this, when sleep was in scarce supply, he would chain-smoke his way through the exhaustion. Now there seemed to be no repelling it. Harris had told him to get some rest, but there were a few things he needed to do first.

Patricia MacDougall, the fourth victim, had last been seen on Sunday afternoon, walking her dog in Holland Park, something she did every day, though usually in the evening. She had been seen drinking a coffee and smoking a cigarette outside the café mid-afternoon. She paid and left. No one had seen her since. A team had been blitzing the park since yesterday, accosting every parkgoer with pictures of her and the artist's depiction of the man seen drinking with Nella Perry in the pub. But no one had seen her leave and no one had recognized the suspect. The dog had also vanished. Foster didn't bet against it turning up dead on someone's doorstep at any second.

Nigel Barnes had begun filing the first batches of descendants' names. With the help of Andy Drinkwater, Foster had sketched out a condensed family tree for the Fairbairns, Darts and Garretts on the whiteboard, their names on the top, lines leading down to each of their living descendants. Those who had been spoken to on the Fairbairn list were marked, as were those whose movements were deemed worth following for the next twenty-four hours. There were still seven descendants to be contacted. None of those they had located matched the fingerprints found at the scene.

As for the descendants of John J. Dart and Joseph Garrett, Foster had decided to put a car outside the house or place of work of each likely victim and follow them for twenty-four hours, without them knowing. Informing them there was a possibility they might be the next victim of a serial killer would create understandable panic. The whole operation yoked together hosts of officers from other investigations and other departments, but Detective Superintendent Harris, scared witless by the mocking of that morning's press, was willing to offer Foster all the support he needed.

As Foster scratched an innocent Fairbairn name from the list, Drinkwater approached him.

'Another one bites the dust,' Foster said, wearily.

Only six Fairbairns were left outstanding. Was the killer among them or was Foster heading down a cul-de-sac?

'What do you want, Andy?'

'Sir, forensics say they've found some DNA on the last victim. On her clothes. Seems the effort of getting her up the stairs to the flat caused him to sweat. They found drops on her shirt.'

This perked Foster up immediately. The pace was beginning to tell; the killer was getting sloppy. Making mistakes he had avoided earlier in his spree, becoming too ambitious.

They had a link. He got in touch with forensics and asked someone to get along to the Hunterian Museum and get a sample from the skeleton of Eke Fairbairn. If it matched the killer's, then the theory that it was one of his descendants was on the money.

His phone went. Heather Jenkins, filling him in on what they had discovered that morning at the FRC.

'Pfizer has disappeared from the records,' she told him. 'Every mention of him and his wife and child.'

Foster cursed their luck. Of all the protagonists in the 1879 case, he felt he was the one who deserved the most opprobrium; perhaps the killer felt the same. Part of Foster hoped the bent bastard's conscience had got the better of him, that he'd left his clothes on the beach and walked into the sea, never to be found. But that didn't explain why his family had vanished, too.

'Tell Nigel to keep working on it,' he told her. 'Wherever he wants to go, whichever archive, it's open for him.'

Foster and Drinkwater arrived at a draughty community hall in Hounslow as the light started to ebb from the day. Foster felt so tired that putting one foot in front of the other was an effort. After paying a visit to the West London Family History Society he vowed to get some sleep. Everyone was in place; they would watch the suspects and their potential victims all night. Each inch of Powis Square had already been searched and was under surveillance. For the first time they appeared to be a step ahead of, not behind, the killer, though it made Foster feel uneasy. Did he have one final sleight of hand?

Inside the hall the air was cool, wintry even. Yet there were rows and rows of people sitting down, a sea of white hair bearing out John Fairbairn's claim that few of his fellow members were below retirement age. Fairbairn, seated in the middle, saw them enter and gave a wave. Foster nodded back. At the front a tall, elderly gentleman in a knitted cardigan was giving a talk, referring to diagrams on an overhead projector. He and Drinkwater stood at the back and listened, waiting for the man to finish so they could begin the task of collecting everyone's prints.

The voice was flat, without tone. Just listening made Foster's head feel heavy. At first, the words washed over him. But then, to keep himself awake, he tuned in to what the man was saying.

'Those who know nothing of history, who are ignorant of the sacrifices made by others to build their country and their family, have no appreciation at all of the struggles and sacrifices involved in making and building something that will last. History gives us a sense of proportion, of the longer view of things. We are self-centred beings at our core. The world revolves around us, around our individual needs. If we do nothing, if we study no subject outside ourselves, we cease to believe that anything else matters. And nothing could be further from the truth.'

Foster was reeled in. He's talking about people like me, he thought. I have studied no one. I have cared about no one but myself. All that matters to me is work, the here and now. I have no sense of the past and no sense of the future. I don't know where I came from, who my people were.

I don't know who I am.

He was roused from this bout of introspection by his vibrating phone. He took it outside. It was the barman from the Prince of Wales, calling from a payphone. He had more information on the man seen drinking with Nella Perry the previous Friday. He wasn't working that evening, but would be at the pub. Foster decided to head straight there. He told Drinkwater something had come up and left him to handle the family history society.

As he left, he checked his watch. It was six in the evening. He remembered the newspaper account he had read of the fifth killing, in which it stated the victim's body had been found as 'the bell of All Saints Church tolled for the first time after midnight'. One a.m. They had thirty-one hours before the killer ended his spree and retreated into the crowd.

Nigel sat in the back of a black cab as it edged forwards with the mass of central London traffic that choked the city every Friday night. The great escape. People watching precious seconds of their weekend tick away as they crawled along congested roads.

The National Archives were his destination. At Kew Bridge the traffic formed a bottleneck to cross the river, and his patience broke. He got out and walked the last half-mile. A soft rain began to fall.

The lights of the archives were on, casting a glow across the shadowed lake. As Nigel approached a security guard unlocked the door, checked his bag and allowed him through. He headed straight upstairs to the main reading room. A young staff member, a pale, pencil-thin PhD student, who looked as if he saw daylight by accident, was waiting to fetch and retrieve. As Nigel had requested, he had laid out a series of ledgers and documents on a reading table. Service records for the Metropolitan Police.

Nigel recognized a problem immediately. In 1881 Pfizer was forty-three. There was a gap in the record of new recruits between 1857 and 1878, almost certainly the era in which Pfizer would have signed up.

So he went first to the Register of Leavers, which began in 1889. Pfizer would have been in his fifties by then; he would have done his time. Nigel hunted through several volumes of dry pages for his name, taking his search up until the turn of the century, well beyond the date he would have retired. No sign of any H. Pfizer. If there were no records of him leaving, there would be no record of any pensions, ruling out yet another source. He checked the lists detailing the deaths of serving officers, which expired in 1889. No Pfizer in there. These records would not solve the mystery.

Foster pulled up outside the pub and parked on a single yellow. He could see through the large glass windows that the Friday-night crowd was out in full, braying force. Inside there was barely standing room. He fought his way to the bar. No sign of the barman behind the counter. In fact, he didn't recognize any of the staff from the previous Sunday.

He tried to recall the barman's name through the fog of exhaustion. He'd said it on the phone. Karl, that was it. He asked one of the other staff, a tall blonde with her hair tied back in a bun.

She motioned towards the door with her head. 'He's not working tonight. But he was here.'

'He's gone to get some money out,' added another

member of staff, passing by with two brimming pints in her hand.

Nothing to do but wait, Foster thought. A couple vacated two bar stools next to where he stood. After hearing what Karl had to say, unless it was so significant that it required immediate action, he was going home, so he ordered a pint. The pub was loud but, given his weariness, it felt good to be surrounded by people, by music, by conversation, by *life*.

The pint came. He took a long slug, feeling the tension ebb. There was a tap on his shoulder. Karl. He was dressed in denim, jacket and jeans.

'Sorry,' he said. 'Cash crisis.'

Foster said he didn't mind. Karl ordered a bottle of lager Foster had never heard of and took the stool next to him. Foster began to feel hot, as if all the blood was running to his head. Tiredness, he thought. His system was fusing; his body struggling to regulate his own temperature. He yawned, unable and unwilling to stop himself.

'Hard week?' Karl asked.

'You could say that,' Foster muttered.

Karl cast a look over his shoulder at the teeming pub. 'Busy in here tonight,' he said.

Foster noticed his right leg danced as he spoke, unable to keep still. He took another sip, not in the mood for small talk.

'What's funny is, that this place is full of young rich kids,' Karl said. 'Princedale Road used to be the epicentre of the counter-culture and political protest of the 1950s and 60s.'

'Really?' Foster said, interest awoken.

'Yeah, just up the road at number 52 is where they founded *Oz* magazine. You know, the one that urged people to "Turn on, Tune in and Drop dead"? Got closed down; the publishers were sent to Wormwood Scrubs on obscenity charges. Then, at number 74, you had the opposite side of the coin in the 50s, the White Defence League, who wanted to keep out the blacks. And, at number 70, there was Release, the first drug-awareness charity. Now we've got two gastropubs and not a lot else.'

'You know your stuff,' Foster said.

'Local history is a bit of a hobby of mine. This area has a lot of stories in its past.'

Tell me about it, Foster thought. 'So what is it you wanted to tell me? Something about Dammy Perry?'

Karl nodded. From the back of his jeans pocket he pulled a pack of cigarettes, lit one and inhaled deeply, as if sucking all the goodness out of it. Foster felt the familiar pang.

'Want one?'

Sod it, Foster thought. Once a smoker always a

smoker. He nodded. Karl pulled a cigarette out and handed it to him. Foster took it, enjoying the feel of it between his forefinger and index finger, rolling it back and forth. It was the sensuousness of smoking he missed as much as the nicotine; the pack in his pocket, tapping the cigarette on the pack, sliding it between his lips, watching the smoke curl in the air.

He leaned forwards. Karl sparked his lighter and lit the cigarette for him.

'Yes, it dawned on me this morning. Don't know why it didn't earlier.'

Foster drew long and hard, taking the smoke deep into his lungs where he held it, filling every space.

'Not sure how significant it is . . .'

Foster exhaled. The world in front of him swam. He felt a firm hand on his shoulder. Karl's, he presumed. He was about to ask what he was doing, but his head felt hot, hotter than before, then like it was filling with water. His chin lolled on to his chest. His body weight went with it, making him lurch forwards. He would have fallen off the stool but for Karl's hand.

'Easy,' he heard a voice say.

Noises swirled; his vision blurred.

'What's wrong?' a woman's voice asked.

'It's OK. He's a mate. Had a bit too much. Don't worry, I've got him.'

The voices sounded miles away.

Then the world went white.

25

Nigel accessed the site where it was possible to search thousands of passenger manifests for ships that left Britain during the 1880s. There was a chance Pfizer had chosen the New World or one of the colonies as a final destination. An experienced Scotland Yard detective would have no trouble in finding well-paid work overseas. There was no Pfizer listed.

He went to the Map Room. On a series of low shelves at the furthest end of the room were deed poll records. A ledger for each year from the 1850s onwards. Nigel decided to start with 1882 under P. He found nothing for that year, or the next.

In 1884 he got his break.

There he was. Pfizer, Henry. February. Below him were Pfizer, Mary and Pfizer, Stanley.

This was not unusual. Many immigrants changed their names. Brauns became Browns and Schmidts changed to Smiths. People sought to avoid the suspicion and the wariness of their new neighbours or, if they had taken British nationality, to declare fealty to their new adopted country with an Anglicized name.

Few did it officially, like Pfizer had. It was not compulsory and it cost money. Often people did not want to draw attention to the change; they might have been unable to obtain a divorce, so just took their new partner's name for appearances' sake and to avoid accusations of illegitimacy being hurled at their children. Yet Nigel sensed that, if anyone would take the bureaucratic route and enshrine the change in law, a policeman would.

There remained one problem. The indexes before 1903 did not give the person's new name, the information he required to trace the bloodline forwards. What he did have was a date. Pfizer might have changed his name by deed poll, but no one was to know unless he advertised it. The most common method was to place a notice in the press. Unfortunately, Nigel was at the wrong place for newspaper archives.

He turned instead to the *Phillimore and Fry Index to Change of Name 1760–1901*. This was the sort of insane, backbreaking project to which genealogists had always been attracted. The two authors had dedicated their working lives to transcription – collecting and collating all kinds of information for the benefit of future genealogists. For this volume they had combed 241 years of names which had been changed by private acts of parliament, or royal licences published in the London and Dublin *Gazette*s, as well as notices published in *The Times*, and put them all in one index.

It was also shelved in the Map Room. He found it and laid it out on the table, turning immediately to P. The entries were typed, listed alphabetically. He scrolled down through the Ps until he saw it.

Pfizer, *see* Foster.

Nigel stared at it for a few seconds, not registering. Surely not, he thought. He found the index entry for Foster. There were several. But there it was. Foster, H: Pfizer, H of Norfolk Place, Paddington, London. The entry had been gleaned from an advertisement placed in *The Times* of 25th February 1884.

He went to the 1891 census. There was Henry Foster, police detective, living at Norfolk Place, Paddington with his wife, Mary. Stanley had obviously flown the nest. By 1901 it appeared that Henry was dead because Mary was living on her own.

This had to be a coincidence. He rang Foster's mobile. It was switched off. He tried Heather. She was on her way to meet him.

'I've found Pfizer.'

'Good.'

'He changed his name,' he said. 'To Foster.'

She remained silent. 'You don't really think . . .' she eventually said.

'I don't know,' he said, interrupting her. 'But we need to get into the FRC again and find out.'

Another taxi ride across town and Nigel was back at the FRC. Heather was waiting for him.

'Foster's gone home to sleep, which explains why the phone is off. Someone's going round to knock him up. Make sure he's all right,' she explained, as if there was nothing to worry about, though anxiety seeped from her pores. She disappeared to make a few further calls.

Nigel went to the death indexes to check on Pfizer/Foster's death. Aged fifty-four, in 1892. Cancer. His only son, Stanley, married and followed his father into the Met, starting as a constable, rising to detective. He had four children, only one boy, Stanley junior. He had only one child, a boy, Martin Foster, before he joined up and met his death at Passchendaele in 1917. Martin carried on the family trade, policeman, and had four children, including two boys, Roger and James.

Roger married in 1959. Nigel turned to the birth indexes from that point onwards. In the first quarter of 1960, the couple had a child.

Grant Roger Foster.

He cross-referenced with the mother's maiden name. Definitely the right child.

He sat down, put his head in his hands. Foster was a direct descendant of Henry Pfizer.

He did not notice Heather at his side.

'It's him, isn't it?' she said.

He nodded slowly.

'Foster's not at home,' she said, voice faltering. 'He was at a family history meeting with Drinkwater earlier this evening. Andy said he got a phone call, something to do with the case, didn't say what, and he left in his car, didn't say where. His phone's off, we're getting the records. We've checked his usual haunts. All the hospitals, too. Nothing as yet.' She breathed deeply. 'He's disappeared off the face of the earth.'

It was relief he felt when he withdrew the knife from the wretch's still-beating heart. Relief that the Lord's work was done; relief that one less drunken fool was able to bespoil His work; relief that now he could turn his attentions to his next task. 'Be ye angry and sin not,' said the Lord. 'Let not the sun go down on your wrath.'

His righteous anger coursed through this earthly vessel. His head pounded with it. Yet the time was nigh when that sun would fall and he would accept the bountiful gifts of the Lord in Paradise.

The drunk was left gurgling and spluttering for his misbegotten life. Through the night he heard the distant wail of the trains rattling to and from Paddington. Those screams and the rustle of the cool wind were the only sounds he could hear. He stood and waited for the drunk to relent in his pathetic resistance to death. When, after one futile heave of his wounded chest, his victim fell silent, he walked away. He checked his pocket watch for the time and left the scene of his final act.

He turned out of Powis Square, on to Talbot Road. He went left, walking past the awe-inspiring temple of All Saints, looming majestically in the fog. It struck once, dolefully. Behind him came the murmur of voices, the short blast of a whistle. Thank heavens for the fog that cloaked and hid him.

His journey took him to the junction with Portobello Road, a street for which he possessed nothing but distaste; his small shop struggled to cope with the markets and bigger stores that were opening along that winding road. A few peelers passed him, agitation on their faces. He scurried on, his hand in his pocket clutching the handle of the knife, passing underneath the railway bridge, turning left and then walking all the way down to Pamber Street.

All was still. Their small house sat silent and dark above the shop. Everyone was asleep. He thought of them up there, warm in their beds, unaware of the craven wickedness of the world into which they had been born. *This world is no place for the innocent and pure*, he told himself.

He opened the door slowly. The smell from that evening's boiled meat still filled the house. He always demanded silence during mealtimes but, that evening, he had relented, allowed Rebecca to tell him of her day. Abigail muttered a few words. Yet, despite his efforts to make conversation with them, Jemima and Esau did not speak. They appeared to enjoy the ham, which was some comfort.

He slipped off his shoes but the jacket stayed on.

This world is no place for the innocent and pure, he repeated.

He put his foot on the first stair, creaking under his weight. He stopped. No sound. He continued, putting no more weight on the ball of each foot than was necessary. As he neared the landing he could hear the soft breath of his children rise and fall in their sleep.

Jemima appeared at the top step like a ghost.

'Segar?' she whispered.

He looked at her. He felt pity, no more. She had borne him three children, but the woman was godless at heart. She prayed only because she knew he would visit his anger upon her if she did not. A simpering creature.

'It is me,' he said.

'Are you hungry? Do you wish to eat?'

He shook his head and stepped on to the landing. He could smell the soap on her. For a second he was transported to another time, a distant land in which he remembered promenading hand in hand through Hyde Park, the sun on their backs, her beaming with joy, him with pride.

A different time, he told himself. I was a different man. The call had not yet come.

'No.'

He brushed past her and made his way to the children's room. They slept in the one bed. Outside the door of his little ones, he listened. Not a murmur.

He stepped in. It was darker in here and he waited until his eyes had adjusted. When they had, he could see Abigail asleep on the left side of the bed, arm hanging outside. Rebecca was on her back, head on the pillow. Both were in a deep sleep.

He walked over. Abigail turned and murmured. When the time came he would spare them the knife and find some other way to send them into Paradise. The idea of hurting his darling twin girls, the only two people on the planet for whom he cared, who made him smile, made him feel of this earth, was abhorrent.

Both girls were bold, yet enjoyed their scripture. Not like Esau. He went to church under duress. A timid boy, he rarely ventured far from his mother's skirts. For the past month he had been unable to look in his father's eyes, terrified by what he saw there.

But where was he now? He looked either side of the bed. He was not on the floor, as he sometimes was, escaping the flailing arms and legs of his two younger sisters. He left the room. Esau was not in his parents' bedroom either; Jemima swore on her life he had gone to bed and not been seen since.

He stopped for a second. Had the boy grown suspicious? Sneaked from the house and followed him? The boy was smart, perhaps too smart. He yawned. It could wait. Esau would return.

In the morning the truth would be found. Then he would use the belt.

26

Foster felt as if he was emerging from the deepest sleep he had ever experienced. Semi-conscious, it was a few seconds before he even considered the effort of opening his eyes. He was lying down, but his body was unable to move. It had yet to catch up with his mind.

What had happened? He remembered the pub. Then nothing. Had he been that tired? Collapsed maybe, brought home. Yet this didn't smell like his room. It smelled musty – a heavy scent of cardboard, like some of the archives Barnes had taken him to. He opened his eyes. The first thing he saw was a bare light bulb suspended from the ceiling by a dirty white flex. There was no other source of light, natural or not. The ceiling was bare concrete, immaculately clean. The walls beneath it appeared pockmarked. As his eyes adjusted, he could see they were lined with what seemed to be eggboxes, an attempt at sound-proofing perhaps.

Foster felt his limbs prickle. Feeling was returning. Why had it gone? He attempted to lift his right hand, but it wouldn't move. Something tight was holding it down, a strap of some sort. Likewise his other hand, his arms, both legs and chest. His clothes were gone, save for his boxer shorts. He tugged hard with his right hand, but the binding wouldn't give. He patted the surface he was lying on. A bed of some sort. There was a flutter of panic in his stomach.

To his left were piles of boxes stretching to the ceiling. To the right were more boxes, some items of furniture, a chest of drawers and a cabinet. Either side of the bed there were perhaps three or four feet of room. However hard he tried to lift his head, he was unable to see what lay behind or in front of him, but he could sense more clutter looming. It was like being surrounded by the entire contents of a house.

There was a shuffling sound from a corner, outside of his vision. He was aware of breathing, a presence.

'Is someone there?' he mumbled.

No reply.

'Is someone there?' he repeated, more insistent.

A figure appeared at his right shoulder. Foster struggled to focus on his face. He made out dark hair, and that the figure appeared to be holding something, but he was unable to make out what.

'Who's that?' he moaned, his voice weak.

No answer. Foster repeated his question. Still no reply.

'What the fuck is this?' he asked louder, trying to move his arms.

The figure continued to stand by him. Then he spoke, voice clipped, without emotion.

'This,' he said slowly, 'is retribution.'

He strapped some tape over Foster's mouth.

Foster felt his insides lurch with terror. He tried to spit out the tape, force it off. It was impossible. The man ignored his muffled cries, moved away out of sight. Foster felt him undo the buckle around his right ankle. Instinctively when it was free, his foot kicked out, but he had no strength and no other limb to fight with. The man held down his leg with one firm hand; there was a scraping noise as he pulled something across the floor, another smaller table of some sort. He lifted Foster's foot so the heel and ankle rested on this new platform; the section of his leg from knee to ankle was unsupported. The man strapped his ankle to its new position.

Foster's vision became clearer. At last he could make out the man. It was Karl. The instrument he was holding above his head was a sledgehammer; Foster watched as he lifted it high. He began to struggle against his bindings, trying to jerk and twist his body out of the way, but he was too tightly pinioned.

'*No!*' Foster screamed, but the tape blocked all sound.

He knew what was about to happen, but could do nothing except wait for the impact. There was a crack as the hammer came down with sufficient weight to smash both his tibia and fibula. The pain roared up from his shin like fire.

He let out a howl of agony no one could hear. Then slipped out of consciousness.

Nigel stared out of the window of the FRC canteen at the grey morning, silently reproaching himself. Had he checked out the change of name sooner, they might have had a chance to warn Foster. Heather told him to forget it. Foster's phone records revealed that the call that had lured him away from the family history meeting had been made from a public phone box on Ladbroke Grove just before six p.m., well before Nigel had confirmed Foster was a descendant. Still Nigel blamed himself. He went over all the details he had soaked up over the past week: the newspaper reports, trial transcripts, the endless certificates and census returns he had waded through, searching for some detail that might lead them to Foster and the killer. Nothing came. Time was bleeding away from them. By the end of that day Foster would be killed. He forced himself to think once more.

Heather, face pale and wan, had gone to join the search. Every cop in London was being called in to help, all leave cancelled. Their leads were turning up nothing. During the night word had come that Eke Fairbairn and the killer's DNA were not a match. Their one hope – that pursuing the descendants of Eke Fairbairn might lead them to Foster's kidnapper and their serial killer – had been extinguished.

Nigel felt useless, knowing of no way he could help. The last victim in 1879 had been found in a small garden square off Portobello Road. That was being watched. There seemed little more for him to do but wait and see whether half the Metropolitan Police could scour the entire area and find their colleague. For the sake of completeness he had finished tracing Pfizer's descendants. Foster was the last of the line, the killer's only choice.

The centre opened, the weekend amateurs filing in to lock away their belongings. Nigel sat watching them come and go, a steady stream of people, a younger crowd than during the week, even a few children among them. Before long the room was filled with people having a coffee, catching up, poring over documents they had collected that morning and planning their day's research.

Phil, the whistling receptionist, walked in, looking around. He saw Nigel and made his way over.

'Hello,' he said in his jovial manner. 'You been here all night, then?'

Nigel nodded, hoping he hadn't found him just to make small talk.

'Have you seen Dave Duckworth anywhere?'

Nigel hadn't.

'Strange,' he said. 'There's a group of American tourists at the front desk. He's supposed to help guide their search. He's half an hour late.'

Probably caught in traffic, Nigel thought.

'Not like him, because these people look pretty wealthy,' Phil added.

'I haven't seen him since yesterday,' Nigel said eventually, remembering the conversation about his client with the rare surname, Kellogg . . .

The thought struck Nigel so suddenly, he almost jumped. Could it be a coincidence? He needed to get to the newspaper library to find out.

Foster drifted back to consciousness, drenched in sweat; only when he twitched did he feel the coruscating stab of pain from his fractured shin. He knew the break couldn't be clean. The tape had been removed from his mouth. He turned his head to one side and vomited copiously. Had he passed out through pain or been drugged once more?

He knew Karl was the killer. He knew he was the fifth victim.

'Why are you doing this?' he spat out between gasps for air, his body craving oxygen.

'As I said, retribution.' The voice remained calm, reasoned. Without malice.

A surge of pain left him speechless. He seemed to lose consciousness for a few more seconds, though it could have been longer. Sweat poured from his brow. He came round again, the last words of his assailant on his mind.

'Retribution?' he gasped eventually. 'What for?'

'If you were more aware of your family history, you would know.'

Foster tried to concentrate on what Karl was saying, to forget the pain. It took every ounce of effort. 'What about my family history?'

'You mean you haven't guessed yet?'

'I'm not in the mood for a fucking quiz,' he hissed, regretting the effort when the pain coursed through him and he vomited once more.

'It will hurt less if you remain still. The whole ordeal will be less painful if you remain still. And keep quiet, or the tape goes back on.'

Foster, feeling faint, fell silent. The soundproofing on the wall, the tape across his mouth; this must be a place where they might be heard. At some stage he knew he must gather his strength and let out the loudest scream he could muster. He might only get one chance.

'If you knew your family history, then you would know your great-great-great-grandfather was Detective Henry Pfizer. The crooked German bastard who fitted up Eke Fairbairn to get the press off his back.'

The words came to him through a fog of agony. Finally, they registered. His ancestor?

The judicial murder of Eke Fairbairn was the corpse in his family's basement.

Consciousness began to ebb away. He could not hear a thing in this tomb. The silence was broken only by the killer's voice and his own wracked gasps of pain. He tried to fight unconsciousness; next time he might not wake up. To remain alert he focused on the shattered limb, going so far as to move his leg, hoping the awful, searing pain would ward off oblivion.

'Pfizer was your ancestor,' Karl said. 'You'll be punished for what he did. Just like the descendants of Norwood, Darbyshire, Pearcey and MacDougall were. You already know this, but before he was executed the police decided to try and beat a confession out of him. That could only have taken place with the sanction of your ancestor. They fractured six bones in his body.'

Six, Foster thought. Five more to go. His whole

body tightened at the thought. He must find a way to get out, to deter the killer.

'Why pick me?' asked Foster. 'There must have been other descendants of Pfizer.'

'No. You're the last one. It all ends with you. And it seems appropriate that you're also a police officer. Thankfully. I picked the most successful of all of them. With Darbyshire, Perry, it was always the wealthiest. Call it class envy, if you want.'

Karl walked into Foster's field of vision on his left, preceded by the smell of stale smoke. Foster remembered the cigarette he'd bummed. Then he knew. That was how the killer ensnared his victims. All were social or committed smokers. Karl found a way to introduce himself, offered them a smoke and that was it – lights out. Inhaling a cigarette doused in GHB would render you helpless in a matter of seconds, reaching the brain quicker than any spiked drink.

'Now, are you ready?' Karl asked.

Foster's mind swam. He thought of his father. The last few moments before he took the cocktail. He had remained resolute and stoical. The look of a man staring at the void and the void looking away. Death came as a release, a balm for someone so eager to escape. Would he be able to face the end of his life with such dignity?

The tape was laid across his mouth. He could taste the plastic. His left arm was unstrapped, laid outwards, wrist facing up, his hand resting on another table. Foster stared straight into the eyes of the killer, not once looking away. Karl did not return his gaze, merely lifted his boot and brought it down swiftly on Foster's forearm.

This time the break was clean. Compared to the nightmarish pain from his leg, his arm simply went numb. Foster never flinched or once looked away from the killer. He made sure his eyes bored into him the whole time he was at his side.

He waited for him to remove the tape so he could use his anger, all the pain, to let out a roar.

Nothing. The tape remained. He lost consciousness once more. He came round, the tape removed, opened his mouth but the noise was weak. He licked his parched lips. Through the haze he thought of another tactic.

'This can be done another way,' Foster whispered hoarsely. 'I know about Eke Fairbairn. I know about the injustice.' He stopped to grimace, catch his breath. 'I know about the beating, Stafford Pearcey's statement, the knife being planted, the judge's summing up. What happened was a travesty. But there is such a thing as a pardon. The case can be reopened. Your ancestor's name can be cleared.'

Karl was back out of sight.

'Eke Fairbairn is not my ancestor,' he said.

Nigel headed for the national newspaper library, making it there in less than half an hour. Inside he ordered the 1879 editions of the *Kensington News*. The story he wanted he'd first seen on Monday, in the issue of *The Times* on the day following Fairbairn's conviction. But it was only a few paragraphs. He needed more detail. When the volume arrived he flicked through to the edition for the third week of May, the first following the trial. A report of the events in court shared the front page with the story he was looking for.

MAN SLAYS WIFE AND DAUGHTERS

Yesterday morning, shortly after seven o'clock, Mr Inspector Dodd of Kensington Division received a report from a neighbour of blood washing under the front door of a house on Pamber Street. The abode was the home and business of Segar Kellogg, chandler shop owner.

Inspector Dodd proceeded to Pamber Street to find no little excitement in a neighbourhood already in foment over the appalling exploits of the so-called Kensington Killer. He went to the door and indeed saw what appeared to be blood on the top step.

He knocked and received no answer. Then he tried the door and found it open. To his horror, behind it he found there a boy, unconscious yet still alive.

His body was awash with blood. Behind him was a trail leading to the entrance to the cellar, from where it seemed the stricken boy had dragged his wounded, mutilated frame along the cold wooden floor before passing out. The detective followed the bloody path down to the depths, where he was met with a scene of utter carnage.

The woman was quite dead, her throat carved open. Alongside her he found the cold and rigid bodies of two children. A short distance away, on the floor, was the corpse of a man with a knife protruding from his chest.

On removal of the body the surgeon's surmises received their confirmation. Mr Kellogg had most likely murdered his wife, stabbed his son in the neck and then smothered his poor little ones before turning his own instrument of murder on himself. No other suspect is being sought.

Neighbours said Mr Kellogg was a devout Christian and abstainer. Detectives have not ruled out the suggestion that he was in the grip of religious mania.

Nigel needed to find Duckworth.

'Then why?' Foster asked, straining now to make himself heard. 'If you have nothing to do with Eke Fairbairn, why are you doing all this?'

There was a sigh.

'The police arrested an innocent man for a crime he didn't commit to save themselves from criticism. On the day that Fairbairn was convicted, the real killer, a man named Segar Kellogg, murdered his wife and two of his children. He slit her throat, stabbed his own son in the neck and smothered two seven-year-old girls. If he had been in the dock – if the police, if your ancestor, had done their jobs correctly – then that family would have lived. An evil man would have swung.

'The son survived. His vocal cords had been severed. He never spoke again. Never recovered from what he had seen. There was some semblance of a life for a short while. He changed his name to Hogg, which has been our family name ever since, got married, had two kids. But it never went away. Eventually he decided he couldn't live with what had happened, the horror of what he remembered. Before he died, he wrote down everything he had seen but had never been able to speak about. How he had followed his father at night and watched him slaughter two men. How fear of his father had prevented him from telling anyone. His regret at obeying that fear and how he hated the forces of law and order for getting the wrong man.'

'Have you heard of forgiveness?' Foster asked.

Hogg ignored him. 'You don't know what it's like living with that mark on you. Knowing those genes course through your veins. That your blood is polluted. The stain has always been with us. I knew that, the day I read the letter written by Esau Hogg. I turned thirty-five in January this year, the same age Segar Hogg was when he murdered his wife and two daughters, and Esau's age when he decided he couldn't take living with the pain any more and hanged himself. I knew then that it was time to finish it all. It ends here with me. There is no one to follow.'

'But what about other members of your family? Presumably they lived a decent life if you're here today. For God's sake, we're more than a bunch of genes; they don't define us.'

'Coming from someone who's merely the latest in a long line of policemen, that's pretty rich. You've never thought there may be something genetic about that?'

Foster clenched his teeth against the pain. He found that if he didn't move, then it was possible to ignore it; helped, he thought, by whatever drugs were still swimming in his system.

'My ancestor may have stitched up Fairbairn. But

that doesn't mean the rest of us are bent cops. There is such a thing as free will. These things aren't preordained.'

'You heard of psychogeography?'

Foster vaguely remembered Nigel Barnes mentioning it. Some bullshit about how a place affects the way people act.

'The theory is that the environment in which you live has an impact on people's emotions and behaviour. I walked the same streets where my ancestor preyed on his victims. I was born a street away from where he slaughtered his family. I learned of what he did and how he escaped justice. How my family has been stained with this ever since.'

'Sounds like an excuse not an explanation.'

Hogg snorted derisively. 'I'd expect little else from a policeman. Funny, the very people you would think might pay attention to theories like this, theories that might help explain the behaviour they have to deal with every day, are the most dismissive.'

Foster dry-retched. Composed himself. 'I don't go in for theories.' He drew a deep breath; he felt himself starting to drift, but steeled himself. 'There are people who live decent lives, there are criminals . . . and then there are weak-minded sadists like you.'

Hogg laughed falsely, almost condescendingly. 'That's enough conversation for now,' he said.

Foster heard him pull a line of tape from the roll. He tried to turn his head but couldn't prevent it being strapped over his mouth. He felt a hand on his chest. He watched as the killer pulled back his fist and slammed it into his side. He felt the air escape from him in a rush, a stabbing pain in his ribs. His body, acting on instinct to protect itself, attempted to twist away, aggravating his other wounds. Another punch landed on the same area as the first. It felt like a hot knife was being thrust between the muscles of his ribs. The area burned.

Make this end, Foster said silently, plaintively to a God in whom he had never believed.

Nigel discovered that Esau Kellogg had changed his surname to Hogg. He'd got married and tried to forge a new life at a house in a notorious slum on the outskirts of Kensington. The couple had two children but, two years after the second was born, Esau ended his life at the end of a rope.

Nigel traced the bloodline, spinning through the generations as fast as possible. The line was weak, but it survived. He reached the present day. Only two descendants remained: a man, who would now be thirty, named Karl Hogg; and a woman of seventy-six named Liza. He had no address for Karl other than the house his parents had been living in when he was born. The last address he could find for Liza was more than forty years old. He would need Heather's help if he was to track them both down.

Nigel called her to pass on what he'd found. She was on her way to Duckworth's flat on the border of Islington and Hackney – to see if he was there, and to speak to him about the client he had mentioned, named Kellogg. Heather suggested Nigel meet her there and give her the details.

When Nigel arrived, Heather and Drinkwater, faces taut, were in Duckworth's small, ordered office. There was no sign of him. Heather was holding an olive-green box file. She threw it down on the table for Nigel to look at. A white tab bore the printed name Kellogg. Nigel opened the crammed file. There was a series of brown paper document holders. The first was labelled with black felt tip: Darbyshire. Inside were original copies of birth, marriage and death certificates, running from the 1870s – the marriage of Ivor Darbyshire, newspaper editor – to the present day. Nigel flicked through to the present. There appeared to be around twenty living descendants. Among their records he found the birth certificate of James Darbyshire.

'The four others are in there. Including Foster,' Heather said.

'He knew.'

'He found out,' Heather said. 'Read this.'

She moved the computer's mouse, kicking the machine back to life. As the screen brightened, Nigel could see the indexed contents of a folder. The cursor highlighted a document entitled 'kellogg letter'. It was created on the Wednesday of that week. Heather double-clicked.

Dear Mr Kellogg,

It has been some time since I last heard from you. I draw your attention to my final invoice, which was sent to you with your last batch of research and for which I have yet to receive payment. I trust my work met with your satisfaction.

While on the subject of my research, I think we both know the reason you asked for it. I have been reading the newspapers and have noticed a striking connection between the people you hired me to trace and those who have been victims of the serial killer in Notting Hill. It is not for me to judge how people use the information I provide them with. But, in this case, I think my concern is justified. With that in mind, I think we should perhaps reconsider my fee and seek to in-

```
crease it sizeably. I have contacts with
the police and national newspapers –
agencies who would both be interested in
getting their hands on the information
that I have provided you with. Confiden-
tiality is sacrosanct in my business, and
is one tenet to which I strictly adhere.
However, in this case, the circumstances
are so extraordinary as to test that
belief. The ball is in your court.

  Sincerely,

  Duckworth
```

Nigel shook his head, unable to believe that Duckworth had attempted to blackmail the killer before approaching the police.

Actually, he could. Presumably the killer knew that, too, and had picked his stooge carefully.

'We've found a post office box address to which he sent the documents. The owner is registered as a Mr Kellogg, 24 Leinster Gardens, w2. There's a team on the way there now.'

'Read me that address again,' Nigel said.

Drinkwater repeated it.

'Tell your team to turn back. That's a fake address.'

'How do you know that?' Drinkwater said abruptly.

'Because that's a fake house.'

'A fake house?'

'When they built the Circle Line, they had to demolish a whole load of houses on the route because it was built so near the surface. Most people were paid off and relocated, and their houses were then knocked down. The residents of Leinster Gardens were richer than some of their neighbours and had a bit more clout. They said, with some justification, that a railway track would ruin the line of the street. The Metropolitan Company agreed to build a fake façade to disguise the fact that there was a big gap where numbers 23 and 24 had been.'

'Shit,' Heather said, with feeling. Then she asked, 'How have you got on tracing the Hogg bloodline?'

'I've found two living relatives.'

'Let's find them. Quick,' Heather said. 'At the moment they're all we've got, and we're running out of time.'

According to the electoral rolls, Karl Hogg's last known address was a purpose-built flat nestling at the western end of Oxford Gardens, a blossom-lined street of four- and five-storey Victorian mansions, most of them long since carved up into flats for young professionals.

Nigel and Heather sprinted up to the third floor

of a red-brick block that was out of keeping with the stately atmosphere of the rest of the street. They knocked on Hogg's door. No answer. An elderly woman in a neighbouring flat was in. She confirmed that a Karl lived next door, but she knew him as Karl Keene. Two months ago he had taken away most of his furniture in a van, though he had returned a few times since. When she asked if he'd moved out, he said he was going away but would be around for the next few months.

'Did he say where his furniture was?' Heather asked.

She shook her head.

'Did he work at all?'

'As far as I know, he worked from home most of the time. He produced his own magazine and a few books, or he used to. He did a lot for the local history group. They're based in the Methodist church on Lancaster Road. I know he used to give talks and produced things for them.'

They ran the short distance to the church. The history group's office was tucked around the back of the building, up a flight of stairs. A large woman in a huge pair of brown-rimmed spectacles sat behind a desk in a small room neatly arranged with books and files. She gave them a welcoming grin as they entered.

'Can I help?'

'We're looking for Karl Hogg,' Heather asked, flourishing her badge.

The woman could not hide her shock. 'Goodness,' she said. 'Karl? We haven't seen him for a while, I'm afraid.'

'How long's a while?'

She took a deep breath and looked out of the window. 'A few months at least. To be honest, I think he's got a bit bored with us. He became disillusioned.'

'Why's that?'

'Well, we're just a small local history group. Most of our members are interested in finding out how their relations lived, and a number are interested in the influx of people who emigrated from the Caribbean, the history of Notting Hill Carnival, that sort of thing. Karl's interests were more, well, idiosyncratic you might say.'

Nigel wandered over to a rotating wire stand featuring a few of the group's publications. He turned it and saw a thick, bound booklet called 'The Sound of the Westway'. The author was Karl Hogg. Inside he could see it was self-published; there was little emphasis on design and clarity, page after page of unbroken prose, no illustrations. A labour of love. He scanned the list of contents. The book appeared to be a treatise on the dark underbelly of Notting Hill and the Dale. Stories of the Christie killings on

Rillington Place, Jimi Hendrix's death in a hotel off Ladbroke Grove, the Rachman landlord scandals, the race riots that plagued the area in the 1950s and 60s, the area's role in the Profumo scandal, the declaration of independence by the residents and squatters of Freston Road, 'Frestonia', the spirit of anarchy and independence and otherness that manifested itself in the music of The Clash, who gave the booklet its title.

No mention of the Kensington Killer of 1879.

The woman manning the counter was still explaining why Karl Hogg had drifted away from the group. 'He became obsessed with something he called psychogeography. I have to say, it went right over the heads of many of our members. He never quite got on to mystical ley lines running beneath the streets, but he was heading that way; it was all-consuming for him, the idea that this area was afflicted – or blessed – with all these past events and would continue to be. He was obsessed.'

Nigel had seen this happen before. Men (usually) traipsing the streets in search of some mythical London soul, convinced that parts of the city had characters and personalities that imprinted themselves on its inhabitants. Nigel had some sympathy for such theories: how else could you explain an area of London like Clerkenwell with its history of agitation and protest? He remembered standing at the site of 10 Rillington Place less than a week before, as the sun drifted down and night followed, yards away from where he had found Nella Perry's body, and the familiar humbling feeling he knew so well: in the presence of history, on the site of an infamous event, picturing what happened there and how its repercussions still echoed down the years. He had sensed, even then, the killer knew all about the area's history and notoriety, even revelled in it.

'Where is he now? Do you know?' he heard Heather ask.

'No one's seen him. Only the other day we were talking about it. How over the last two or three years he became a solitary soul. Before then, you used to see him in the pubs, on the street, walking, talking to everyone: he claimed to be listening to the music of the streets. But then he became withdrawn, odd. He had a few grand dreams and schemes, but they came to nothing.'

'Any places he used to visit regularly? Local pubs, perhaps?'

'The Kensington Park on the corner of Lancaster Road and Ladbroke Grove. Horrible, grotty pub, but he liked it. John Christie drank in there, he always told us, as if that was going to change anyone's mind. Other than that, his Aunt Liz lives in a tower block at the top of the Grove. He used to pay her visits.'

'Thanks,' Heather said, and turned to leave.

'I did hear he'd taken a bar job.'

'Where?'

'The Prince of Wales.'

Foster came to, the drug wearing off, the pain rushing in, bursting through. He had watched while the killer had injected him. Was this the dose that ended his life? But he regained consciousness, a mixed blessing. He tried to move his shoulder but was met with a burning flash of agony in his right wrist as he flexed his hand. He tried to cry out but the tape was in place.

'I broke your right wrist and right ankle while you were out of it,' Hogg's reedy voice said. 'You should thank me for sparing you that experience. Keep still. We have only two more breaks, then this is over.'

Foster tried to remember where those wounds would be inflicted by recalling the injuries inflicted on Eke Fairbairn, but his mind, scrambled by pain and narcotics, refused to concentrate on one thing for more than a few seconds. Any notion of time had long since gone.

He seemed to drift once more. When he returned, the tape had been removed. Foster, disoriented, muttered woozily. Each word was an effort. Hogg ignored him.

There was a muffled noise from behind one of the boxes.

'Everyone is waking up,' Hogg said.

Foster heard him opening a bottle of some description. From the corner of his eye he watched as he went behind the pile of boxes. He could hear a man groaning, the voice soft and confused. The killer let out a low shushing noise, then re-emerged syringe in hand.

'Who's in there?' Foster said. There had been only five victims in the 1879 case. Was this a sixth?

'It's someone who gave me a helping hand over the past few weeks. Unwittingly. Though he did grow to be suspicious. However, I picked him well: rather than running to the police, he demanded money for his silence.' He smiled. 'He'll get his payment later.'

Foster fought to keep conscious. He guessed the fracture to his leg might be compound, the pieces of bone having pierced the skin. Without instant treatment it was probably well on the way to becoming gangrenous. Even if he got out of here, saving it was unlikely. He let his head rest back. Bound and drugged, his body broken and battered, he could see no escape.

'Did you bring them all here?' he asked. Foster wanted to know as much as possible. Not that it mattered now.

'Except Ellis,' Hogg said, out of sight. 'I kept him at a place I rented. Cost me an arm and a leg in sedatives but it was worth it, though I got the dosage a bit wrong. Killed him before I had a chance to do it. You live and you learn. For the rest, this place was ideal: you can bring the van in, it's secure, no prying neighbours and I've soundproofed it so no one can hear you scream.'

'Were they all alive, like this, when you . . .'

'Yes. On the same bed. Drugged, but they felt it. I wanted them to.'

Foster felt his gorge rise. The anger gave him strength. There was no way he was going to lie here, tortured and waiting to die.

'You aren't killing to avenge anything,' Foster spat out. 'Those people were innocent. You're doing this because you enjoy it, you sadistic bastard. Just because you think you have a reason – and some pseudo-intellectual horseshit about being affected by the air – it doesn't make you better than your ancestor. In fact, you're worse.'

He paused there, he had to, the effort too much. As he recovered his breath, summoning the will to goad the killer more, he sensed him at his side.

'You know what the most painful bone in the body is to break, don't you?' the voice whispered directly into his ear.

Foster did not want to hear the answer. 'Fuck you.'

The killer, face red with anger, reapplied the tape. Then he raised the sledgehammer and brought it down with full force on Foster's collarbone. He felt it break instantly in midsection; a bolt of fiery pain powered through his neck and shoulder and down his right-hand side.

Foster issued a cry that came from his boots.

As he writhed, the killer went out of view, returning with a syringe, which he stabbed into Foster's arm.

The light was beginning to drain from the day as Heather and Nigel sped to the Prince of Wales. The staff sketched in the final few minutes before Foster's disappearance. How he came in search of Karl Hogg, shared a drink with him and collapsed, presumably drunk. A member of staff claimed he appeared woozy when he arrived, though Heather assigned that to exhaustion. When he slumped at the bar, Hogg said he'd overdone it and would take him home. He then took him to his vehicle, a small red van, and drove away. Foster's car was still where he had left it, parked a short distance from the pub.

Hogg was paid cash; he worked there Friday and Sunday lunchtimes; the only contact they had for him was a mobile-phone number, which was switched off. He was not a registered owner of a vehicle, which closed off one avenue, and he didn't seem to own a credit card.

'The last of the bohemians,' Heather muttered, sardonically.

An address came through for Liza Hogg. Nigel and Heather raced round there, Nigel unable to prevent himself from staring at the digital clock, illuminated on the dash, ticking over. It was ten in the evening when they arrived at Liza Hogg's flat in a tower block on the eastern side of Ladbroke Grove, looming over the Great Western running in and out of Paddington. Heather knocked at the door. No answer. Heather swore. She knocked again. Silence. Nigel peered through the window beside the door into a dimly lit kitchen, the only colour a pair of yellow rubber gloves draped over the taps.

They were just about to start knocking on the neighbour's door when the light went on. There was a rattle of chains, and the door opened a fraction.

The worn, pinched face of an elderly woman peeped cautiously through the gap. 'Yes,' she muttered, wearily.

'Mrs Hogg?'

The woman nodded.

Heather flashed her badge. 'Sorry if we've woken you,' she said softly. 'We need a quick word, nothing to worry about.'

Liza Hogg invited them in, flicking on light switches as she passed them in her dressing gown and slippers. They followed her through to the sitting room, where three cats had made a bed of the sofa. Liza shooed them away.

They sat down, Nigel and Heather on the small, threadbare sofa decorated with a faded floral pattern. Nigel kept quiet – he felt awkward even being there, but Heather had insisted he came.

Heather apologized for barging in. 'We're actually interested in the whereabouts of a relative of yours.'

'I've only one,' she said slowly, as if still escaping the clutches of sleep. 'You mean Karl?'

'Have you seen him recently?'

Liza shook her head. 'He doesn't visit me much these days.'

'He used to?'

'He used to live with me. After all that happened.'

'All what happened?'

Liza, more awake it seemed, sighed deeply. 'Where do you want to start? The poor lad hasn't had an easy life.'

Heather and Nigel exchanged a glance.

'Go on,' Heather urged.

'His father raised him and his brother for a while. But then he was driving back from work one day when a drink-driver lost control and smashed into him. He died. Karl took it very bad. He was close to his dad. And to his brother. He came to live with me; his brother went to university. They were strange lads, the pair of them. His brother, David, had a lot of problems. He took his own life at university. Hanged himself.'

Nigel had witnessed much of this tragedy while researching the bloodline at the FRC, but it was only here, coming from the mouth of an old woman, that he saw just how bleak it had been. As if their blood had been tainted.

'Karl withdrew completely when he moved in. Sat up here staring at the walls. Didn't want to do anything with life. The only thing he was interested in was our family's history. You see, we've a rather chequered past.'

'Yes,' Heather said. 'Did Karl know about that?'

Liza nodded. 'We *all* knew about that.'

'You said Karl got interested?'

'To say the least. All he did was research that. He'd go to the sites of the murders. All day and all night he walked. It was the 1980s; a lot was going on around here. Finally he came out of himself, starting to write about the place, its history. Became obsessed with that, too. At least it stopped him reading and rereading the letter.'

Liza got up and shuffled to a drawer in a bureau at the far side of the room. She opened it and rustled around. Time seemed to stand still. Nigel could not bear it. Come on! he thought to himself, casting an impatient glance at a wooden clock on the mantelpiece. Eventually the old woman emerged with a piece of yellowing paper, neatly folded.

'This is the letter I showed him.' She handed it to them. 'It's the suicide note written by Segar's son, Esau. Karl used to read it almost every night.'

Heather opened it up carefully. The paper was fragile, the folds worn almost to the point of disintegration. Nigel leaned in so he could read it too. The writing was a scrawl, though still legible. There was no introduction, no signature, but it looked to Nigel as if it was genuine.

I knew he killed. I cannot relate what it was that drew me to that conclusion. The look in his eye, the hours he began to keep, a sense of awful foreboding. As the police discovered each victim, it became clearer to me that my father was responsible. I could point to no evidence save his night-time excursions and the cold glimmer of hatred in his eyes. He had long since stopped communicating with me. I disappointed him, that was clear. I did all I could to keep out of his path.

One night I heard him leave. I climbed from my window to the street below. The fog was thick, blanketing the city, muffling its sounds. I simply listened and followed his soft wolf-like tread. I shadowed him all the way until he grabbed some poor soul staggering back from a night of drink. I heard a muffled cry and then watched him fall. My father turned, I ducked away, then he made his way back home.

I failed to get back before he did. The next morning he asked where I was. I concocted a tale of meeting a friend, though I knew it would earn me a beating. He only stopped when my mother begged him to. I lay on my bed on my front, weeping as my mother tended the wounds to my back and backside from the strap, praying to whichever God for the peelers to come and take him away. But they never came.

From that day he sank further into insanity. He made us pray four times a day. He beat me incessantly. Then came the night. He urged us to follow him down to the cellar. Each night since, I remember the damp smell, the cold floor, then the noise . . . my mother gurgling, spluttering, choking on her own blood. He grabbed me and plunged the knife into my neck, eyes wide as saucers and brimming with mania. I remember nothing else.

I was struck dumb from then on, forever to keep the dark secret quiet in my heart. Until now. Until this day when I end my own wretched life. I carry that man's blood. With me it ends. It is my fervent dying hope that those who proceed can live without this stain on their souls.

Heather folded the letter back up. 'You said he doesn't come by very often these days,' she said.

Liza shook her head. 'Once or twice a year. Not quite sure what he's up to. He hasn't written one of his books in a while; he usually brings me a copy, but hasn't done for at least a year. While he wrote them he seemed OK. I think he thought the world would listen – it didn't. But the last time I saw him, he said he was working on another project.'

'Do you know what he does, where he goes, any friends?'

'Not these days. He used to spend a lot of time around the site of the house.'

'The house?'

'On Pamber Street. Segar Kellogg's house.'

When Foster surfaced, he couldn't speak. His mouth gaped helplessly wide, wedged open to its furthest extremity, as if stuck at the midpoint of a yawn. He tried to bring both tiers together but his jaw felt locked in place. From the bottom of his field of vision, he could just make out a metal plate on his top lip. He took a few desperate breaths through his wide-open mouth, the air rushing in gulps, drying his throat in an instant. There was a fleeting moment of panic when it felt as if his throat would seize and he would not be able to breathe.

By inhaling through his nostrils he managed to regain control. Not my teeth, he thought. With his tongue he flicked at the top and bottom rows, only able to reach the latter. They were covered by what felt like a strip of rubber. Some contraption had prised open his mouth.

'Unfortunately, I won't be able to take any more questions from the floor,' he heard his killer's voice say, 'the floor now being unable to ask any questions.'

Foster struggled against his restraints like a wounded, cornered beast, instinct and preservation kicking in once more, damning the pain each minor movement caused.

This wasn't how he thought it was going to end. Not like this. A heart attack one night, maybe. Or some bullet from a suspect they had forced into a corner. All of these he had considered when lying in bed, or mulling over a glass of red. But not being tortured by a fucking maniac. If he had a gun and the use of his hands, he would have no hesitation in blowing his own brains out.

'The item you are wearing is called, rather bluntly, a mouth opener. I've adapted it a bit, but it's used in sadomasochistic circles in pursuit of helpless degradation and absolute control. God bless the Internet.'

He leaned in closer; Foster could feel his warm breath on his face.

'You can't see, but there are two screws here.'

The contraption moved. The screws were at either side of his mouth.

'If I turn them clockwise they bring the two metal plates that are covering your upper and lower sets of teeth closer together.'

Foster felt the contraption loosen and his jawbone relax with an ache.

'But if I turn anticlockwise . . .'

He felt the screws turn. The gap between the top and bottom of his jaw became wider once more.

'If I keep screwing like this, then eventually your jawbone will break – very slowly.'

He continued to turn, thread by thread. Foster felt the strain on his jaw as it was pushed back to the position it was in when he woke up. The skin at the side of his lips had split. Breathing was a struggle once more. Foster felt himself fading, unable to get the air he needed because the widening of his mouth tightened his neck and constricted the airway.

The fight was leaving him, his thoughts starting to drift . . .

The barbiturates had come from the street. A drug dealer, who passed them information from time to time, said he would get hold of them for the right price. Three days later they met in a car park and he was handed the vial.

'You sure you know what you're doing here?' the dealer had asked. 'My mate says that's some heavy shit.'

Foster reassured him. Did not tell him it was for his own father.

That night his father wanted to do it. His affairs had been put in order, nothing was left undone. They sat at the kitchen table as the night fell and drank a bottle of Château Montrose 1964. Rain had decimated the crop that year, but the Montrose was picked before the storms came, a true rarity. His father had long been saving it.

He drank it in a state of reverie. Before he took the first sip, he stared long and hard at the beautiful red hue, then buried his nose in the glass and inhaled deeply. A look of contentment was written across his face. When he took a sip, so did Foster. The wine was like liquid velvet, the acidity correct, the tannins gentle and mellow. It was the silkiest wine he had ever tasted. His father savoured each drop like it was nectar of the finest fruit.

When he finished the glass, he stood up. Not even allowing himself more than one glass in the last few minutes of his life.

'Don't do it, Dad,' Foster said, voice breaking.

'This life holds little more for me,' his father said. 'The cancer will kill me in a year. It will eat and eat away at me. I would rather retain some control and choose the time of my leaving.'

'What changed, Dad? You were so full of fight.'

His father held up his hand to quieten him. 'Don't give me the first degree,' he said slowly. 'Euthanasia means "easy death" and I want it to be that way. Respect my decision. There are some fights you can't win and there are some fights you don't want to win. Now you can leave if you want. I'll understand. You're implicated enough as it is.' As he stood up, he looked at Foster. 'One day you'll understand.'

His father went upstairs. Foster followed, not quite believing this was happening.

In his room, his father plumped up some pillows and lay down. Next to the bed on a table was the vial. Foster climbed on to the bed; tears stung his cheeks. Helplessness. There was nothing he could do. Fear. This man had always been there.

Nothing was said. They hugged. His father told him he loved him and was proud of him. Foster, breaking down, returned the gesture.

His father edged backwards on his throne of pillows. Then he picked up the vial, turned the top and emptied seven white pills into the palm of his hand. He looked at Foster, smiled, eyes wet. Then he threw the pills into his mouth and took a hefty swig of water.

*

'Now, this may hurt.' The killer was back, his voice dragging Foster from the brink.

He started to turn the screws.

Heather's car slammed to a halt on Bramley Road. On the way, as they careered through the narrow, streetlit warren of Notting Dale, she had phoned through for an armed response team to assist them. Then she turned to Nigel.

'Foster will keep himself alive as long as possible,' she muttered, her jaw firm.

Her faith in him appeared unshakable. Nigel was desperate to believe her. It was only a half-hour from midnight.

They jumped out, Nigel clutching an Ordnance Survey map from 1893 and a small torch. He marched forwards, checking their position against the map, trying to work out where Pamber Street might have been. Above them the Westway, which carved through the area like a concrete river, pulsated with evening traffic. They walked along a short road leading down to an underground car park, Heather and the team following Nigel's steps.

Nigel could see as he passed a series of five-a-side football pitches that Pamber Street was no more, one of the streets razed when the overhead motorway was built. The map told him that Pamber Street had lain north of the Westway. With his finger he traced the angle of the road and looked up at one of the characterless brick blocks of flats that studded the area. He veered towards one. In the distance he heard a van pull up at speed. He turned to see it disgorge a troop of armed response officers. More should be on their way.

'Keep going,' Heather gasped. 'Find the flat.'

Nigel headed straight for a block that appeared to stand on the same patch of ground as Pamber Street. Few of the flats were illuminated. There was the thud of footsteps on the ground as the armed team caught them up. Nigel and Heather reached the entrance and made for the stairs.

'Where now?' Heather asked breathlessly.

'Number 12,' Nigel said, bounding up the stairs. The number of Segar Kellogg's shop. Instinct told him his descendant would have picked a flat of the same number. They reached the second level and made their way across the corridor linking the flats. The armed team was now alongside them. Nigel stopped outside number 12. No one said a word. Nigel stepped back. His eyes glanced to his right, where he could see lights and vehicles descending on the area from all sides. Then they met Heather's. Her dark eyes were wide with fear, expectation. He felt his heart beat firm and insistent against his ribcage, as if attempting to force its way out.

The team of four men took up their positions, strapping on pairs of night-vision goggles. The flat was silent, no light from within. On the silent count of three, one officer battered the door and it fell with a sonorous thump. The others poured through shouting. Heather followed them, and Nigel's curiosity ushered him through in her slipstream.

The men marched around the flat screaming warnings. Nigel, his eyes not yet accustomed to the light, braced himself for the sound of a gun. Nothing came. The small living room was empty. The single bedroom, too. They burst through into the kitchen: nothing. The air was fusty, sweet-smelling. In the darkness he heard Heather's voice.

'Are you sure it was number 12?' she screamed, her tone accusatory.

'Yes,' he whispered hoarsely.

He was certain. He felt himself shrink visibly. Another group of officers appeared in the doorway. One of them flicked a light switch, lighting the room, making Nigel squint.

In the middle of the small, spartan sitting room was a large, white fridge-freezer; the only item in there save a wooden chair. Nigel and Heather looked at each other. One of the ART pulled the fridge door open. Empty but for half a carton of milk. He pulled the first drawer of the freezer open. Nothing. Then the second. Immediately he stepped back. Heather moved in, Nigel at her shoulder. He could see a bed of ice stained watery-red. On it lay a pair of hands and what appeared to be a wig, though a flap of blue-black skin betrayed its true origin.

Darbyshire's hands, MacDougall's scalp. They had the right place.

'Too late,' Heather drawled numbly.

The ringing in Foster's ears was incessant. It drowned out everything: the voice of his potential killer, the quickening beat of his heart, even his own pathetically shallow breaths. Speaking was too much effort. The pain in his body from his many wounds had drifted away. Indeed, he could not feel his body at all. The only sensation was the ringing. Suddenly it stopped. He felt light, ready to float free. Peace and contentment flowed through him.

Then he felt the bed beneath him once more, as if slammed back into his body, aware immediately of the agony from his suppurating leg and shattered collarbone in particular. He opened his eyes and gasped: the pain from his ripped jaw shot through his entire body, yet he was incapable of emitting anything other than a low moan in protest.

For those few seconds he wanted to be calm and peaceful once more, away from his wracked, fragmented body and the smell of old cardboard.

'Thought you'd done a Graham Ellis and jumped the gun,' he heard Hogg say.

The voice was nearby. What was he doing now?

Foster could sense a presence to his left.

'Not long now,' Hogg added. 'Then it'll all be over.'

Foster had no more fight. He closed his eyes, seeking the soothing balm of unconsciousness. There came the first stab of pain on the thumb knuckle of his right hand. A thin piercing stroke with a knife. He knew at once what it was.

The number 1.

Nigel stumbled out of the flat, needing air, the image of the severed body parts repeating in his mind. Policemen poured past him as he made his way down the stairs, mingling with a trail of confused residents forced grudgingly from their flats a few minutes before midnight, many in their nightclothes. Nigel did not know what to do with himself. Foster was certain to be dead; the killer had won.

He turned and glanced back at the functional brick building, ignoring the chaos around him. Two centuries ago, under a similarly brooding night sky, at the same hour, Esau Hogg had followed his father and watched him slaughter an innocent man. A few days later, within fifty yards of where Nigel now stood, Esau's father had ushered his family to the basement beneath the shop, and butchered them.

The basement, he thought.

His eyes were attracted to a sign to one side of the block, black on white in giant lettering: 'STORE MORE'. A road wound down underneath the council block, ended by a black garage door. Some sort of self-storage facility. Using the torch, he checked the 1893 map, folded and bundled into his coat pocket. Then he looked back at the block of flats. The road on the 1893 map was at a different angle from the other streets that branched off the main road. Tracing it with his finger, Pamber Street seemed to follow the contour of the road leading down to the underground storage unit. He ran towards it. Outside the entrance was a security guard.

'Is anyone in there?' Nigel asked, gesturing with his finger at the door.

'No,' the guard said. 'There's only me on duty. What's going on here?' He gestured to the mêlée around the block of flats.

'Police work.'

The security guard raised his eyebrows. 'You police?'

Nigel decided to lie. He nodded imperceptibly. 'I need to get in there,' he said, indicating the entrance behind the guard. 'It's important,' he added.

The security guard weighed up his decision.

'Once you've let me in, you need to go and find Detective Sergeant Heather Jenkins and tell her to meet me in here,' Nigel continued with as much authority as he could muster, not wanting to give him time to think about it too much.

The gleam in Nigel's eyes, his desperation, appeared to sway the security guard. He turned back and unlocked the door, letting Nigel in.

'Where's unit 12?'

'First floor down. Take the lift.' He disappeared into an office for a few seconds, returning with a set of bolt cutters. 'Only the customers have keys. You'll need these.'

The security guard turned and left. Nigel headed down into the storage area, turning right from the brightly lit parking bay through a giant set of double doors, towards a lift.

'Nigel!' a voice hissed from behind. It was Heather, out of breath from exertion. She had followed him out of the flat, caught him up. 'Where are you going?'

He told her about the family being murdered in the cellar, and how he had re-examined the map.

She looked at him coolly. 'I just passed the security guard. He's adamant there's no one in the entire complex.'

Nigel shrugged. 'There might be something in there that can help us.'

Heather glanced at the bolt cutters, the glimmer of a smile on her lips. 'Where did you get them?'

'Playing the cop opens a few doors. Literally.'

Heather unholstered her radio and spoke, giving her position and asking for back-up. 'Come on,' she said.

The pair ran to the lift, went down a floor, alighting on a long corridor that stretched for about a hundred yards. The walls on either side were white steel, broken at regular intervals by bright yellow steel doors. The only silence was the gentle hum of the air ventilation system. Nigel walked down the hall, to a point where the doors were less tightly spaced, indicating bigger storage units. He turned and gestured to the last door on the left. No number on it. They stopped outside, looking at each other. Still only the distant hum of circulating air.

'It's not locked,' Heather said.

All the others they had passed had been.

Nigel looked at her. The bolt cutters he had were

no use now, but he felt his grip tighten on the shaft. Heather reached down and grasped the metal door handle. Slowly, without making a sound, she pushed it down and pulled. The door opened.

'Bloody hell,' she said simply.

There was a wall of boxes blocking the doorway like bricks.

From beyond came a noise, the sound of something being knocked over. Followed, Nigel thought, by a low moan.

Heather flashed him a look, eyes wide. 'He's in there,' she hissed. She looked behind her, along the corridor. No sign of back-up.

Nigel looked at the wall of boxes blocking their path. Without another thought, he took a short run and pitched himself headlong. He met a box square on, felt it give on impact and the whole edifice shift. A searing pain went through his shoulder. The top rows of boxes came down with him as he burst through the makeshift barrier.

'*Stop! Police!*' he heard Heather scream out.

He was lying on one side and managed to look up, seeing a dark-haired man with a knife charge across the crowded room towards them. Behind him a supine figure lay almost naked on a trestle. Nigel pushed a box out of the way and jumped to his feet, intercepting the man's path to the door and Heather.

He swung the bolt cutters back like a baseball bat and struck at the figure. They hit the man square in the chest, making him stagger backwards and drop the knife. His eyes flared with anger and he jumped straight to his feet, launching himself at Nigel. Nigel did not have time to swing the cutters once more, but used them to fend off his attacker. His face was contorted with agony, sweat streaming from his brow, teeth bared. He was doing all he could to repel the attacker, but his crash through the boxes had wrenched his shoulder and he could feel his grip on the bolt cutters giving way.

The man wrestled the cutters from his grasp. He swung them back behind his head. Nigel lifted his arms to protect himself from the impact. There was a deafening crack that echoed through the vault. He lowered his arms and saw the man on the floor, in black jeans and white T-shirt, slumped against a box. There was a small hole in his forehead, only now beginning to gush blood. The man's eyes were open, but he was obviously dead.

Nigel felt his legs weaken and he slumped to the floor, staring ahead, ears still ringing from the shot, cordite in his nostrils. There was a silence that seemed to last for an age before all hell broke loose. Policemen funnelled in, guns at the ready. Nigel instinctively held his hands up to show he was not armed; he saw their anxious eyes scour the room in search of another assailant, then relax when they saw it was empty. One beckoned Nigel over towards them.

Nigel began to tread gingerly but Heather, ignoring the warnings, sprinted past him, to a corner of the room. He turned and saw the pale, lifeless figure of Foster lying on a makeshift trestle. Nigel followed her. Foster's leg was at a grotesque angle, clearly broken. The rest of his body was covered in welts and bruises. He was absolutely still.

'*Grant?*' Heather screamed, standing over him. 'Oh, my God! Grant!'

27

A steady drizzle blanketed Kensal Green Cemetery. Suitable weather for a funeral, Nigel thought, as he gazed across the verdant churchyard. Where is everyone, he wondered? His only companion was the priest, alternating between impatiently checking his watch and anxiously looking for some clue from Nigel as to the whereabouts of the rest of the mourners, and two pallbearers, who had disappeared behind some foliage for a smoke.

Beside the grave, on a trestle, lay a vast coffin – it needed to be, given the size of the body occupying it, Nigel thought. Beside it was a mound of earth, dug the night before, covered with artificial turf-like cloth. Nigel thought about calling Heather on her mobile; she and the rest of the team should have been here by now.

'Sorry, but I really do need to get away by eleven,' the priest muttered apologetically.

'It's OK,' Nigel said, looking towards the main path that cut through the heart of the graveyard. 'I see someone now.'

It was Heather and Andy Drinkwater, dressed in black. They disappeared from view behind a tree. When they emerged the other side, Nigel waved, then stopped dead when he saw who was with them.

Foster.

He was in a wheelchair pushed by Drinkwater. Nigel had thought he was still in hospital. Last week he had spoken to Heather to see how he was, and she'd said he was improving, but that the medical team treating him thought he would be there for some time. He appeared to have lost some weight over the last three weeks, but then, he was having to suck most of his meals through a straw. As he came nearer, Nigel could hear him muttering like a ventriloquist through his broken jaw.

He was berating Drinkwater for being a lousy driver. 'Jesus, Andy. You can forget it, if you think you're ever getting behind the wheel of my car.'

It was the first time Nigel had seen Foster since his kidnapping. He was surprised to see him looking so well. The breaks had all been clean, apart from the fracture of his right tibia and fibula. They'd inserted a series of screws and a metal plate. The operation was deemed a success, though Foster would not be doing the 100 metres any time soon, and he would be left with some pain and aggravation. The jaw had been badly broken, but the other fractures were on their way to being healed. The main worry was his psyche: How would he recover from his ordeal at the hands of Karl Hogg?

'Nigel Barnes,' Foster's voice said through clenched teeth as he reached the grave.

Nigel offered his hand in greeting. Foster took it and gave it a tight squeeze that indicated to Nigel he had not lost much strength.

'Didn't expect you here,' Nigel said.

'Yes, well, only right and proper, given the part my family played in this poor bugger's demise.' He took a deep breath. 'Thanks for all you did. Without you, it might be me in there,' he added, looking at the coffin. He turned back. 'Not sure that wouldn't have been preferable to knowing my ancestors were German, though.' Foster flashed a smile through gritted teeth. 'Promise me one thing. Don't go jumping through boxes when you have no bloody idea what's on the other side.'

Nigel looked sheepishly at Heather, who was nodding theatrically. After the paramedics had taken Foster to hospital and forensics descended on the scene, Heather had walked up to him as he sat against the wall in the corridor of the storage unit, shell-shocked. He thought she was going to check whether he was OK, perhaps offer him a blanket.

'You stupid wanker,' she said, with feeling. 'Don't

ever, ever try to be the hero again. He could have had a gun and shot us both.' She had dropped to her haunches, so their eyes were level, and put her hand on his shoulder. 'That's what I'm supposed to say. Unofficially, well done. Karl Hogg had already carved the reference on the knuckles of Foster's right hand. He was holding the knife he was going to stab him with. Had we waited for the ART, it might have been too late.' She paused. 'You feel OK?' Her hand went to his cheek. It felt warm.

'Jenkins,' a voice cried out.

It was Detective Superintendent Harris, surveying the scene.

Heather smiled at Nigel, took away her hand and stood up. 'Yes, sir . . .'

'Here come the Fairbairns,' Heather said now, pointing across the cemetery at a couple in the distance dressed in black, arms intertwined.

The Home Office had granted Eke Fairbairn an official pardon and the Royal College of Surgeons had agreed to release his body for a proper burial.

'When was Karl Hogg's funeral?' Nigel asked.

'A week ago. Cremated. Only his Aunt Liza was there,' Heather replied.

'Good riddance,' chuntered Foster.

Foster had been unconscious when they found him. Another twenty minutes and he might have died of his injuries. Nigel had asked Heather how much of his ordeal he recollected. No one knew. He'd refused counselling.

Forensics had gone through every box and container in the storage unit. The knife Karl Hogg brandished at Nigel was the one used to stab his victims. He was about to push it through Foster's heart. In the fridge-freezer in his flat, forensics found a small box containing enough GHB to fuel the appetite of the clientele of a London nightclub for a month. They had been through reams of CCTV footage from the storage site; Hogg was a nightly visitor, drawing up at his unit in a van, loading and unloading boxes. On occasions they had even helped him with heavier packages, providing him with a forklift truck and driver, unaware of their macabre cargo. The staff became so used to his lengthy visits that they stopped noticing his comings and goings.

In one corner of the unit, behind a wall of boxes, Dave Duckworth had been found drugged up to his eyeballs. He had spent a few days in hospital before being arrested and charged with aiding and abetting.

'He's going to plead guilty,' Heather said. 'Five years, probably. If he's a good boy, out in three or so.'

Nigel winced at the prospect of fat Dave coping with the regime of prison life and the attentions of his cellmates. Couldn't happen to a nicer lad, he thought.

John Fairbairn and his wife had made it to the graveside. They nodded a greeting to them all, then fell into conversation with the priest. After a few seconds, he stepped forwards and began to intone.

'I am the resurrection and the life, saith the Lord . . .'

When the coffin was lowered, and the short service over, they bade farewell to the Fairbairns. Eke Fairbairn's life had been brutal and short, his lingering death a travesty. Yet here he had finally been laid to rest. The past had been closed.

Drinkwater pushed Foster away from the graveside.

Nigel fell into step with Heather, a slight lurch in his stomach. 'You on duty?'

'Why do you want to know, Nigel?'

'Been having a few dreams recently. Bad ones. Wanted to speak to someone about them.'

'I'll get you a number,' she said.

That wasn't what he had in mind.

'Anything else?'

Nigel took a deep breath. 'Just wanted to see if you fancied a drink sometime. Now that it's all over.'

She glanced at her watch. 'Quite fancy one now, to be honest. Let me tell Andy. He can take Ironside back on his own.'

She hurried forwards to catch up with her colleagues. The Fairbairns and the priest were already on their way out of the cemetery. Nigel turned around to take one last look at the grave of Eke Fairbairn. The drizzle halted, the sun edged out from behind the massed ranks of spring cloud.

In the distance he heard the playful caws of three crows.

If you enjoyed THE BLOOD DETECTIVE,

read on for a taster of Dan Waddell's second novel

BLOOD ATONEMENT

Extracts from the opening chapters follow here . . .

(To be published by Penguin in 2009)

The candle on the ledge guttered as it neared its end, shadows dancing on the wall. Beside her Sarah sensed the rhythmic rise and fall of her sisters' chests. Henrietta's and Emma's ability to fall asleep as soon their heads lay on the pillow infuriated her, while she tossed and turned seeking sleep that took an age to arrive.

Not tonight though. She lay rigid, pinned down beneath layers of blankets, not wanting to move and so drown out the muffled voices from the adjoining room.

Her future, her whole life was being discussed in there.

She could hear her mother, softly pleading, occasionally sobbing. Her father's sonorous voice in response, calm and unyielding.

'I do not mean to disobey you, Joseph,' she heard her say. 'But he is in his sixtieth year. Does that not seem wrong to you?'

The low rumble of his words was more difficult to decipher. Sarah eased herself from under the weight of her covers and crept silently to the door, the breath from her nostrils frosting in the crisp night air. She shuddered. The December night was hellish cold but the undergarments beneath her night clothes warded off the worst of the chill. She eased the door open and slipped into the dark hall. The words were more audible out there.

'Sarah is only fourteen!'

'You were only fourteen, Harriet, when your father pledged

you to me.' Sarah sensed her father's impatience. Her boldness had reaped it many times.

Her mother choked back a sob. 'May the Lord forgive me, I must protest. You were only nineteen, Joseph, nary a few years older. Not two score years and more like Hesk—'

'Enough!' Silence.

Lord no, not Hesker? Sarah thought of his enormous stomach, bulging eyes, sagging, bewhiskered jowls and flabby wet lips, habitually moistened with a flicking pink tongue. There was a metallic taste in her mouth now, testament to her rising bile. She felt sick.

'The matter is agreed. I will hear of it no more.'

'But Joseph —'

'Harriet!' The voice was resolute, commanding. She knew then that her mother's protest was at an end. A hot tear ran silently and slowly down her cheek. She retreated quickly back to her room before her father left for his. It had been a long time since he had favoured her mother's room as his place of rest.

At her bedside, she fell to her knees and burrowed her salt-wet face in her hands. The Lord was her only chance of reprieve.

'Our dear heavenly Father, I thank thee for the blessings bestowed on me and my family. The food on the table, the bounty in the fields, the health of our livestock. The manner in which Joseph junior was spared when plague-ridden in the summer and it seemed all hope was vanquished. I thank thee for those and many other blessings. I beg here for thy mercy. If it be according to thy will that I be wed to Hesker Pettibone, then I beseech thee

to think again. I apologize for my insolence, but I request with all reverence and humility that I not be married to that disgusting fat old hog – I seek thy forgiveness for that ungodly description. Should thee ignore my plea, so help me heavenly Father, I will not answer for the actions I henceforth take. Amen.'

As Sarah climbed back into bed, her ice-block feet seeking a source of heat, she heard the soft whimpers of her mother in the room next door. Strangely, it gave her strength.

I would rather be cast into the fiery pit than live a life of quiet desperation and suffering, she thought.

Nigel Barnes stopped walking and brought his hands out from behind his back, holding the skull. He did it too quickly. The skull wobbled in his right hand, which was itself shaking, and almost fell to the floor. He looked at it, silently counted to three, then composed himself and looked forward.

'He has remained silent too long,' he said. One-two-three. 'Now it's time to hear his story.'

The cameraman brought his equipment down from his shoulder. 'Good,' he said impatiently. 'Only problem with that one was I clearly saw you mouthing "one-two-three" before you delivered the last line.'

'And I nearly dropped the skull.'

'And you nearly dropped the skull. Also, when you were walking to camera, I could see your eyes glancing down at the mark.'

Nigel cast his eyes to the floor. Three feet in front of him was an 'X', scratched into the cemetery path by the cameraman's trainer. He'd been looking at the shape for most of the twenty paces rather than the camera, yet had still ended up missing it. He sighed.

'You also look very ill at ease.'

Because I am, thought Nigel. What sort of person could walk and talk to a camera with a fake plastic skull in his hand and feel comfortable? Probably someone who had spent their life practising for such a moment in front of a mirror. The only thing Nigel had done in a mirror was squeeze spots when he was younger.

'Mind if I have a ciggie before we go again?'

The cameraman nodded. 'I need to make a call or two anyway.' He looked ruefully around at the graves on either side of them. 'Think I'll go and make them on the street,' he added. 'Seems a bit disrespectful to do it here.' He put the camera down at Nigel's feet and loped off, giving his sagging jeans an upwards tug as he left.

Disrespectful, Nigel thought, sitting back on an anonymous gravestone. Unlike smoking a cigarette. He produced his fixings from his pocket and rolled a smoke. He lit it and exhaled loudly and studied the clichéd, stilted script they had given him to memorize.

The call had come in a week ago. In the summer,

encouraged by Scotland Yard's press office, he'd given an interview to a Sunday newspaper about his role in the Karl Hogg case. 'The Gene Genius' it had proclaimed. 'The Family Historian who helped make a savage killer history'. Nigel had groaned when he read it, embarrassed by the way his role had been exaggerated, worried by what the officers who worked on the case would think of it. Would think of *him*. Then the phone started ringing. Radio, television, the odd magazine, he was too polite to say no. Not when he learned he could make some money from it. He downplayed his role, praised the police. 'Every bit the modest hero, aren't we?' a DJ from Radio Shropshire had told him, winking as if he knew what Nigel was doing. Come to think of it, what was he doing?

One of the calls had come from a TV company. They were making a pilot for a series investigating burial sites unearthed during building development. The idea was to take the remains and find out who they belonged to, how the people died, dig out their stories. Tara, the producer, called and said she'd seen the piece and that Nigel seemed ideal. They had met in a coffee shop off Oxford Street and over lattes she ran through the idea and asked if he'd be interested in taking a screen test. Why not? he thought. A chance to get away from rooting around in other people's pasts. Or at least doing it for more money and getting recognized in the street. He felt flattered. Particularly when she said they were looking for a photogenic young historian with what she called 'phwoar factor'.

So here he was, in the middle of Kensal Green cemetery on a drab morning in October, performing the televisual equivalent of patting his head and rubbing his stomach, and proving terrible at it. Mike the cameraman, now stepping back through the cemetery, hands plunged deep into a green combat jacket, had been very patient, but Nigel knew that all four attempts had been amateurish at best.

Mike hoisted the camera back on to his shoulder.

'Let's go again,' he said.

Nigel flicked his fag on to the grass and twisted his heel on it, shivering against the cold. He should have worn more than his tweed jacket, but felt it was the 'look' they wanted. He made his way back to the grave of Alfred Rossiter, 1829–1892, which marked the start of his walk. He flexed his shoulders, drew in a breath and turned around. One-two-three.

'The dead are always with us,' he said, and started to walk. 'Sometimes closer than –'

'Cut!' shouted Mike.

'What *now*?' Nigel asked, perplexed.

'You've forgotten the bloody skull!'

*

Detective Chief Inspector Grant Foster, emitted a weary sigh as he crouched over the woman's mutilated corpse. During his convalescence, human nature had not taken a turn for the better. He rose to standing, wincing slightly at the bolt of pain searing up his leg from the metal plate holding his right shin together.

The victim's throat had been cut. From the pool of dried blood on the floor, it was clear that the murder had taken place several hours ago. The killer was long gone. His eyes were drawn to the rest of the bedroom. A bed with white sheets and yellow duvet and pillows; a bedside table with a lamp, a stack of paperbacks and a radio alarm clock; a battered pine chest of drawers, its surface teeming with vials, bottles and cases, above it a large mirror. A whole wall was given over to cupboards filled with clothes, shoes and handbags. There was a fragrance in the air that he could not pinpoint but there was a hint of lemon to it. A pile of clothes lay in the corner with a pair of discarded shoes. There were no signs of struggle. Just a woman in her mid to late thirties lying dead on the floor, a gaping wound from ear to ear.

Foster rubbed his face with his right hand. It was his first week back. He'd insisted on being on call. That call had come at 2 a.m., a blessed relief from lying in bed listening to the blood pounding in his ears, waiting for sleep that rarely came. He climbed into his old suit, realizing only then that he could fit his thumbs into the gap between his gut and the waistband, forcing him to dig out a belt and pull it to the tightest notch. He had anticipated a gang killing, probably some hapless kid stabbed in the street in Shepherd's Bush or Kensal Rise. Instead he'd got this – a woman lying dead in a cluttered bedroom, in a lavishly furnished Victorian terrace, on a quiet, affluent street in Queens Park, a middle-class ghetto between Kensal Green and Kilburn.

Detective Sergeant Heather Jenkins walked into the bedroom with a scene-of-crime photographer at her shoulder. 'Mind if I . . .' she said nervously.

'Fill your boots,' Foster said.

He turned to Heather. Her hair was scraped and tied back off her face and she looked pale and worn. Bad news, he thought.

'The victim's name is Katie Drake,' she said. 'Thirty-seven years old. An actress. Her neighbours found her. They had a set of keys. They were alerted by a friend of Katie's after she and her daughter failed to turn up at an ice-skating rink to celebrate the daughter's fourteenth birthday.'

Foster felt a shudder of apprehension. 'And where's the daughter?'

'We don't know. She's missing.'